The Last Voyage

Brian D. McLaren

The Last Voyage

First published in Great Britain in 2025 by Hodder Faith
An imprint of John Murray Press

1

A CIP catalogue record for this title is available from the British Library

Trade Paperback ISBN 9781399814140
ebook ISBN 9781399814164

Typeset in Sabon MT by Hewer Text UK Ltd, Edinburgh
Printed and bound in Great Britain by Clays Ltd, Elcograf S.p.A.

John Murray Press policy is to use papers that are natural, renewable and recyclable products and made from wood grown in sustainable forests. The logging and manufacturing processes are expected to conform to the environmental regulations of the country of origin.

Carmelite House
50 Victoria Embankment
London EC4Y 0DZ

www.hodderfaith.com

John Murray Press, part of Hodder & Stoughton Limited
An Hachette UK company

The authorised representative in the EEA is Hachette Ireland, 8 Castlecourt Centre, Dublin 15, D15 XTP3, Ireland (email: info@hbgi.ie)

Contents

Part I

End Your Life as You Know It

1
Not So Pure

Gabriela Mercedes Coroy glanced at her eyes in the rearview mirror. *Strange to see*, she thought. *Tears. Everyone thinks of me as smart and cheerful, not sad and fearful.*

She paused before putting the car in gear, watching herself watch herself in the mirror. For the first time in her twenty-seven years of life, Gabriela had lied to her mother. Forever this would be true: that her final conversation with her mother was a lie. It wasn't just the goodbye that broke her heart, but also the lie.

She tried to reassure herself as she drove through the old neighborhood toward the highway, dodging skinny dogs and bags of trash in the rutted gravel road. *It was only una mentira piadosa, a white lie, a pious lie*, she told herself. *The lie was morally necessary.* She felt an empty ache in her stomach.

She turned south onto CA-1, following the faded sign for Guatemala City. Only the *mala* remained legible. *Reverse graffiti*, she thought.

She tried to reassure herself. If her mother knew the truth, many lives would be at risk. So, her mother must believe this lie, truly believe it, for her own sake, for Gabriela's sake, and for the sake of Gabriela's companions.

All the world's poor knew what Gabriela and her mother knew: that the world was ruled by oligarchs. American, British, Russian, Chinese, Saudi, Brazilian, whatever . . . they were all remarkably similar. The oligarchs kept government officials, whether elected or appointed, like lap dogs on short leashes. Their pet politicians protected them, licking their hands, performing their tricks, attacking their enemies when commanded to do so, passing laws to protect and enhance their interests. In return, the oligarchs made their pets moderately rich. They rewarded their hungry little egos with tasty treats. And they assured their re-election. If the politicians didn't comply, the oligarchs had convincing methods of punishing them, and cheap replacements were always easy to acquire.

The oligarchs themselves were connected to one another by networks of threat and obligation, and their networks were intertwined with global crime syndicates, not to mention local criminals, private militia, and, of course, pliable political parties. Behind them, there were lines of smiling religious leaders eager for handouts in exchange for providing moral camouflage for the nearest oligarch's decadent behavior.

Nearly every oligarch on Earth was surrounded by this nervous, eager, nodding flock of yes-men, little men (and a few women) who gained a fortune and lost their souls by telling their bosses what they wanted to hear. As a result, most oligarchs lived inside invisible bubbles of narcissism, echo chambers of arrogance, from within which they could go for decades without anyone daring to disturb them with a contrary opinion.

Yes, there were a few clear-minded exceptions, and they were the ones who worried Gabriela. These outlier oligarchs knew that the jig would soon be up for them, as for everyone. The global ecosystem that had taken billions of years to evolve had tilted suddenly into disequilibrium, a victim of human overshoot, and soon the highly profitable economic pyramid maintained by and for the oligarchs would collapse and decay like a corpulent corpse.

That's why information on how to escape the coming catastrophe was, for the savvy, the most valuable commodity on Earth.

And Gabriela was one of the few who held this information.

She had been chosen as one of the ten for the last voyage.

That's what put her mother in such danger.

Gabriela instinctively hunched her shoulders and gripped the steering wheel more tightly as she felt again the precarious nature of the situation she had brought her mother into. She again looked in the rearview mirror, but not to see herself this time. An oligarch's emissary could be driving behind her at this very moment, ready to make his move.

She reached up a hand to touch her necklace. Each simulated gemstone hid a cyanide tablet she could bite into and swallow if she were captured. A similar bracelet dangled from her wrist. She had been given permission to make this visit on the condition of wearing this deadly jewelry. It was worth the risk to see her mother one final time, even though the goodbye entailed that lie.

More frightening to Gabriela than biting a fake gem filled with real cyanide: at this very moment, an oligarch's emissary could be pulling up to her mother's house.

She tried not to imagine the scene: his fancy car, anonymously white, so out of place in front of her mother's humble casita in Chimaltenango . . . his manicured hand stretching out from an expensive suit, knocking on her door with some lie of his own, pretending to be a reporter, or an official from the Guatemalan government, or perhaps someone from Gabriela's lab in Boston. He would speak perfect Spanish. He would be cradling a breath mint between his upper teeth and cheek. He would smile and compliment her for her beauty, for her immaculate home, for her pretty pink flower box at the front door with its gerbera daisies – red, yellow, salmon, white. He would ask for information about Gabriela's whereabouts, politely at first, but that would change when he didn't get what he was looking for.

Her mother was incapable of deceit. That's why Gabriela had to tell her mother a lie so convincing that she would repeat it with complete sincerity. Then the emissary would recognize her mother as another poor and simple peasant who knew nothing, a pure, innocent soul. It was Mami's ignorance and purity that would save them both.

I am not so pure, Gabriela thought, *not so innocent*.

Gabriela had rehearsed the lie a hundred times before telling it, and now she reviewed it one last time: *Un oligarca de Colombia me ha contratado para dirigir un programa secreto de investigación cientifica*, she had said, feigning pride and happiness. An oligarch wanted her to use her skills in genetic engineering to help save coral reefs in the Caribbean, and he would pay her extravagantly. *Es una oportunidad tan emocianante!*

Gabriela tried to comfort herself with the rationalization that there was some truth to the statement. She was indeed going away on a voyage, and an oligarch of sorts was involved, and coral would even be a minor character in the story. But here was the lie: her voyage would not take her to the nearby Caribbean. It would take her across an expanse vast beyond her mother's imagination.

Why did she have to add that little joke, which only made the lie sweeter, and therefore more bitter? "No te preocupes, Mami. No es como si me fuera a Marte," Gabriela had laughed when she said it: *Don't worry, Mom. It's not like I'm going to Mars!*

The joke was perfect, because Gabriela was always joking, always making her mother laugh. The joke was the final touch that made her lie such a masterpiece of deceit.

"Es peligroso trabajar por esas personas," her mother warned, wagging her index finger, but smiling as she did so: *it's dangerous to work for those people*. But instead of discouraging her only child from going, she gave permission with her favorite motherly advice: "Ten cuidado, querida. Vuelve segura." *Be careful, beloved. Come back safe*. And then she added, "Siempre me haces sentir orgullosa." *You always make me proud*.

That, of course, was the one desire that most shaped Gabriela's life: to make her mother proud, to bring her joy. And when a large sum of money showed up in her mother's bank account shortly after Gabriela's disappearance, it would fulfill another great desire: to keep her mother safe, just as her mother had always done for her.

I am not so pure, she said to herself once again, because coexisting in her heart, along with her shame for lying, Gabriela had to admit there was something egotistical. She not only took pride in trying to protect her mother from danger; she also took pride in the elegant plausibility of the lie itself.

Gabriela had been a scientific prodigy from her adolescence. She had been chosen at sixteen to be part of a special program – funded by an oligarch donor – for gifted students from poor countries to attend Harvard University in the U.S. Starting in 2045, she studied genetics in hopes of saving living things from the ecological catastrophes sweeping the Earth. Amphibians were her favorites, having captured her curiosity as a little girl when she learned of the extinction of the golden toad in nearby Costa Rica. She remembered the windowsill of her bedroom back in those days, stuffed animals lined up in a row, all of them frogs, toads, and salamanders, big ones, small ones, lifelike, comical, one playing a ukulele and wearing a straw hat, one named Kermit, although she didn't know why. Her mother had saved them all in a box that she kept in her closet, among her old shoes, even after all these years. Before leaving her mother's house, Gabriela had retrieved Kermit. She glanced over at him, sitting in the passenger's seat with his lanky green legs crossed.

The great amphibian die-off accelerated as it spread across the globe, the effects of habitat loss, pollution, climate change, the chytrid fungus, and other pathogens. Her dissertation advisor convinced her to shift her research focus from amphibians to corals. "Save something that can still be saved," he said. "And save something an oligarch might find fundable. Something that isn't slimy."

A brown girl who escaped the barrio of her childhood – she was exactly the kind of harmless person an oligarch would make the beneficiary of a crumb of his largesse, especially if she had a charismatic subject of study, something shimmering and colorful like a coral reef. After all, what gift can an oligarch give to the person he loves most, when that person already has everything? The feeling that he is a friend of the poor, of course, and a friend of nature too! That's a gift truly worthy of an oligarch . . . worthy to be given to himself and received from himself.

Gabriela was not naive. She understood why nearly all oligarchs engaged in philanthropic projects: largely as a public relations strategy, to enhance their brand, and usually to distract from their other more unsavory clandestine activities. They loved to make a show of saving the Earth and helping its downtrodden with their right hand while their left hand was despoiling the Earth and crushing the downtrodden.

Gabriela hoped against hope that her plausible lie would protect her mother from *esos bastardos sucios* if the imagined emissary ever came.

Just over an hour later, she pulled into the parking lot of her shabby hotel near La Aurora airport. Used condoms, plastic grocery bags, beer bottles, crushed batteries, hypodermic needles . . . the parking lot hadn't been cleaned for months. *My poor Guatemala*, she said to herself, looking at her eyes once more in the rearview mirror. *Her finest hotel looks like this*. She was still sniffling, still trying to convince herself that the lie she'd told was, if not morally justifiable, at least a necessary evil.

That's all that's left to us these days, she thought, *the lesser of evils. What a world*.

She grabbed Kermit and rushed upstairs to pack her small suitcase. Then she sent a message on her bracelet: *Ready for pickup*. For ten minutes, then twenty, she sat on the side of her bed and stared out the hotel window across the blue smoky hills of her beautiful country, simply gazing, hardly thinking. Pollution, fires in the hills . . . the smoke seemed worse every time she returned to visit her mother. The smoke brought back bitter memories.

Then, suddenly, she winced. A stark realization pierced her musings like a burn to skin. She ran her finger along a disfigurement on her left ear, a scar that reminded her every day of the love of her mother in this dangerous world.

Who am I kidding? Gabriela asked herself. *There is no protection for my mother. The emissary will not know of my mother's pure heart. He will think she is just another clever liar, intentionally hiding the truth, trying to deceive him. He will threaten her, frighten her with stories of bad things that happen to people who oppose his boss. Since Mami is still an attractive woman, even at forty-eight, he may do even worse. Whether the emissary believes she is hiding information or not, he will kill her in the end, because emissaries, like the oligarchs who send them, deal in death. Human life means nothing to them. The poor are simply the shit in which they grow their money. That's all they care about, money, money and power, money and power and pleasure. Who am I kidding? I was not protecting her. I was only protecting myself and my colleagues.*

She couldn't let these thoughts continue. The pain was too great. *Mami's only hope*, she thought, *is that the oligarchs never find out the truth about her daughter.*

She went to the bathroom to splash water on her face. As she held a threadbare pink hotel towel to her face to let it dry, she felt a ping in her implant.

She still wasn't used to the implant in her ear. Implants were a luxury of the rich, as were com bracelets like the one she now wore along with her cyanide-tablet-gemstones. She never could have imagined having either of these technological luxuries when she was a little girl in the barrio back in Chimaltenango.

Her bracelet shivered. Silva was waiting out front, the screen said, waiting in a black sedan. *Our staff will pick up the rental car. Just leave the key at the front desk*, it said. All the details would be taken care of.

Off to meet my fellow travelers, Gabriela thought. *Off to training. Then off to . . .*

She didn't know where the training facility would be. Perhaps in Kenya, but probably not. Maybe somewhere in Europe, maybe New Zealand. Everything was shrouded in secrecy, as it had to be. Secrecy was as necessary to their training as Gabriela telling lies to her mother.

She forced a smile toward her image in the bathroom mirror. *Time to look like a professional woman*, she said to herself, *not like a little girl crying for her mother*. She picked up her small suitcase, put Kermit under her arm, left her room, entered the hotel elevator, and touched the button that said *vestíbulo*.

Es hora de terminar mi vida como lo conozco, she murmured. *Time to end my life as I have known it.*

As she slid into the back seat of the black sedan, she had one of her favorite jokes ready. "Hey, Silva, I have a story for you. There was a photon checking into the hotel just as I was checking out."

Silva, middle-aged with straight hair too blond to come out of a bottle, looked in the rearview mirror and made eye contact with Gabriela. "A photon? Imagine that," she replied, raising her eyebrows without smiling.

"Yes!" Gabriela said. "A very beautiful, sexy, voluptuous photon. The porter asked the photon if she needed help with her luggage, but she said . . . are you ready for this? . . . she said, 'No, I'm traveling light.' "

Gabriela laughed even harder than Silva, partly because she really loved that joke, but mostly for the pure joy of meeting grief and fear with good courage and good cheer.

2
Black Holes All the Way Down

I shall be alone, lugubrious, saturnine, Colfax thought. *A pitiable Lear, a superannuated artifact, musty and passé, solo and without solace, talking to myself circuitously, bereft of all but words.*

He sighed, then looked at his bracelet to check the date: November 5, 2056. Another cold and damp morning, the sky a featureless November gray. Snow was falling against yellow-gold maples and green pines, a subdued Sunday in Seattle under a low ceiling of heavy clouds.

Colfax wanted someone to listen to him, maybe even to appreciate his brilliance. He needed someone's attention, maybe even admiration, to pull him out of the great deep suck of self that he always felt when he was alone. But if that was not possible, then he wanted a drink, his favorite companion in solitude, just one, perhaps two. *Straight vodka would be good, maybe a twist of lemon. But then again, perhaps not.*

He made some coffee instead. He stared out the kitchen window across the backyard, patches of grass cupping mounds of wet snow. A handwritten letter lay on the kitchen counter next to a box that had been filled with homemade chocolate chip cookies, each topped with a triangle of three cashews. They had been sent by Hailey Clark, Colfax's almost-ex-almost-fiancée.

The night before, Colfax had devoured all but one of the cookies and then despised himself for it. He picked up the letter and re-read it for the fifth time.

He paused on the last sentence: *I'll call Sunday morning when the boys are at gymnastics.* He knew she would. So, he waited.

The snow melted as it hit the window, the drops zig-zagging downward. The window slowly morphed into a mirror, the drops blurred, and Colfax saw his own face, his goatee mostly snow now, his hairline receding, leaving a sparse drift of comb-over. *I was much thinner when alcoholic spirits were my primary source of nutrition*, he thought. *Now I bear the similitude of a bloated ostrich, but without a neck*. He found his bulkier visage dreary and distasteful.

Hailey was my last chance at preserving any illusion of being something other than an abdominous, disconsolate dotard, he said aloud, something he had been doing more often lately, finding strange comfort in the sound of his own odd, unrhythmical voice and his love of big words. *This loneliness feels like a black hole inside a black hole within a black hole. Infinite gravity all the way down, an infinite ravenous insatiable abyss.*

He sipped his coffee and looked through his translucent reflection. The mirror again became a window, seemingly streaked with tears. The bird feeder in the yard was almost empty. A solitary female cardinal, a drab rust in contrast to her mate's bold brightness, hunted for sunflower seeds, flicking millet to the ground. A dark-eyed junco was less fussy and foraged for millet in mud and snow. *They used to be ubiquitous, but no longer*, he thought. A rush of lesser goldfinches flew in, but they soon left without finding anything worth consuming.

For four winters, I accompanied Ann here in this house in her descent into cancer, he thought. *The hardest and best endeavor of this peevish, aggrieved, selfish life of mine.* He recalled the nine months after her death, trying one day at a time to fill the bottomless emptiness with something other than booze. Then came Hailey. *She was my robin, my Capistrano swallow, my harbinger of hope*, he thought. *She needed me to help her recover from a living Otto as much as I needed her to help me recover from a deceased Ann. And she was certainly the best editor I ever had. My book would only have been read by a few academic peers if not for her ability to make my esoteric arcane prose more . . . prosaic. What a gift she . . . has been.*

Another November in Seattle. Cold. Damp. Gray. Empty. With more of the same to look forward to for the foreseeable future.

Colfax's com bracelet disrupted his grim thoughts with a ping in his implant. It was Hailey, as promised. He pressed the button on his bracelet, and in the receiver implanted in his right ear, he heard the familiar click followed by the intimate sound of Hailey's breath, which meant she was whispering directly into the mic in her bracelet. A shiver ran up his neck.

Finally, she broke the silence. "I'm sorry," she said softly. "You understand. I had to write because I couldn't bear to . . ."

"Yes," Colfax interrupted. "I cannot blame you. The cookies were a generous gesture, a spoonful of indulgence to mollify the bitter medicine in the letter. I was a sentimental dolt to think this age gap could be overcome . . ."

"No, you know it's not that, Colfax," Hailey said. "It's not . . . it's, you know, my situation. I have responsibilities that you understand as a parent too. When Otto asked to reconcile, it . . . it's for the boys. I can't put my happiness above . . ."

"Our happiness, Hailey. Remember I am, or at least once was, a significant variable in this equation," Colfax said, and instantly regretted doing so. She was audibly crying now.

He tried to repair the situation: "I apologize, sincerely, Hailey. That was uncalled for. I was being . . . petulant, petulant and self-centered, as usual. Of course I am cognizant of your competing loyalties. Two dependent progeny and a marriage of long tenure . . . not something you could easily discard, especially now that Otto has returned, petitioning for mercy and promising to amend his ways. I was often in his position, beseeching Ann for mercy *again*. And of course you are predisposed to forgive, as Ann was. I would not have forgiven me, if roles were reversed, but like Ann, your nature is different from mine, morally finer, no doubt. In you, the quality of mercy is not constrained. That is yet another reason I . . . love you." He decided to stick with present tense. "And those cookies were indeed delectable."

"You finished them already, didn't you? You're worse than my boys," she replied.

"I saved one," he said. "An act of hope."

And then she was crying again.

Colfax spoke: "So this is the terminus, the end of a short but very beautiful odyssey. This is farewell. For good." His inflection sounded more like a question than a statement.

"For the best," she replied, her voice quivering, "for all of us. We couldn't have lived with ourselves, Colfax, if we hurt my boys for . . . us . . . I'll always, always . . ."

"Please," Colfax interjected. "No need to say it. We both know. There is no need to say anything more. We have always . . ."

"That's what makes this so hard," she said.

Suddenly Colfax heard a man's baritone. "Who *is* that?" the voice interrogated. "Why are you *crying*?" Colfax couldn't tell if the tone was protective or accusatory.

The call ended with a click in Colfax's implant. A second shiver ran up his neck.

Before he could register grief, the smoky savor and silky texture of whisky danced on his tongue, even more enticing than vodka. He hadn't felt this tempted since Ann descended into her final coma and he descended into a three-day binge that landed him in the hospital two floors below her. His daughter, Eve, had to plan the funeral without him. *Even now, I am little more than a self-pitying, self-absorbed dry drunk who binges on chocolate confections, full of self-execration, and deserving every bit of it*, he mused aloud. *Simultaneously a decrepit has-been and an immature punk. Pathetic. Despicable.*

The snow was falling more steadily. The flakes seemed to Colfax to be in a relentless rush to find some surface on which to liquify.

He opened the box on his kitchen counter and extracted the last cookie. He broke the cookie in two, then four, and then crushed the fragments into crumbs and watched them fall from his left palm into the box. He carried the box toward his front door.

He put on his coat, then his wide-brimmed hat. The silence of snowfall always drew him outdoors, especially when he was in pain. He stood on his front step and shook the box and scattered the crumbs on the snow. Perhaps they would feed the hapless Bewick's wren he had noticed a few days earlier. More likely though, they would be consumed by dark-eyed juncos. *Perhaps a bit of chocolate will lessen their sorrow*, he thought.

But what of my sorrow? Have I not already surpassed my lifetime quota? he muttered as he placed the empty box beside the door and locked the keypad from the outside. *Ah, but there is no such thing as an upper limit for pain*, he answered himself, just above a whisper. *There will always be more to be had. An endless supply of mournfulness, desolation, and melancholia.*

Before long, he'd walked far enough that there was a half-inch of wet snow on his shoulders and the brim of his hat. He kept meaning to walk away from his favorite bar on Ballard, but his feet seemed to be on autopilot. Of course, it would be closed so early on a Sunday morning, but even so, it drew him. Even though he was more of a cursing man than a praying man, he began chanting to himself, his words keeping rhythm to the gentle crunch of his steps in the wet snow, *Grant me the serenity to accept the things I cannot change . . . I loathe those words*, he thought, *yet I somehow find them necessary, so I intone them like a superstitious conjuration.*

His bracelet pinged his ear implant again. It was a different ping; this time, signaling an encrypted coms app. In lieu of a number, the screen on his bracelet read, *UIC Manhattan*. What unidentified caller from New York would use encryption to call him on a Sunday? Curious, he pressed the button, hoping it was not a reporter. He was sick of reporters, sick of politics, sick of fame, sick of controversy, sick of fighting the oligarchs and their kleptocracy, sick of deadlines and interviews, sick of every damned thing except birds. And, to his shame, cookies. And, let's face it, spirits.

He tapped his bracelet. "Colfax Innis," he groaned.

"Colfax, old man. Thurman here. It's been a long time." It was the same gravelly voice, but it sounded a little more . . . weary. Weary. That was it.

Colfax couldn't hide his shock: "Thurman? Thurman! Has it been fifteen years, sixteen? Since our twenty-fifth Vanderbilt reunion, yes? Why this unexpected contact? Are you not ruling the world with your cronies from a private bunker somewhere in Nunavut or Greenland or Tasmania, watching civilization self-immolate in a tragicomic clusterfu—?"

"I'm in Seattle at the moment, and hardly running with the crowd that rules the world," Thurman interrupted. "More like running from them. Might we meet for coffee?"

"Hell yes. But when?"

"How about now?"

"From where are you calling?"

"Look behind you, old man."

Colfax turned back and saw through the snow a white Tesla Model 99 appear, ghost-like, descending the hill. It decelerated and came to stop just ahead of him, in front of the old familiar bar. The passenger door opened, like a bird lifting one wing. Colfax tapped the snow off his hat and coat and got in, with no idea where he was going.

3
Assurance Colony

When they entered the coffee shop, Thurman picked a table in the corner at the front, away from everyone else. Colfax noticed that Thurman chose a seat with his back against the wall. *Is that so he can monitor who enters through the doors? Was it merely a jest about running from the oligarchs?* Colfax wondered. Thurman powered down his bracelet, leaving Colfax to wonder if this was an act of courtesy or security.

Once they settled, they picked up right where they left off years ago, as good friends often do. They reminisced about college, about Nashville bars and parties to which they were disinvited, girls they dated, not mentioning Ann, who had briefly dated Thurman before becoming Colfax's girlfriend and, later, wife. Then the tone changed.

"When I heard about Ann's diagnosis, I planned to call, but I never did," Thurman said. "I kept putting it off because . . . well, I regret that. I truly do. I didn't know what to say, to her, to you. I should have called. I failed you both."

"We never expected you to call," Colfax replied. "We knew you were otherwise occupied, and there was nothing to be said, really. Or done. After a slow initial onslaught, conditions at the end deteriorated more rapidly than any of us could have expected." They were silent for a beat, then Colfax added, "Years ago, Ann and I used to sit in this very coffee shop on Sunday mornings and read about your work with Suntec. Back then, I was still under the employ of the EPA, may it rest in peace. I often regaled my staff with tales of our para-academic adventures and your professional achievements. I would inform them that you had done more to delay the catastrophe than we had. I took pride in telling them you were once my friend."

Thurman shook his head, appearing uncomfortable with the adulation. "Still your friend, Colfax. Always, no matter what."

Colfax continued, "What you did was disruptive, revolutionary, Thurman. Making Fifth Gen solar energy so affordable was a start . . . your creation of co-ops with mass buying potential and low-interest loans, your decision to manufacture the best panels and batteries in disadvantaged areas, your commitment to license only installation and maintenance companies that were minority-owned. Then, beyond all that, you announced you would gradually divest ownership to your employees. And, from the start, you plowed your profits into that tree-planting initiative. How many did you plant: was it nine billion to match the human population?"

Thurman shook his head. "In Suntec, we didn't count trees. We counted forests. And the difference mattered. In the end, I came to realize that the fossil fools in Congress would simply count all the trees I was planting to justify sucking more oil and gas out of the ground. I remember that a journalist called it *policy-based evidence-making*. They started with a pro-carbon policy and then turned everything into evidence to justify it."

"I too have ample experience with their craven idiocy," Colfax interjected.

Thurman nodded. "So you do. A strange addiction, carbon, and as fatal as any opioid. I kept fighting, and I kept losing, all these years." He cradled his empty mug in interlaced fingers, as if weighing it. Colfax noticed the skin of his fingers, light brown and wrinkled; the watch on his left wrist, expensive and titanium; his nails, perfectly manicured; his left hand, still no wedding ring.

"And you never married," Colfax observed, with a nod toward Thurman's hand.

"No, no. There's someone I'm . . . close to. For many years now. But marriage, no, no, not for me, nor for her. No point, really."

"So, are you still running Suntec? I looked for information about you a couple times, but you went as dark as an oligarch, as they say. I didn't expect a call when Ann passed. I knew you cared. We both knew."

"I did care, though I didn't show it, and I had gone dark, as you say, out of necessity," Thurman replied. "Privacy became essential for my current work, and actually for my survival. Extremely so." With that, he unobtrusively pointed to his bracelet, and then to Colfax's, a universally understood gesture. Colfax quickly powered down his bracelet, and Thurman continued. "I still own a fraction of Suntec, but soon that final fraction will be transferred to employees. They elect their own management, so I have no duties there. I am primarily involved in a different venture, but that involvement is dark because that venture is . . . out of favor. Seriously so."

Colfax understood *out of favor*. An organization would go *out of favor* if it failed to play along with more powerful or ruthless corporations. Going out of favor was dangerous, because all the top oligarchs had access to ubiquitous CCTV data and other net communications. They used facial A.I. and voice recognition software to track one another constantly. If they wanted an out-of-favor competitor to disappear, all they had to do was tip off an E.S. or *extermination service*, as they were called. E.S.s were always happy to perform the surgery, as they called it, maybe using a sniper, maybe a drone. Business was competitive and risks minimal, so the costs weren't high.

"Are you able to . . ." Colfax asked, without asking.

Thurman paused, then leaned in slightly. "I'd like to. But I need you to agree to confidentiality."

"Of course," Colfax said. "Understood."

"I need it in writing, old man," Thurman said.

"You have employed that curious epithet for me since our undergraduate years," Colfax replied, "when I was not at all old."

Thurman grunted out a chuckle. "Back then, you looked young, but you talked and acted old. Now at least the two match."

Thurman reached into the inside pocket of his black jacket and pulled out an old-fashioned envelope, with two pages of single-spaced print tri-folded neatly inside. "Actual paper. I know it's quaint. And the agreement is unenforceable with the current state of the legal system. But it's our protocol, our tradition, really. And it's important that you only sign it if you vow on whatever is sacred to you, which I assume would be either a dictionary or a pair of binoculars, to maintain absolute confidentiality. Permanently. I'm serious. Lives depend on this." He gave Colfax a "do you understand?" look with his eyebrows.

Colfax scanned the papers. "Do you by chance have a . . ."

Thurman grunt-laughed again and pulled an old-fashioned pen out of his jacket. Colfax was about to start signing, but Thurman interrupted. "I need you to read the whole thing. Every damned word. In my presence."

"Tedious lawyerly boilerplate," Colfax complained as he read. As he scratched a hasty signature onto the last page, he felt a sudden wave of seriousness or queasiness, or both, then he folded the pages back into the envelope, and handed it to Thurman.

Thurman placed them on the table. "You were asking who I work with. The answer is highly relevant to this visit. It's Macopro, Colfax. I work with Macopro."

"Christ. Jesus H. Christ. Mars Colonization Project. Holy Christ," Colfax replied, leaning in, trying to restrain his volume. "I am duly impressed, although not fully surprised. It strikes me as a good fit for a man of your genius and daring. Back in the early 40s, Macopro was always in the news, especially right after that *Excelsius* disaster. You have kept your involvement secret all this time."

"So far, at least. I have been there since '37," Thurman said, and then added nothing.

Colfax continued, "So you were involved during the whole Robot Fleet period, and then for the first landing in '44. And then *Excelsius*. Astounding. They always talked about that Ukrainian woman, that oligarch's widow – I have forgotten her name, but they never mentioned you. Then Macopro itself seemed to disappear from public consciousness. I honestly have not given it a thought for years now. I assumed it was . . . passé, I suppose. Plus, so much inanity has befallen us on Earth that Mars naturally faded . . . out of sight and out of mind, to use a grotty cliché. I am reminded of the space station when we were younger, before the Satellite Wars in the late 30s. It passed four hundred kilometers above us sixteen times every day, but months or years could pass without the average person ever thinking about it. I suppose even the most extraordinary things become invisible when they become routine. Baseline syndrome, I believe, is the psychological term for the phenomenon."

"As you can imagine, for someone involved on the inside, it has been far from routine. Let's just say a lot has befallen us," Thurman continued.

"So, you say you remain *involved* with Macopro, as in currently. How involved?"

"Let's just say I'm very involved."

"Which explains your secrecy. But it fails to explain this meeting, unexpected for me, but evidently part of a premeditated plan for you. This is not merely a social visit to re-establish friendly contact with an *old* friend."

"I wish it were. I've followed your work, Colfax. And your losses. Not just Ann. I was worried about you in the previous . . . administration." He leaned in and lowered his voice. "President

DePaul was a fool to fire you and shut down the EPA when we needed it most."

Then Thurman imitated the previous president's exaggerated southern drawl perfectly: "*We will no longer destroy this fragile economy for the sake of the environment whose God-given purpose is to serve humanity. We must protect jobs and economic growth from every leftist-socialist-wokist-ecoterrorist threat.* What a mountain of extinct-in-the-wild elephant shit that was."

"He was a damnable buffoon. A cretin. An ignoramus," Colfax spat. "To hell with him and the whole damned politicult."

"You, too, kept fighting even though you kept losing," Thurman replied, his voice mournful. "You have remained steadfast and valiant in our long defeat. You're lucky you weren't disappeared. So many have been. You didn't have the same means to go dark, as I did."

Colfax glanced around before responding, lowering his volume. "The devastation inflicted upon our nation and world by that putrescent mound of arrogant feculence DePaul and his puerile, sycophantic cronies will require centuries to recover, if . . . if . . ." Colfax stopped mid-sentence, as if the subject weren't even worth the breath. "And, from the looks of things, whoever wins this week will be worse."

"If you only knew, old man," Thurman replied. "If you only knew."

Talk like this, both men knew, was dangerous, but sanity and integrity depended on taking risks to speak freely, even if in whispers. Now that they had "re-established the norm" by taking the risk of speaking plainly and from the heart, Colfax changed the subject. "My professional demise as a bureaucrat has, at least, delivered an upside. When I left the directorship, I started writing, which I have come to love. Ah, the simple joy of speaking freely, without bureaucrats blanching."

"I read *Dawn or Twilight?* It was thorough. And depressing. And courageous," Thurman said. "I'm probably its only reader who would say its only flaw was understatement and excessive optimism. I never expected you to be such a talented writer. You were always so . . . public, and dynamic. It's hard to imagine an incurable extravert like you holed up for long enough to produce a book. But then again, you always had the best vocabulary in the room, and you never tired of showing it off. Frankly, I was surprised by how understandable the book was."

"I was assisted by a superb editor," Colfax interrupted.

"Well, you and your editor deserved all the accolades *Dawn or Twilight?* won you, Innis. Didn't you win the Gifford?"

"Funny. I hardly noticed all the laurels. They brought me no joy. Nothing mattered after losing Ann. Winning the National, then the Grawemeyer, then the Gifford and the Gates and the Benioff and the Ping – those should have been highlights of my life, but they got swallowed up in all the loss. Damnable cancer. Damnable disease with its fucking finality."

That's when the conversation turned.

Thurman leaned forward and said, "Colfax, I'm here about a matter of urgency. I'm here to ask you to undergo another loss. I'm here to ask you to consider *ending your life as you know it*."

Colfax immediately got the feeling Thurman had rehearsed that curious line. Or perhaps he had used it on other people too. He looked Thurman in the eye and said, "You want me to commit suicide? I know I can be morose on occasion, but *really*, Thurman."

"No, no, not that at all, no," Thurman said firmly. Then he placed his palms flat on the table and his voice dropped to an even lower register than normal, somewhere between a growl and a rumble. "I'd like you to consider becoming part of Macopro yourself. And not on Earth. I want you on Mars."

Colfax's brows raised, but other than that, he didn't move a muscle.

Thurman continued, "It's a one-way trip, Colfax. There's no return voyage. Everyone who goes understands that. Emigration is permanent. It means leaving everything behind. Absolutely everything. That's what I'm here to ask you to consider."

"Mars? What? Me? Why?"

Thurman restrained a chuckle so that it sounded like he was clearing his throat. "That's the first time I've ever heard you utter four monosyllables in sequence. This must be how your editor felt, reducing your habitually inflated, pretentious, ostentatious diction to intelligibility. I feel a great sense of accomplishment about that."

"If it makes you feel better, I could add that I feel I have been escorted into an ambuscade, rendering me gobsmacked and nonplussed in stupefaction."

"That's more what I expected you to say," Thurman replied, faintly smiling. Then his countenance turned and he seized Colfax's gaze. "Innis, old man, I am completely serious. I am asking you to consider a final adventure, a final voyage. I articulate that word *final* with intention. You have to understand that and count that cost."

Colfax paused, letting that phrase sink in.

He repeated it out loud. "End my life as I know it. Terminate my quotidian existence. A final adventure. A last voyage. I was not even aware that you were sending people anymore."

Thurman nodded, pursing his lips. "Only once more."

Colfax felt a flush of something he didn't know how to name. Did he feel . . . wanted? Needed? Significant? He found himself trying to suppress both his shock and his . . . pride, yes, that was it. He felt flattered. He had to consciously work to suppress a smile.

"Well, at least your unexpected proposition comes at a propitious moment," Colfax said, gazing into his empty coffee mug as if it held something terribly interesting.

"There's never a great time to ask someone to consider ending their life as they know it," Thurman replied. "And, believe me, I've had plenty of practice."

Thurman's voice seemed even more raspy than Colfax remembered it, but its slow, musical pace was exactly the same, still pure West Tennessee.

Colfax looked up from his empty mug and scanned the perpetual perfection of Thurman's appearance. Hair and mustache: perfectly trimmed, pert as a kingbird. Black shirt, jacket, and pants: perfectly chosen, mysterious as a raven. Posture: perfectly erect, like a blue heron. Hands: perfectly folded on the table, like a guinea fowl on her eggs. Expression: perfectly inscrutable, yet fully present and potentially fierce, like a goshawk looking down from a branch. Demeanor: perfectly calm, perfectly centered, perfectly aware, like a swallow-tailed kite riding an invisible wind current. Even his coffee mug seemed perfectly positioned, like a barred owl on a branch. *The man is ready for anything, but waiting for nothing*, Colfax thought. *He is a Zen master.*

"Well, Thurman, life as I once knew it already came to an end, almost two years ago," Colfax said. "First with Ann, then with work. Each time it appears that I might re-acquire something resembling a life, another disappointment kicks it out of my pitiable grasp. Right up to this weekend. Right up to this very morning. Which is why this is a fortuitous occasion for this kind of proffer. The coincidence is shuddersome – spooky, unsettling, haunting."

"The only thing more annoying than the pretentiousness of your fancy words is the condescension that comes when you define them," Thurman replied. He appeared mildly annoyed. Or amused. Or both.

Several customers left and the coffee shop grew strangely quiet. Colfax felt the comfort of the gentle sounds of spoons and mugs on tables, and he stared again into the depths of his coffee mug. He was buying time and Thurman was allowing him to do so. The calm was suddenly interrupted by the raucous hiss of the espresso machine.

Colfax still didn't know what he wanted to say, so he started talking, hoping to find out. "Thurman, after losing Ann, I was despondent. Dangerously so. The neck of a bottle was my barrel of a gun. Then I got involved with someone, someone I cared about deeply, and still do care about, but now I have lost her too. Really, that leaves only my daughter. And Eve is doing quite well," Colfax mused. "I am sure you remember her, though she must have been but a young pre-adolescent last you saw her."

For some reason, Colfax felt eager to change the subject from Mars. He started rambling about Eve, her work teaching ethics and philosophy at a Franciscan medical center nearby. "That would surely be the hardest thing about such a venture," Colfax said. "Saying goodbye to my daughter." Without warning, his eyes teared up.

Thurman looked down at the table. "You wouldn't be saying goodbye to Eve, old friend," he said.

"You just called this a one-way trip."

"Colfax, I've already spoken to Eve," he said. "She was the one we originally approached about this mission. She would like to go, but . . ."

Colfax opened his mouth and said nothing.

Thurman continued. "Eve hasn't said yes because she doesn't want to leave you . . . alone, here, so soon after losing Ann. She asked me if I would consider including you. I told her there are no plus-ones. She countered by asking me if there's a more brilliant scientific mind that we could have on Mars than you. It was hard to win me over, but she succeeded. And frankly," he leaned in again and spoke just above a whisper, "if you write another book like *Dawn or Twilight?*, I doubt you'll be safe here. So, you may not be choosing between safety and danger, but between one kind of danger and another, on one dangerous planet or another."

Thurman continued, "If you say yes, Eve will say yes, but our invitation to you is contingent on her saying yes. This is a *conditional* recruitment on my part, requiring an *unconditional* commitment on your part." He lowered his head as if to say, "Do you understand that?"

Colfax slowly nodded. Unexpectedly, he felt a flash of anger, its origin unknown. "When did you speak to Eve? Why has she refrained from mentioning any of this to me? Why would you need a scholar of ethics and comparative religion such as her for the Mars settlement? They are all scientists, all engineers. I would be at home there, but not Eve with all her religious . . . *connerie*." He translated his Anglo-Saxon crudity into French.

Thurman's eyes darted around the room. Colfax realized he had been speaking too loudly. Once more Thurman leaned in and whisper-growled: "Eve and I have been talking about this option for several weeks. I asked that she not speak to you about it until I spoke to you first. We have protocols in Macopro."

Colfax again shook his head. "I am sorry, Thurman, but . . ."

Thurman interrupted. "The normal costs of transporting one person there – they're astronomical, no pun intended: around ten billion Americredits per person. And this last voyage will be twice that. Our recruitment process for each mission is very, very, very tightly controlled. Especially for this mission. No one applies, Colfax. No one finds us. We find them. Every potential crew member is screened for nine competencies before they even know they're candidates: physical health, mental health, genetic health, the specific gene set associated with radioactive resistance, genetic diversity, emotional maturity, social intelligence, fluency in English, capacity for progeny." He counted off those requirements on his fingers, and then commented, "You are the first, and actually, the last, non-repro to be recruited for Mars . . ."

"Non-repro?"

"Non-reproductive resident, Colfax. Not that you couldn't – your present reproductive ability is none of my business, but, well . . . all the others we've transported are young and they've agreed to produce progeny when the colony can provide a quality of life conducive to the thriving of children. From the start, we have been building toward minimum viable population."

Colfax once again followed a tangent. "It feels peculiar to hear you speak of minimum viable population, since I have spent the last ten years trying to warn the public about its opposite, maximum viable population. If we want the whole human population to live at a European standard of living, the maximum viable population on Earth is no more than 2.5 billion. Fewer would be even more advantageous."

"Yes," Thurman replied. "I remember that number from your book. I thought your proposal for reaching that goal in less than a hundred years was . . . bold. It wisely avoided the racist tropes of twentieth-century population arguments, and it seemed both comprehensive and doable – if only we had political leaders who actually gave enough of a damn to cut the strings of their oligarch puppet-masters . . . and if we only had religious leaders who didn't bury their heads in bullshit and insist on putting their religious self-interest above the common good. Neither of which we have. Which means Earth's human population will surely be reduced through other means, less intentional and less pleasant means. Anyway, the situation on Mars is very different."

"Of course it would be," Colfax replied. "In avian studies, we typically use the fifty/five hundred rule: fifty individuals to avoid short-term genetic inbreeding and five hundred to avoid long-term genetic drift. I would imagine the minimum viability numbers for humans would be similar. But ecologists only speak of minimum viable population when we are dealing with a species that is already on the verge of extinction. Is that how you are now thinking about the Mars colony, Thurman? An *assurance* colony for a species on the brink?"

Colfax's gaze met Thurman's. Thurman didn't blink. Colfax swallowed hard.

4
Bitter Coffee

Thurman ignored Colfax's question. "Look, old man, if we were only concerned with genetics, we would only recruit women for the project, since in this era of sperm banks, frozen ova, intrauterine insemination, and genetic engineering, men are rather unnecessary, strictly speaking. In fact, our final voyage will include a reproductive tissue bank of frozen ova from hundreds of thousands of women and frozen sperm from over a million men. But eggs and sperm aren't worth much without living women with uteruses to bear new life, and caring adults to raise . . ."

"Just when I thought I could not possibly feel more superfluous . . ." Colfax interrupted. "But I suppose there is a kind of poetic justice to male superfluity, after all these millennia of male supremacy." Colfax shifted in his chair and continued. "Does this mean you screen out non-hetero and nonbinary individuals? It would seem a shame to reverse all the progress that has been made over the last century in assuring equal rights for sexual minorities, especially because we now see that diversification of gender identities is in fact an important evolutionary and social adaptation."

"Mmmm," Thurman replied ambiguously. "Sexual orientation is not an issue for us. Who residents pair with romantically is their business, as is their gender identity. What we need is simple: for all the women, whatever their orientation, to be willing to bear children, and for all the men to be equal partners in caring for future generations. Theoretically, we would need about 2.1 births per woman on average to sustain population, but practically, we need 3 or 4 per woman to grow our population to get us to the five hundred baseline you mentioned. Ultimately, I would like to see communities of five hundred or so multiply around the planet. Minimum viable population and multiple assurance colonies . . . they are always on my mind."

"How do you handle male–female ratios? In avian ecology, we generally use a one to three or one to four ratio," Colfax asked.

"A hard sell among humans, at least for the women," Thurman continued. "Our original plan was for a population of about two hundred and fifty over the first dozen voyages. Once we reached that, we had hoped to proceed with pregnancy and birth on Mars, all while continuing to build the population to five hundred adults through ongoing recruitment over another dozen voyages, two every launch window. But since circumstances have . . . changed, now we're working with a more minimalist minimum viable population. Frankly, we have more men than we need, and barely enough women."

"And the total population on Mars now?" Colfax asked. "What would it be?"

"Let's just say around two hundred, under a hundred males and over a hundred females," Thurman mused. "So, our margin is . . . far less than ideal. We need every resident to be concerned about bearing and raising healthy offspring, and we're counting on every woman to be reproductive. That can change in the future, when our population crosses five hundred, but until then, procreation will be, frankly, a matter of survival."

"Yes, I would imagine that nobody wants to be the endling . . . the last survivor in a stranded, shrinking, aging population," Colfax replied. Suddenly he realized something. *Thurman must not know about Eve.* Colfax blinked but didn't speak as this realization spread to his gut.

Thurman continued. "You'll be the only one on Mars over sixty, or even over fifty, our elder statesman, if you will. Our first four voyages were mostly men, for a variety of reasons. Some are in their forties now. All our subsequent voyages have had a strong majority of women, and nearly all our female residents are still in their twenties and thirties, with adequate years of fertility ahead of them. The project's biological clock is definitely ticking. The numbers, whether for minimum or maximum viable population, are equally unmerciful."

Colfax nodded thoughtfully, but his mind was racing. He was surprised Eve hadn't told Thurman about her condition. He knew she was impeccably honest – compulsively so, and he could imagine her neither lying nor concealing relevant information like that. *I have fewer scruples*, he thought, so he said nothing and tried to change the subject.

"Putting procreation aside, then, what exactly are the competencies you are hoping I might bring?" Colfax asked. "Would I supply any tangible benefit beyond reducing my daughter's anxiety?"

Thurman replied, "Unfortunately, there won't be much in the way of bird life on Mars, so your ornithological background will be wasted on chickens, quail, and ducks – chosen for their nutritional value, not their biological interest. Your ecological background, on the other hand, along with your understanding of evolutionary biology, could be very valuable in designing, building, optimizing, and maintaining the growing numbers of greenhouses we'll need to keep ahead of our population. By the way, if you're conjuring images of terraforming Mars, you might as well give them up now as science fiction. Mars is so lacking in both atmosphere and magnetosphere that all future life there will be contained in some way. For now, think greenhouses and underground dwellings. Lots and lots of greenhouses and underground dwellings."

Colfax made a mental note to refresh his memory on the magnetosphere and its role in terraforming.

Thurman continued. "Your ability as a writer could help us. Up until this point, we've done far too little in terms of writing the history of this project. I would love to have you keep a record of your experience during the voyage and after your arrival. Simply having someone there I know and trust who can serve as . . . I suppose an *elder* would be the word, and a chronicler . . . that would mean a lot to me personally. A pity we can't send your editor too, to be sure that what you might write would be readable."

Colfax's eyebrows raised momentarily, but then he overcompensated with a scowl. "So. It appears I am not actually *needed*," he said, "but you will find something for me to do so you can procure Eve's presence. That still confounds me, by the way. Mars Colony is a community of scientific prodigies, and Eve is bright in her way, but she will never be a real scientist. Unfortunately."

"We need Eve precisely because she's a theologian-ethicist-philosopher and an expert in comparative religions. She's a . . . spiritual prodigy, you might say. An ethical prodigy. And, as with many prodigies, it appears her father doesn't appreciate the full magnitude of her brilliance."

The look on Colfax's face showed a mix of incredulity and disdain. He was thinking, *Religion has caused enough damage on Earth. Please do not be a pillock and inflict religion upon Mars.* But he didn't say it.

"Innis, I know you've never approved of your daughter's interest in religion," Thurman said. "I suspect you've never even understood it."

"Interest in religion?" he replied. "Holy God, Thurman, she devoted her goddamn life to the enterprise. She was a goddamned fucking Evangelical for a while. Now she teaches ethics and spiritual care – whatever that is – to med students and social workers at a goddamned Franciscan teaching hospital. That is far more than an *interest* in religion. It is a comprehensive fucking rejection of everything I stand for."

Thurman gave Colfax a stern look. "Funny. I seem to remember you telling me in college that you thought I was a 'goddamned fucking luddite' for believing in 'all that sententious anti-intellectual religious horseshit.' I imagine it hasn't been easy for Eve to be Eve and follow her own path as a spiritually oriented person with you as her dad. I understand her life decisions have been a painful embarrassment to you. You always were a proud and controlling bastard. You let Ann give you a daughter, but you don't appear to have given your daughter much of a life of her own, free from your judgments."

Colfax was about to defend himself, but Thurman raised one finger.

"I fully understand your disdain for that vocal religious minority that opposes everything we both have worked for. Their short-sightedness and narrow-mindedness are as repulsive to me as they are to you, old man. They put the cult in *politicult*, as they say. But for reasons Eve can better explain, we need her, and she wants you, and so do we – so do I – too."

Colfax shook his head. "One lesson my father taught me by his consistent example: religious people can do outrageous harm and remain oblivious to it. I will never understand what lacuna in my parenting led Eve to—"

Thurman interrupted, speaking with more intensity, but still restraining his volume. "As I see it, your daughter's religious aptitude, your father's religious pathology, and your religious aversion are three entirely different things. But that's for you and Eve to work out. The issue on the table now on this snowy Sunday is whether you are willing to accompany her, and not just accompany her, but support her, as the first Martian theologian/ethicist. If you decide not to go, I just hope you can convince her that you'll be fine staying here. Because, my friend, Macopro needs her. Mars needs her. With you or without you. People like Eve are hard to come by these days."

Colfax nodded, signaling a change in tone. "Of course I will discuss this with Eve. And I apologize for my opprobrious blathering."

Thurman picked up the confidentiality agreement and handed it to Colfax. "Take this and bring it to Eve, at your earliest convenience, please. She's expecting to hear from you. Today. She'll tell you what I haven't, and, be assured, there is much that I haven't told you. Make this happen today. Understood?"

"Understood," Colfax replied. They stood, gathered their coats, and at the door, Colfax powered up his bracelet, held it up to the scanner bot, and pressed "Pay." He entered the amount on the bot screen, heard the familiar digital voice say, "Thank you for using Americredits, and God bless America, the last great hope of mankind!" They stepped outside.

Out on the sidewalk, Thurman pointed subtly to his own bracelet. Colfax powered his down again. Thurman groaned, "Miserable politicult. Makes me sick every time I hear that woman's smarmy voice. Anyway, thanks." He offered to drive Colfax back to his house.

"No. I shall walk. I do enjoy the snow. Strange to be getting so much of it these days with the planet at 2.7 degrees above the old norm. If you get your way, I might never see snow again. I need to see how this . . . settles."

"We do have a time frame," Thurman said.

"Which is?" Colfax asked.

"There is real urgency," Thurman said flatly.

"I have a fortnight to decide? Ten days at least?"

"Two days, but one is better. We launch in six weeks, and for at least four of those weeks, you'll be in pre-flight quarantine, not to mention training, intense training, especially for a man your age. If you decide to go."

"That is ridiculous. That is insufficient time for a decision of this magnitude, Thurman. Even if I decided today, I would have some investments to liquidate, and a short manuscript to finish, a home to sell, and a magnificent vehicle for which to find a worthy buyer. If I say yes, I will have to wait until the following launch. Six weeks is too soon. I need no less than six months."

"Innis, did you not hear me? *This will be the final voyage.* There will be no more." He stepped closer and said with a finality that invited no further questions, "Your investments will be worthless to you anyway, sooner than you might think. We have people who can take care of any essential matters."

"So, if I accept your proposal, my decision will be as final as a myocardial infarction. Life as I have known it literally terminates in six weeks."

"Less, actually, because of your need for intensive training in an undisclosed location. You said it already ended, Innis."

"Indeed. But still, Thurman. This pathetic little performance is all I have."

Thurman glanced down at his bracelet. "I'm sorry, but I have a pilot, a private jet, and two of my colleagues waiting for me. They just flew up from Guatemala, and we still have miles to go before we sleep."

"You oligarchs do love your private jets," Colfax snarked. "And your luxury vehicles."

"I never drive the same vehicle twice, Innis. There is no joy in being out of favor."

To Colfax's surprise, Thurman opened his arms and embraced him. Colfax responded awkwardly. Thurman sent his contact information to Colfax's bracelet, then put on his leather gloves and walked across the street to the Tesla. It lifted its wing and he slid effortlessly inside. *He has hardly aged*, Colfax thought, *except that his hair and mustache are now white as whalebone, not unlike my own.* Colfax remembered a portrait hanging in Thurman's living room when they were teenagers – the twentieth-century Civil Rights leader Howard Thurman, the grandfather of Thurman's father, as Colfax recalled, and the source of his first, middle, and last name. *Same long face, same sad, deep, curious, kind eyes*, Colfax thought. *Same understated brilliance.*

Thurman drove away without turning or waving, disappearing into the snow as if into a mist. There was no engine sound, just the hiss of tires on wet pavement.

Thurman Howard Thurman. Mars. Eve. Beyond belief.

The snow was falling more slowly now, big flakes. *It feels enchanted,* Colfax thought. *Chimerical. Phantasmagoric.*

He walked along Ballard, and was halfway home when he powered on his bracelet and hit "Call" as he had done hundreds of times in recent months. "Hailey, direct to voicemail," he said aloud. His implant pinged.

"Hailey, this is just to say . . . you made the correct choice. I was not sufficiently strong to make it, and I had so much more to gain and so much less to lose than you. I simply wanted to tell you . . ."

And, in the snow, he choked back a sob and disguised it as a cough. He composed himself and continued. "You will never know what a gift you have been in my life. You have brought nothing bad to my life. Only good. Only good. From start to finish. Without you and your . . . your love, I do not think I would have survived these years. Thank you, Hailey. No regrets, no hard feelings. I hope things work out with Otto. For his sake, for the boys' sake, and especially for yours. I . . ." He wanted to say more but couldn't, because he knew if he spoke, he would cry, and if he cried, he wouldn't be able to stop. Better to stop now. "Thank you," he finally managed. "I thank you. Be good to yourself, Hailey. Do it for me, please."

He pressed "End." *Fitting*. It was 11:05 a.m.

He looked up. He was once again standing directly in front of the bar where he spent so many hours and nearly ruined his life a few years back. A neon sign announced *Open* in orange. A little voice pinged like an implant deep in his lower brain.

Just one more time, for old times' sake. Just for an hour. No one will know, the familiar voice said. *It may be your last chance.*

He felt a chill run across his shoulders. He walked slowly past the bar, hesitated, then leaned forward, briskly marching straight home. *No thank you. Not this time.* He concentrated on the complex bitter aftertaste of dark roast on his tongue. That, and the growing feeling that he had to urinate.

5
Dusk

Colfax messaged Eve: "Coming over shortly. You understand why." He immediately received an *acknowledge* ping.

He took an unhurried hot shower and put on some dry clothes. As he closed his closet door, he felt a pang. *It would be a real loss to part with such a fine wardrobe*, he thought.

A few minutes later, as he eased into his new car, he had a similar thought: *I have dreamed of this fine vehicle since I was a young lad. This McLaren makes Thurman's Tesla look pedestrian. I will miss it . . . if I go.* He deactivated the auto-drive and depressed the accelerator hard, just to enjoy the power of the electric motor pressing him into the top-grain leather seat. The roads were virtually empty. He made the forty-five-minute trip to Eve's apartment in less than thirty-seven minutes. *Odd*, he thought as he activated auto-drive to park the car. *Eve has never owned a car. Never even desired one. She knows not what she is missing.*

He sat in front of Eve's building, reminding himself of Thurman's words to him about Eve, and he coached himself to avoid needless offense: *Try not to insult her and her religious lunacy . . . religious interests.* But his mind quickly returned to its familiar circuit of well-worn ruts, wondering how a daughter of his ended up believing superstitious *connerie*.

He checked his car clock as he powered down: 3:34 pm. The snow had slowed, just tiny flurries now. The whole world looked black, white, and wet through his windshield. A thick blanket of Seattle gray hovered over the treetops, strangely luminescent, bottom-lit.

He walked up to Eve's condo. Before he could knock, Eve opened the door and offered a cautious smile like a little girl who just got caught sneaking an extra slice of pie. She wore the blue and gray wool sweater Colfax bought her mother on their last trip to New Zealand a decade earlier. He noticed Eve's ruddy cheeks, a genetic signature from her Nordic ancestry. *Her hair looks even more blonde than her mother's was*, Colfax thought, *if such a thing were possible. No wonder my brother nicknamed her Hay Bale.*

"I wanted to tell you, Dad. I really did. You were the one person I wanted to talk to most about this. You know how I hate secrets," Eve said, reaching out to hug him. Then she pointed to her wrist. *Off?* she implied.

"Off." Colfax nodded, adding, "Are you going to invite an aging gentleman in out of the snow?"

She led him by his wrist into her condo. Colfax paused as he always did as he entered. Eve's whole living room wall was a window facing west, overlooking docks and boats, rocks and water, to cloud-shrouded mountains across Puget Sound. *Eve never could have afforded this if it were not for the life insurance check after her mother's death*, he thought, congratulating himself for his financial foresight.

They stood side by side, taking in the view. Eve slid her right arm around her father's waist, and he gently touched his left hand to the small of her back.

A mixed flock of black scoters and buffleheads swam just offshore, along with a red-breasted merganser and a pied-billed grebe. A shearwater – he couldn't tell which species – dropped in to join them. *They are uncommon here in the Sound*, he thought, *much more common offshore*. Then he reminded himself of the latest statistics: *Much more common is hardly an applicable phrase for any birds, when total bird populations have plummeted by six billion over the last eighty years.* Along the rocks, a lone willet and a few dowitchers and plovers walked and scurried, pecking among the sand and stones. The tide was past halfway out. *About the same as the bird population*, he thought.

"Counting plovers again?" Eve asked, giving him a squeeze.

"Not counting, just noticing," he replied. "I am not certain how many more I will see in the future . . . for reasons you understand."

She squeezed him a little harder.

"Why birds, Dad?" she asked, resting her head on his shoulder. "Why have they intrigued you so much?"

"Ten thousand species," Colfax replied. "At least there were when I was younger. And five thousand of them are, or were, songbirds. All of them – from shoebills to penguins to hummingbirds to hawks to sparrows – are descended from a few species of winged dinosaurs after the Cretaceous extinction event. They have adapted to nearly every habitat on Earth. They are, to me, the most amazing phenomena of evolutionary history, present company included. Their intelligence, their profound pulchritude, their habits and culture . . . We humans may not survive our self-inflicted Capitalocene extinction event, but if the birds somehow survive, I can only imagine what they will become in thirty or sixty million years with us out of the way. If . . ." Suddenly, unexpectedly, he choked up. For the second time in one day, he faked a cough to cover his emotion.

"Let's talk," Eve said, leading Colfax over to the couch. "We don't have much time."

Eve lit a fire in her small fireplace to Colfax's left. *She knows how to arrange the kindling and paper so it lights fast with one match*, Colfax noticed. He remembered teaching her that skill on their camping trips when she was a child. The fire crackling, she moved to the kitchen to make some tea. She returned a few minutes later with Colfax's favorite, orange spice herbal, with real honey, hard to come by at any price these days because of the ongoing insect die-off. She probably got hers from the protected apiary inside the university greenhouse where she volunteered each week.

"Do you have the papers from Thurman?" she asked, still standing. Colfax produced them from his jacket pocket. She scanned them and gently placed them in the fireplace, page by page, then sat beside her father and watched them burn.

"That was all for emotional effect?" Colfax asked.

"Macopro protocol," she replied. "I think of it as a corporate ritual. Which means, yes, all for effect."

"Emotional impact is likely more efficacious than the legal system these days," Colfax said.

Eve sat sideways on the couch, facing her father, looking serious. "Here's what happened, Dad. It was October first. I had just finished teaching an ethics course in emergency self-triage for my social work students. You know, addressing moral injury and the like. God knows the few social workers left have their work cut out for them these days. This impeccably dressed man was waiting at the doorway as I was coming out of class. He asked if we could talk. At first, I thought he was a government investigator of some sort, which made me nervous, since I sometimes re-establish the norm in class. Then he told me his name and explained that he had been friends with you and Mom since college, and then I remembered you mentioning him and Suntec over the years, and I vaguely remembered meeting him once or twice. I trusted him enough to get in his fancy Tesla. He took me to a little restaurant way up in Everett. We both turned off our bracelets and he re-established the norm with a few choice statements about the oligarchs, and I reciprocated. Then I breathed easier."

Colfax nodded and she continued. "I assume he told you that he is the co-owner of Macopro."

He half nodded. "*Co-owner* was not the term he used, but I am not surprised."

"And did he tell you anything else, like why he wants me on the team?"

"No. I remain curious about that. He said you would explain. Everybody knows Macopro is about scientific research, not . . . your line of work."

"Well, it's not quite that simple," Eve said. "When Macopro was a big deal in the news back in the early 40s, it was pitched as a pioneering project, with the goal of establishing a Martian colony for scientific and technological purposes."

Colfax nodded. "As I recall, they had aspirations of a major mining operation of some sort. They had evidence from the unmanned *Voyager* landings that certain minerals that were rare and valuable on Earth would be commonplace on Mars."

"Yeah. Think about that, Dad. It really made no sense. It made way more sense when they started mining on the Moon. I mean, don't lunar rocks have way more useful elements, and who could ever imagine shipping anything back to Earth from Mars? Nothing could be that valuable. The whole PR campaign was really implausible. But the newsfeeds loved covering it positively. We humans have projected our wishes and dreams onto Mars for millennia. So, the newsfeeds loved to evoke old romantic pioneer myths, the Martian gold rush, boldly going where no one has gone before. That sort of clickbait got lots of views."

"So, its actual purpose was?"

"I need to give you some backstory to answer that. The original co-founders were Simon Kuyper, part of the old Trump crime empire, and Vagit Deripaska, a Russian oil tycoon and an old confidant of Vladimir Putin back in the teens and twenties. I'm sure you'll remember their names. They conceived of Macopro as a life raft, a back-up plan if the oligarchs destroyed human civilization, something they felt their associates were all too capable of doing. They wanted to create a haven on Mars to weather the coming storms on Earth."

Colfax lifted his eyebrows, partly in disbelief, partly in surprise. "You just named two of the most notorious oligarch families on Earth. I cannot imagine a Kuyper or Deripaska doing anything remotely humanitarian. They were death angels, not saviors."

"I'm not saying they were humanitarians. They envisioned Mars Colonization Project as their private retreat so their families and cronies would have safe passage to Mars if things got too bad here. And you can be sure the only ticketholders would have been white, rich, right-wing, and loyal. It makes sense, really: who else could have amassed the resources to do something so audacious? Who else could have pulled the strings to make it possible politically? Who else would have seen at close range how dangerous their fellow oligarchs were? And who else would have been so invested in old-fashioned Russian American white supremacy?"

"Ah." Colfax replied. "You remind me of that time a certain American president wanted to purchase Greenland. In a time of runaway global warming, everyone, it seems, needs a cold and desolate land to call their own. Those are the oligarchs we know and loathe, full of unalloyed and voracious self-interest."

"It wasn't *purely* self-interest, at least not for everyone," Eve replied. "It turns out that Vagit was at least partially legit. You may recall he was a major donor to the mammoth de-extinction and reintroduction project in Siberia in the 20s and 30s, and that success seemed to inspire a real curiosity in him about science. He said in an interview once that walking the tundra changed him, that he had a kind of mystical experience under the Siberian sky watching the first mammoth herd resting under the Northern Lights. Weird to think, really, that a man like him may have had an experience like that. Anyway, he read the American science-fiction writer Octavia Butler, and he sincerely bought into her 'multi-planet species' Earthseed idea. That got him interested in the theoretical possibility of terraforming, even though Mars is a terrible candidate because of its high radiation bombardment and lack of atmosphere. I think his interest in Mars exploration was real, and I think his concern about human futures was sincere as well. That was Deripaska. But Kuyper – he was a typical American oligarch, incapable of thinking long-range or common-good. Pretty early on he started planning how to kill Deripaska so he could own the whole project himself."

"Why would he do that?" Colfax asked. "Other than penurious narcissism?"

"Actually, it was more a matter of Girardian rivalry. Kuyper was happy to use some Russian money, but he had no intention of sharing Mars with a rival. He wanted Mars as a hideout for his gang of rich American right-wing thugs. Eventually, they would return and . . . rule the world, or whatever was left of it. They had no idea back then how difficult it would be – if not completely impossible – to survive on Earth after even a year on Mars plus the two years in space to get there and back. Anyway, that's the plan Kuyper developed way back in the late 2020s: escape during the collapse, then return to capitalize on the disaster."

"The vultures of anti-Christ," Colfax said, disdain fully engaged.

"Funny you use that language, Dad. Remember the Reverend Jerry Hodgkins, Jr.? He was that televangelist who led that white Christian nationalist cult, and he teamed up with Kuyper for a while. He convinced Kuyper's people that the whole Macopro project was foretold in the Bible. They equated a voyage to Mars with something they called the Rapture, where they would rendezvous with Christ above the clouds, and then they would return to Earth to launch the Second Coming. They would slaughter their remaining enemies and rule the world as God's anointed overlords. Hodgkins was really the founder of the modern politicult."

"Yet another reason I have eschewed religion so religiously," Colfax replied. "Politics was insalubrious enough before religion added its ostentatious sanctimonious putrefaction."

Eve was used to her father's snark and wordplay. She tried to see it as an odd hobby, as her mother had always done. "Anyway, Simon Kuyper got Deripaska poisoned, but Kuyper made one critical mistake. He told his wife. Do you remember who she was, Dad?"

"No idea."

"Does the name Josefina Vargas ring a bell?"

"Sorry. I seem to be failing your exam in popular culture," Colfax said. "I would perform better on an avian identification exam."

"Well, she was from Brazil. She started as an actor in adult entertainment films, then made her billions in the virtual sex industry. Josefina was actually an intellectual of sorts. She believed in the importance of Macopro, and she was furious at her husband for killing Vagit Deripaska. She leaked information about her husband's whereabouts to either a competing oligarch or to a band of ecoterrorists who hated Simon and wanted to take him out. That's all it took. Simon Kuyper disappeared, and then, a few months later, Josefina Vargas did too. They say she killed herself, but of course, that's unlikely. She may still be alive somewhere, hiding."

"Why have I never heard about any of this?"

"Nobody hears anything about oligarchs that they don't want to be heard. After all, they own all the corporate newsfeeds and they disappear anyone who crosses them. As they say, 'Dark . . .' "

"As an oligarch." Colfax finished the aphorism.

"Anyway, Josefina took two very important steps before her disappearance. First, she secretly transferred the Kuyper holdings in Macopro to Vagit's widow, Ekaterina Deripaska, a brilliant Ukrainian woman whom she had come to trust. Then, she took out a huge loan from Piter Putin, one of Vladimir Putin's many secret sons. Piter was an old man in those days, and one of the richest men in the world, thanks to his father's need to hide his money in other people's accounts. Apparently, Piter was a fan of Josefina's film work. Anyway, he loaned her a lot of money and she secretly transferred all those borrowed funds to Ekaterina as well. And then guess who Ekaterina Deripaska hired to help her run Macopro, after its founders were both dead?"

"Thurman Howard Thurman," Colfax said, snapping his fingers. "But how would she be acquainted with Thurman?"

"As founder of Suntec, he was known and respected around the world. He was one of the few oligarchs who actually produced anything productive and legal, since most of them just bought and sold debt or used commercial real estate to launder money from their main businesses – you know, hacking, weapons, drugs, sex trafficking, stolen intellectual property, political payoffs, kidnapping, website ransom, identity theft, that sort of thing. Ekaterina needed to find someone with the brilliance to help her run Macopro, with the experience to navigate among the oligarchs, and with enough decency to be trusted. Not many people qualified. In fact, Thurman was probably the only candidate."

"So, Thurman and Ekaterina are now business partners?"

"Yes. She's a lovely human being. Tough, but lovely. Her ancestors survived Stalin's genocide by starvation back in the early 1930s and then Putin's war of the 2020s. With that in her family history, you can imagine that she has honed her survival instincts."

"You have met her," Colfax asked, although it sounded more like a statement.

"Yes. And you will too, if you agree to be part of this mission. In case Thurman didn't tell you, she and Thurman are . . . more than business partners."

The pieces were falling into place. Colfax got up and walked over to the window. "Thurman kept referring to this voyage as the last one. And he talked about minimum viable population. What is that about? Is he assuming that Mars will soon have the only remaining population of humans? Is there a deadly asteroid headed toward Earth that nobody has told me about? Are all those disaster movies coming true?"

"No. Or yes, in a way, except that we're the asteroid," Eve replied. "It's exactly the components of catastrophe that you wrote about in *Dawn or Twilight?* – climate change and all the other consequences of a dirty economy, plus the concentration of wealth and power among the oligarchs, plus the social control they gain by owning social and mass media, plus the fear and resentment they generate and direct, plus basic human susceptibility to fascistic authoritarians and their conspiracy theories, plus all the weapons at every level of every society."

"It was one thing to write about it as a possibility. But to hear you and Thurman speak about it as an imminent incoming actuality is . . ." Colfax shook his head. "You are certain he has not become a conspiracy theorist, a kook. It happens to brilliant people too, you know."

Eve replied, "That's what critics said about you, Dad, when your book came out. They said you were like a reincarnated Meadows and Randers from *Limits to Growth* in 1972."

"*An erudite luddite anachronism* – those were their exact words," Colfax interjected. "Much less politically dangerous than *wokist, leftist, socialist, eco-fascist*, which that governor of Florida used to ban me from the state . . . a state I had no interest in visiting anyway, except in hopes of seeing a swallow-tailed kite."

"Look, Dad, Thurman has access to the private machinations among the oligarchs. He told me that more and more of them are shifting their wealth out of traditional currencies, so that when those traditional currencies fail, they'll be holding whatever still has value – agricultural lands, water rights, political connections, newsfeeds, antibiotics, privatized infrastructure, weapons . . . and I guess remote real estate. Ecological overshoot leads to financial and currency collapse, Thurman says, which leads to social collapse. At some point, everybody turns against everybody for a crust of bread or cup of uncontaminated water . . . not just nation against nation, but within each nation, the police against the army, the army against the navy, spies against journalists, the courts against Congress. Every religion, every race and ethnic group, every social class, every branch of the military, every neighborhood and individual fighting for survival against everyone else."

"A total excrement cyclone," Colfax mused, his back still to his daughter.

"Yeah," Eve replied. "Who would have guessed that traditional currencies were the last vestige of mutual trust holding the human community together."

"Human community?" Colfax asked. "That may be an oxymoron. The etymology of the word is often mistaken for shared unity. It actually means shared munitions, shared weapons. Lasting human unity remains, alas, aspirational. You mentioned René Girard earlier. He knew."

Eve got up and joined her father at the window, looking out over the Sound. "If Thurman is right, the shitstorm is coming decades sooner than you predicted in *Dawn or Twilight*?"

"So that is where the life raft fits in," Colfax said. "The most remote and safest real estate of all is on Mars. And therein lies Thurman's urgency. The hull of the *Titanic* is already breached. And Thurman predicts that the ship will sink . . . how soon?"

"If he has a specific prediction, he doesn't say. But if he felt it were safe to wait twenty-six more months to the next launch window, I'm sure he wouldn't have made this the last voyage. This is not Plan A, not for anybody." Eve turned toward her father, watching him process what she was saying.

Colfax continued to stare across the water. "So, if we remain, we cannot expect the future Earth to be a continuation of the present Earth. Earth's future looms tenuous and tenebrous at best. I should have called my book *One Minute to Midnight*. Your scenario does not leave us with much of a choice, does it? We should abandon this sinking vessel while we still have the means to do so."

"There's more you need to know first, Dad."

"There is more you need to know too, Eve."

It had grown dark. The lights on the docks and boats twinkled star-like in the crisp night air. On the other shore, windows in distant houses blinked on, each reflected as a vertical dash across the water, some long, some short, like a series of shimmering genetic sequences or Morse code messages. Above the Sound, vaults of clear, dark sky with their own codes and messages opened between the low, luminous clouds.

"You go first," Eve said.

"My news is neither planetary nor interplanetary. It is purely personal. But strangely relevant to our decision. Hailey and I are . . . no longer a couple," Colfax said. "We officially terminated our relationship this morning, oddly enough. Just before Thurman contacted me with his end-of-life invitation. The timing was . . . spooky."

"Oh, Dad. You really cared about her. I could tell. She sounded like a lovely person, and you told me how much you had bonded with her boys. I was really looking forward to meeting her. What happened? It wasn't because of . . ."

Colfax felt his anger flare. He clenched his jaw and kept his gaze directed out into the night, focused on the shimmering lights in the middle of the Sound. "No. It was not," he snapped. "I have remained meticulously abstinent, in terms of alcohol, that is. It was her husband. He missed their young sons and returned, hoping for a 'relational restart,' to use his rather mechanistic term. Of course, Hailey, the loving and compassionate person she is, felt predisposed to forgive and forget all the previous relational restarts, feeling that one more try would be best for her boys. I imagine it would be hard to walk away from the West Coast's top-rated brain surgeon to take a risk on an unemployed and superannuated writer who walks on thin ice with the oligarchs' favorite politicians."

He cleared his throat and kept speaking, still not looking at Eve. "For her sake, I hope this time is different. At least I will not have to choose between her and you – if we choose to evacuate this planet plagued by human rivalry and folly, that is." Then he turned briefly, catching her eye and looking away again. "But maybe an evacuation is even worse. How will it feel for the two of us to leave behind everyone we care about to . . . to endure the kind of chaos that is surely coming? How will we not be plagued during every waking moment with survivors' guilt?"

"Well, it's not like we're getting evacuated from a war zone to a five-star resort. There's plenty of trouble on Mars too."

"No doubt," Colfax said. "It is a harsh, cold, nearly airless and sterile planet, high in radiation, and with something lacking in its magnetosphere, I understand. Which reminds me of something I need to ask you."

6
Universe 25

Colfax realized he was not quite ready to bring up his daughter's infertility. He needed a diversionary tactic. "I have an idea, Eve," he said. "We could both use a walk. Let us find something to eat. We can keep talking over dinner. All I have put in my gastrointestinal tract all day is a nimiety of coffee."

Eve walked into the kitchen for a tissue and blew her nose. "Nimiety? I've heard your fancy words all my life, Dad, but I've never heard that one."

"Nimiety is the opposite of dearth or paucity," Colfax said. "Everyone knows that."

"Not me. Didn't Mark Twain say never to use a five-dollar word when a fifty-cent word would do?"

"Did he not also say that the difference between the almost right word and the right word is the difference between a lightning-bug and lightning?" Colfax replied.

As they put on their coats and headed outside, they bickered playfully about whether that was an actual quote from Mark Twain or merely a quote attributed to him. The sky was clear now and the snowmelt had frozen quickly, so the snow crunched sharply beneath their feet and there were patches of black ice everywhere. Eve held Colfax's arm. *Just the way Ann used to*, Colfax thought. *I do not recall Eve ever doing this before.*

"Ms. Khung's Thai Garden?" Colfax asked as they left her cul-de-sac.

"It's your favorite, I know," Eve replied. "Let's hope it's open in this weather."

They walked down to the waterfront in silence, each in their own thoughts, and then turned three blocks north toward the restaurant. The air was cold, their breath visible. But as soon as they opened the door to Ms. Khung's, they were bathed in golden light and warm, humid, scented air. *A veritable baptism in the name of the basil, the curry, and the holy coconut*, Colfax thought, *the only kind of baptism I shall ever desire.* Just inside the door, four large koi swam slowly in a large aquarium, one orange, one silverish, one gray-white, one almost scarlet. Their body-mass seemed too great for the volume of water to sustain. A welter of philodendron vines dangled over the edges of the aquarium, giving the restaurant more the feeling of an unkempt jungle than a garden.

Eve observed, "We're Ms. Khung's only customers on this icy night. It's just us and the koi."

Ms. Khung appeared. She immediately recognized Eve and offered her a table near the back. "It's warm back there, you'll be more comfortable," she said, pointing. "For my best customer only!" But Eve politely declined and took a table near the front instead. She seated herself with her back to the wall, just as Thurman had done at the coffee shop. "You learn these things," she said to Colfax, nodding toward the door.

They ordered cha yen and their usual main dishes without looking at the menu, and then Colfax leaned forward.

"So here is the question I have been waiting to pose: why you, Eve? Why did Thurman want a person with your . . . background? You mentioned there was trouble on Mars. Something must have happened that made Thurman want to recruit someone like you for his last crew – at the last minute, relatively speaking."

"Come on, Dad," Eve said. "People have had spiritual needs since before we were homo sapiens. Jane Goodall and her students reported something like awe in chimpanzees before they went extinct in the wild, and biologists observed quasi-ritualistic behaviors in wild elephants when herds still roamed the African savanna. Even corvids have shown signs of ritual behaviors. You shouldn't be surprised, as a scientist, that there would be an ongoing interest in spirituality. Just because we're changing planets doesn't mean we're changing our human makeup. That's basic anthropology."

She was sparring with her dad, reviving an old sport they had played since she was young. Colfax parried and riposted.

"Come on, Eve," he said, mimicking her tone. "The same could be said about warfare. I hope they are not bringing rocket launchers or land mines to Mars too. And money: there is another construct Mars could live without. As I see it, the three – religion, money, and senseless violence – are often closely intermingled. Since they are not bringing a military historian or a banker, I cannot imagine why they would bring a theologian, especially because, according to Thurman, it costs over ten billion Americredits to transport one person. I repeat: *something must have happened*."

"*Touché*. OK. Are you ready for this? Brace yourself." Eve said, switching to a whisper: "It's—"

Ms. Khung came with two tall cha yens. As soon as she left, Eve continued.

"It's suicides, Dad. *An epidemic of suicides*."

Colfax frowned, shook his head, and froze for a moment. "Is that why Macopro went dark – to keep that news quiet, because . . ."

Eve finished his sentence: "If people knew about the suicides, it would have been next to impossible to recruit new crew members. Nobody wants to travel millions of miles to join a community where . . ."

Colfax shook his head again. "Except for dolts like us? What could be behind this so-called epidemic? The loneliness of missing loved ones left behind on Earth? Some deficit in nutrition or some environmental toxin affecting their brain chemistry? Sustained stress, perhaps conflict-induced, a hell-is-other-people scenario in the tradition of Sartre's *No Exit*?

Maybe some problem with a lack of sunlight, or too much artificial light? Radiation perhaps, affecting the brain or endocrine system?"

"Bravo for the quick list of options. Any of those may have played a small part," Eve replied. "I don't think there's one simple explanation. It's probably a matter of complex conditions, not simple linear causes. As you can imagine, I've been immersing myself in the literature ever since Thurman approached me."

"Do you care to summarize your findings thus far?" Colfax asked, dropping his head to look at her over the rims of his glasses.

"The first major scientific study of the subject was conducted by the great sociologist Émile Durkheim back in 1897. His—"

"Of course. *La Suicide* was one of the urtexts of sociology," Colfax interrupted, still looking over his glasses.

"Yes. That's true. And although later scholars have certainly critiqued some elements of his work, Durkheim is still a starting point for serious research. His findings were fascinating. Just one example: he found that in France where he did his research, Protestants committed suicide more than Catholics. He hypothesized that Catholics had tighter social connections and more social obligations. His conclusion was that one major cause of suicide is a sense of social detachment. When people feel socially isolated, their lives feel meaningless and so they—"

"I would think that in a community of a few hundred, people would feel deeply connected to one another," Colfax interrupted.

"Well, Durkheim also found that the opposite extreme also led to suicide. If the regulations and constraints imposed by a society were too great, some people commit suicide as their only escape from a sense of excessive regulation."

"So, neither a *nimiety* nor a paucity of freedom from social obligation are salubrious for mental health," Colfax summarized.

She ignored his vocabulary lesson and continued, "Back in the 20s, there was a lot of talk about *suicide clusters* and the Werther effect, the idea that suicide could be . . . contagious in some cases, not medically, but psychologically. On the medical side, researchers found some correlation between suicide and a shrunken hippocampus, especially the left hippocampus. But none of that research has proven practically helpful for the Mars community in figuring out what's going on there and what to do about it."

"They are brilliant scientists. Have they posited their own hypotheses?" Colfax asked.

"Of course. The Lead Triad – that's the elected group that oversees governance for Mars Base – have sent me lots of documents about their theories. One suggested that something happened to them when the Earth was no longer visible, a kind of planetary homesickness. A few became interested in Ernest Shackleton and his aborted expedition to the South Pole back in the early nineteenth century. I remember someone wrote, 'We're on a dangerous voyage without a Shackleton.' They seemed to think that the lack of strong leaders in the community somehow—"

Just then Ms. Khung returned with two more cha yens. "Free for you. On the house. The cook, she's slow tonight. So, the cook is me! I'm the cook, server, cashier, everybody! Nobody shows up to help me!"

Eve rearranged the dishes to make room for the drinks. But Colfax didn't want to lose their train of thought.

"And you are their substitute Shackleton?" he asked. "That sounds like a lot of pressure."

Eve made a face. "Their point was that Shackleton understood the importance of morale, but it's nobody's actual job to attend to morale on Mars. A few have wondered about *leisure*. You can only work and sleep so many hours a day. What do you do with the other hours on Mars? It turns out that being sedentary for long periods is also correlated with suicide. On Earth, we have a highly developed culture to help us engage in active leisure. But that's harder on Mars, where you can't simply go outside for a walk or a game of tennis."

Colfax tried to disguise his skepticism. "Do I not recall from the old vids that residents had an abundance of – what did they call them, enrichment activities. Games and sport and recreation and such. And do I not recall a documentary where they did a lot of dancing, which must be quite exhilarating in low gravity. I would think they would have had plenty of meaningful recreational activities for their spare time."

"Yeah. All that happened, for a while. But think about the words you just used, Dad: spare time, enrichment, recreation, meaningful activities, leisure. Doesn't that sound kind of . . . like they're in day care or prison camp or something? If leisure activities are the things you do to kill time when you're not working . . . maybe there's a connection between killing time and . . ." She didn't finish the sentence. "I mean, if you need to fill your leisure hours with so-called 'meaningful enrichment activities,' what does that say about the rest of your life? You only need enrichment if something is impoverishing you. You only need to intentionally schedule meaningful activities if your life lacks meaning in general. You only need programmed recreation if you're being . . . I don't know, systematically depleted somehow."

Colfax still felt intellectually resistant to something in what Eve was suggesting, and he translated his resistance into a barrage of questions: "What could be more meaningful than being on the frontier of human scientific exploration? And what could be more meaningful than survival itself, not just individually, but as a species? And if the meaningful work on Mars Base were not enough, did Aristotle not say the purpose of work is leisure?"

Eve shrugged. "I'm not trying to argue philosophy with you, Dad. I'm just telling you what's going on. It seems to me that survival was the preoccupation for the community at the beginning. But after basic survival needs were met, the equation changed. After some residents have been on Mars for a Martian year or so, they start to feel like they're gorillas in a zoo. Trapped. Flat. Impoverished. Soon, more and more residents start . . . 'pacing the cage,' is how Thurman put it once. They just stare into space . . . from their bunks, at the windows, out on the surface. Then they might take an excursion away from the base and never come back. On purpose. If you want to talk philosophy, Camus said that deciding whether life is worth living is the ultimate question of philosophy. And Thomas Hobbs said that leisure is the mother of philosophy. Maybe on Mars, people have the time, space, and leisure to become philosophers and grapple with the ultimate philosophical question."

Colfax rubbed at his goatee with his forefinger and thumb and then took a sip of his cha yen. Then he scowled and said, "I gainsay your point about leisure and philosophy. Philosophy most emphatically does *not* lead to suicide. The famous philosopher-suicides like Socrates and Seneca chose suicide only because they were about to be executed for daring to question the powers that be. Their act of self-termination was a final act of defiance against those in power, which made it a highly meaningful act, in my opinion. Have you been constructing a hypothesis of your own? Some form of acute depressive disorder?"

"It's too soon to call it a hypothesis. I would call it a hunch. I've been focusing on suicide studies from the 2020s through the 2040s, and one sentence from an article by a social psychologist has haunted me. She was recounting how many teens took their lives because they felt nobody really loved them. Their parents were busy and had their own problems. Their peers were competing for who could attract the most attention on social media. In the absence of feeling genuinely loved by others, they seemed to give up on themselves. Here's the sentence that I can't shake: 'The less people care, the more people die.' "

"You are positing that . . ." Colfax phrased it as a question.

"Everything that shapes people these days . . . the competitive stress of late-stage capitalism, the quest for a unique professional contribution in an unstable economy, the stress we feel when our trusted social institutions are being corrupted and dismantled . . . it leaves us all feeling that we have nobody but ourselves to depend on. Instead of turning toward each other, we turn away, or we turn inward, and I think – I expect that you will call this naive or 'touchy feely' – but I think that a culture of stress, competition, independence, and isolation has made us deficient in creating a culture of care, both on Earth and on Mars. And when cultures stop caring, people start dying."

Colfax frowned and looked down. But the critique Eve expected didn't come. Colfax looked into his second glass of cha yen. "Ah, now I remember. There was a name I was momentarily unable to retrieve, but it just came to me: John B. Calhoun. Does that name tintinnabulate any recollections for you?"

"It doesn't ring a bell, if that's what you mean," Eve replied flatly.

"Calhoun was a researcher in mental health in the middle of the last century. He worked for the National Institute of Mental Health and conducted his research in a barn in Rockville, Maryland, as I recall. He studied rats and mice. He constructed what he called *rodent utopias*, designed in every detail to provide for all their needs. His findings were . . . disturbing, to put it mildly."

Eve nodded and waited for him to continue.

"In his rat utopias, he found that the rats would congregate in the part of the environment where feeding took place, and as their population grew, they would . . . they would disintegrate socially. He contrived the inelegant term *behavioral sink* to describe the barbarity into which they descended. Most notorious was an experiment with mice that came to be known as Universe 25. What unfolded was, as you might suspect, the very opposite of utopian: it was wretched and chthonic. In Universe 25, the colony descended into brutal self-destruction and ended in extinction. You, or I, or perhaps we, should be certain to look into that research. Perhaps there would be some corollary."

Eve raised her eyebrows and nodded, as if to say, "I'll have to look into that." She mused, "Calhoun seemed to take a more biological approach, but the Macopro team seems to have taken a more psychological approach. They started where you did, Dad. They assumed the suicides were an expression of depression. And they offered all the therapies and medications you'd expect. But the residents on Mars didn't describe their experience as depression. They described it as *thinking*. Thinking about the meaning of life. Thinking about why anything matters, why survival matters. Thinking about values, about what has value. Thinking about why humanity ended up in the mess it's in. So, one by one, residents started deciding that there just wasn't any purpose or meaning to human existence. Not on Mars. Not on Earth. They'd . . . check out. And they would do so with what an on-planet psychologist called a 'flat affect.' No tears. No dysphoria. No big drama. Just a calm, rational decision to . . . turn out the lights. Less of a behavioral sink and more of a suicidal think."

Ms. Khung glided in with two steaming plates of food. Eve and Colfax took a few minutes to distribute their portions.

As they began to eat, Colfax picked up the conversation.

"So, is that why Thurman recruited you? Are they resorting to *religion* as a suicide deterrent? Instead of a Shackleton, they need . . ."

"Not religion, exactly, Dad. *Meaning*. The residents say they need meaning. They're brilliant scientists, all of them. But they can't cook up meaning in an equation or a test tube or a data set . . . or in a square dance class."

The two ate in silence for a few minutes, each in their own thoughts. Finally, Colfax spoke: "If this were not so tragic, it would be fascinating simply as a biochemical mystery to solve, a matter of brain chemistry and neurological wiring. Just how many suicides are we talking about?"

"Unfortunately, the numbers keep increasing," Eve said. "Macopro has been launching manned voyages for about twelve years, a launch window every twenty-six months, two launches per launch window . . . that's twelve launches with twenty to twenty-five people per launch. There should be well over two hundred and forty people living on Mars. But there are about two hundred. One hundred and ninety-seven last I heard."

Colfax nodded. "That is shocking, indeed. It's as if two of the twelve voyages had crash landed. And there is a strange irony here as well. Earth is nearing ten billion, which is four hundred percent of our carrying capacity at current consumption levels. But Mars is slipping down toward minimum viable population. And this is not a matter of disease or accidents or . . ."

"Not one fatality due to disease. Not one fatality due to an accident. Nothing since *Excelsius*. Screening and training and safety protocols have been excellent. You know, the famous Macopro Method. Triple-triple . . ."

"This is appalling. Nonsensical," Colfax interrupted, arranging his silverware to bring some sense of order to his exterior world.

Eve was firm. "Look, Dad, people don't talk about it much, but even here on Earth more people die in an average year from suicide than from war, crime, and terrorism combined. In this century in the U.S., four times as many soldiers have taken their own lives as died in battle. And in the general population, twenty people attempt suicide for every one who . . . succeeds. Even so, the highest suicide rate in any country is less than one tenth of one percent. But get this: on Mars over these last four or five years, it has been around four percent per year. That would be like over a billion people on Earth taking their own lives in the same period."

"I am . . . incredulous, or nearly so," Colfax replied. He took another sip of his glass of cha yen and then cleared his throat. "How are people . . . doing the deed?"

"Most methods are remarkably similar. As I said, they're well thought out and done discreetly. No desperation, no drama. The people who take their lives do their best, by and large, to minimize loss of equipment and avoid needless inconvenience for their fellow residents. Several have gone out into the Martian desert and dug their own graves to save others the extra work. Then they typically just . . . remove their helmets. Death comes quickly. Their blood decarbonates from the low atmospheric pressure, which causes an immediate stroke. Then their lungs freeze from the frigid temperatures, and they're gone after a deep breath or two. Their excursion suits are undamaged and reusable. Most of them leave a message so their remains will be easy to find and their suits easily recoverable. Some of them send their last words to the whole community. A final act of communication."

Colfax dipped his head and once again eyed his daughter over the top rim of his glasses, his tone mocking: "And what might their message be? I shall waste Thurman's ten billion Americredit investment because I am having a bad day? I am going to rob the only off-Earth human assurance colony of all my expertise – and all my genetic material?"

Eve looked down. She hesitated, motionless, for longer than seemed appropriate to her father. "There's something else I've been thinking about, another quotation that haunts me," she said quietly, followed by another long pause. "It's from an early twentieth-century English historian, or I guess better said, a philosopher of history, Arnold Toynbee."

"Of course, Toynbee," Colfax interrupted. "Everybody is familiar with him."

"Well, I wasn't. But I came across something he said when I was researching suicide. It upset me when I read it, and I still don't know what to do with it. He said that great civilizations aren't murdered. He said they take their own lives."

Colfax shifted in his chair. He was about to argue, but Eve continued: "I think . . . I think the suicides may be unconscious enactments of that realization. If I put Toynbee's conclusion together with the youth suicide research I mentioned earlier . . . if a civilization stops loving, perhaps its people decide that life within it is not worth living. I'm not saying that's a fact. But it is a hunch, my best hunch at the moment."

7
Ovaries

Colfax closed his eyes for a moment and leaned back. "I find that hunch a bit . . . clichéd. Romantic, perhaps, but not actionable. Whatever the accuracy of Toynbee's civilizational analysis, turning a historiographic generalization about civilizations into a matter of specific individual enactment is simply . . . unwarranted."

"You asked me what I was thinking, and I told you," Eve said. "I didn't ask you to critique what I was thinking, but you critiqued it anyway. Do you want me to say thank you?"

"Be that as it may," Colfax said with a slight wave of his hand. "It appears that Thurman is shipping you to Mars as a kind of meaning specialist. But really, would it not be better to send a social psychologist rather than someone associated with religion? Or a trained philosopher, perhaps a semiotician, some sort of reverse nihilist," Colfax asked, although once again he didn't phrase it as a question.

"Well, technically, I *am* a philosopher – of ethics and comparative religion," Eve replied, "and my dissertation research left me more conversant than most in semiotics. And reverse nihilism is not a bad definition of my work, Dad. As for sending in psychologists and psychiatrists, they tried that already. The suicides kept happening and no amount of psychological intervention seemed to help. In fact, one of the psychologists . . ." Eve didn't need to finish her sentence.

"That is stunning, indeed. Chilling. Perplexing. So, Thurman thought of you. You are a kind of Hail Mary recruit."

"I wouldn't put it that way, but I see your point. Apparently, he read Mom's year-end letters every Christmas. He knew about me and my research interests. He told me he needed somebody whose deepest desire was to . . . save people. And he couldn't go public with a job announcement. You know, *Wanted: Expert in Religion, Philosophy, and Spirituality Required to Stop an Epidemic of Martian Suicides*."

"Hence your recruitment."

"Yes. He was very coy at first. He didn't tell me about Macopro. He told me he was the founder of Suntec and now was working on another venture that needed someone with my background. I could tell by the questions he asked me that he'd already read my published work, including my dissertation. It was a little unsettling how much he knew about me."

"Look, Eve, we both know you are indeed amazing, but you are also young and I suspect a lot of others in your field have published twice what you have."

"Dad, this is a colony in crisis, not a grad school looking for faculty. Sheesh."

"I remain unable to ascertain why a comparative religion and ethics PhD would be helpful to suicidal secular scientists on Mars." Colfax emphasized *secular.*

"That's where it gets . . . interesting. You're right, Dad. Not a single person in the colony is what you would call traditionally religious. Some have grandparents or even parents who were Catholic, Protestant, Muslim, Jewish, Hindu, Sikh, Buddhist, Mormon, whatever . . . but every single resident with a religious background is non-practicing in the traditional sense. So, nobody wants a priest or chaplain. They want something very specific: a scholar with a wide knowledge of all human religions, with a scientific bent and a background in ethics. Ethics is really important to them because when they start reproducing – which they need to do relatively soon, they'll need a moral framework to teach the next generation."

"Ah. Would you mind refreshing my memory regarding the title of your dissertation?"

"*Towards a Research-Based, Stage-Relevant, Culturally Integrated Ethical/Semiotic Framework for Post-Conventional*

Human Moral/Spiritual Formation: Criteria, Approaches, and Models. Has a nice ring to it, doesn't it?"

"As if you wrote it for suicidal scientists on the Mars colony," Colfax said, not quite disguising his irony.

"Dad, your snark is wearing thin. I might as well tell you what Thurman described as one of my primary qualifications," Eve responded. "He said that if I could survive having you as my father, then I could connect with the scientists on Mars. He feels that your antagonism to my spirituality is what prepares me to be able to connect with and relate to the Mars Base community."

Colfax felt ambivalent as to whether he should be flattered or insulted. He frowned as a vote for the latter.

Eve was still talking: "Macopro leadership has given up on someone parachuting in – pardon the pun – and fixing the suicide problem. They don't even want me to come in and solve the meaning problem. They want me to help *them* solve the meaning problem. Here's how Thurman put it: 'They're pretty sure that the meaning of life consists in seeking for the meaning of life.' It turns out they're not unhappy when they're thinking about the meaning of life. It's more that they lack . . . support. I guess you could say they know more about exploring outer space than inner space. The language and methodology of science works so well for their professional lives, but for their personal lives, it seems to be . . . less than sufficient."

"No. That is absolutely fallacious," Colfax said, slapping his right palm on the table with enough force to make the silverware bounce. "I can testify on a stack of copies of Darwin's *On the Origin of Species* or Sibley's *Guide to Birds*: Science fills life with meaning. When you know how unlikely it is that the right proteins would come together to form amino acids . . . how unlikely it is that the necessary planetary conditions would remain constant long enough for sentient life to develop, not to mention intelligent life . . . how unlikely it is that extinction events would be sufficiently but not excessively deleterious to allow for certain new species to survive when other dominant ones went extinct . . ."

"Dad, you and I both know all that, and so do they," Eve said. "The scientific unlikelihood of our existence makes some people feel – I don't know, lucky, like they're cosmic lottery winners. They're happy to exist against the odds in a meaningless mechanistic universe, for a while at least. Other people feel blessed instead of lucky, as if they've been given a gift, as if the universe has been rigged for life to evolve, which leads them to believe in the existence of a lively, generous, creative transcendence or presence. But for other people, the unlikelihood of their existence makes them feel like a cosmic accident, a joke, a mistake, a non sequitur, a flickering candle in a strong wind. Their conscious quest for meaning leaves them feeling out of place in a meaningless universe, like they're an evolutionary anomaly that doesn't fit in its environment. And, as you well know, only those who fit survive, so their need for meaning leads them to . . . to diagnose themselves unfit for survival. So, they check out. They precipitate their own extinction."

Colfax smiled as he often did before offering a devastating critique: "I do not mean to discourage you, Eve, but all your theories so far sound . . . insubstantial. Interesting, perhaps, and at least peripherally relevant, but far from compelling. Are there any other findings in your literature review that may sharpen the diagnosis? Anything more . . . empirical?"

"One other line of thought might ring a bell for you. I mentioned that four times more soldiers have died from suicide than from combat so far this century. Various people have been studying that phenomenon. And they've come up with a term, *moral injury*, to describe what they think is happening among soldiers. When soldiers commit an act during war that goes against their moral code, they feel guilty, but in a complex way. They feel guilty for doing something their government ordered them to do, or something they never would have done if they had not been in a war their government sanctioned. Not only that, but when they witness something morally wrong done by a fellow soldier or by their government in general, they feel complicit in an evil that they cannot repair or atone for. Something deep within them breaks. They want to be a good person, a good soldier, but that route is forever closed for them."

Colfax was again rubbing his thumb against his goatee.

Eve continued. "If that sounds familiar, Dad, it's because it sounds very much like what you described in *Dawn or Twilight?* Page three hundred and seventeen. You wrote—"

"I remember what I wrote," Colfax interrupted. "I wrote that every member of our civilization is morally compromised because we depend on fossil fuels even as we call for their abolition. There is no innocent place from which we can speak or act or advocate."

Colfax put down his chopsticks and stared out the window at the empty street, and across it at the expanse of dark water. He was uneasy and he didn't fully understand why. In addition, he was still not sure how to address Eve's fertility issue and felt an urge to change the subject. "You know, it would be a shame for you to leave this planet without mastering avian identification. Your warblers are still quite lacking."

"My lack in that area is not owing to your lack in trying to teach me, I'll guarantee that. There are just too many species of small brown birds," she replied, then added, "and a *paucity* of chances to observe them these days."

"Fewer every year, I fear," her father replied. "Fewer insects means fewer warblers."

"But seriously, Dad, when Thurman told me I had to 'count the cost' of those I'd be leaving behind, I told him I couldn't go unless you came. I love you, you know."

"You were worried I would start drinking again if you suddenly disappeared." Colfax said, testing his hypothesis as he stared at Eve's face for any glimmer of confirmation. "You feared I would be swallowed down the drain of my own behavioral sink."

Eve stared back, unflinching. "I'd be lying if I said that thought didn't cross my mind, Dad. God knows you've given me reason to worry. But this goes way beyond that. I actually need you, Dad, not just for emotional support, but for your brilliance, for your expertise, for your perspective – especially because it's so different from my own. What they're asking me to do is hard and . . . can I say it's of historic importance without sounding grandiose? It's not just that I need you; I think the colony needs you. They need us. I don't think I can . . . save them. But maybe *we* can. You and I as a team, Dad."

"We both know there are already plenty of scientists on Mars at least as astute as me," Colfax replied. "And you know I have absolutely nothing to offer on religion, except that I stand consistently against it, thanks in large part to my own father and his particularly odious form of it."

Eve nodded gently. "You're right about there being amazing scientists on Mars Base: engineers – lots of them, for sure; physicists and materials science people; computer designers and A.I. experts of all kinds, loads of them; a few doctors and psychologists for the residents; smelters and thorium-salt reactor operators and electricians; agriculturalists to handle food production. But so far, there's not a single ecologist. And I think – and Thurman now agrees – that ecology needs to be at the center of the Martian culture as it develops. Not just ecology as a field of study, but as a set of values, a way of seeing."

"The survival status of koi in both aquaria is indeed precarious," Colfax said flatly, nodding toward the aquarium nearby.

"Dad, if human beings on Earth completely destabilize the global ecosystem, as they seem hell-bent on doing, they destroy themselves. That makes the Capitalocene extinction event the single most important moral lesson to build into the surviving human culture on Mars. Otherwise, humans on Mars will repeat the tragedy of Earth. If humans survive, it's even worse: imagine a million years from now how many precious worlds our unreformed species could conquer, exploit, and destroy on an interplanetary rampage. Our species could become a plague across the galaxy. We really could. Remember those *Star Trek* reruns you made me watch when I was a kid? We could be *The Borg*. That's why I need you to help me help them build an ecological culture on Mars, an ecological society with an ecological ethic, so humanity won't make the same disastrous mistake on our second or tenth or hundredth planet that we're currently making on our first. We can put everything you advocated in *Dawn or Twilight?* right in the center of Martian values. Isn't that something we can work together to build?"

Colfax froze for a moment, as if realizing something. "It sounds like you have already said yes, in your heart, if not on paper. It sounds like you are ready to do this."

"Yes, I want to do this. It is terrifyingly final, but I feel it is . . . what is mine to do. Yes, Dad."

"Well, there is one remaining problem I need to address," Colfax said. "It may be serious."

Eve squinted.

"Why did you choose not to inform Thurman about your . . . condition? I find it hard to imagine you concealing your diagnosis from him."

Eve put her hand up to her throat. "I don't know what you're talking about."

"Thurman told me that all recruits agree to procreate. He said I would be the only non-reproductive person . . . *non-repro* was his inelegant term for it. Evidently, he knows neither about my potency nor your infertility."

"Oh, no," Eve said. She grimaced and her cheeks again flushed crimson in that utterly Ann-like way. "He never asked . . . he must have assumed. Nobody asked. I never saw anything in writing. And they never asked for my medical records, I guess because . . . because I shifted the focus to you. Thurman must have been so focused on you, my father, that he forgot to ask about my potential children, theoretically speaking. Oh, good Lord. This could ruin everything."

Colfax thought she was about to cry, and he felt clumsy offering comfort. "Thurman must know, Eve. He is not one to overlook things. He pre-empts mistakes rather than making them. Is that not the essence of the Macopro Method they became so famous for: triple-triple checking every detail?"

Eve bowed her head, her eyes closed. "What do I do, Dad? Do I tell him? If I do, I risk him cutting us both from the roster, which means . . . we're both stuck here with all that's coming. If I don't tell him, if I keep a secret, how can I live with myself? Talk about ethical quandaries. Shit."

Colfax reached over to take her hand, but her fingers felt limp in his. "I have no doubt that your brain and your . . . spirit . . . are worth more to Thurman and to the project than your . . . ovaries."

Eve pulled her hand back and held her cloth napkin to her face with both hands. Colfax got up and came to Eve, kneeling beside her. She turned and nestled into her father's shoulder. Colfax could feel her warm tears on his neck. He stroked her hair and remembered what he used to say when she cried as a little girl. "Eve, Eve," he began. "This is a tough moment. But it is just a moment, and we shall get through it . . ." He left off the final word, "together," hoping that he could say it in unison with her as they used to do when she was small.

"Maybe this whole thing is a waste of time. Maybe when Thurman finds out I'm a non-repro, as you say, he'll rescind the invitation. So maybe the only thing we'll do together is be stuck in the hell that's hurtling toward us here, and it will be my fault, or at least my ovaries' fault." Colfax felt his daughter's body stiffen and tremble slightly as she cried in silence.

The two women I love the most, he thought as he stroked Eve's hair, *both crying in my ear on the same day.*

"Listen," he said. He took her by the shoulders and then put his hands on either side of her face, so her eyes were looking directly into his. "Listen, Eve. Thurman wants you on this voyage, whatever your reproductive capacity. I know Thurman. We shall be non-repro together. The Innis singles. A veritable lineage of Martian monks, you for God and me for science."

"This is serious, Dad. What should I do?" She sounded more like his little girl than she had in years. "What should I *do*?"

"I know what I would do," Colfax replied, returning to his seat and clearing his throat.

Eve looked blankly at him, waiting for him to answer.

"Absolutely nothing. Thurman did not ask. You need not tell. Any lack of inquisitive diligence on his part does not obligate you to wax loquacious."

"But how would I feel to be halfway to Mars and have this information come out. Or how would I feel in twenty years to be the only woman who never . . ."

Colfax squinted as he did when calculating numbers in his head. "Your presence among about a hundred other woman only increases their individual reproductive responsibility by one percent. Or to put it more concretely, it only obligates two women out of ninety to have three children rather than two. I'm sure there are far more than two who will do so gladly."

Eve looked across the room at the koi suspended in the water. "You think math will make me feel better about this? Maybe we're wasting our time. Maybe when I tell Thurman . . . maybe this will be the second time infertility will be a deal-breaker for me."

"Colin was a bastard," Colfax said, intentionally mispronouncing her old boyfriend's name as *colon*. He again reached across the table to take Eve's hand. "He was a cretinous rodent, and you have been far better off without him."

"I loved *Colin*," Eve said, withdrawing her hand and correcting the pronunciation. "So please don't try to make me feel better by insulting someone I loved."

Colfax tried to repair the damage. "OK. Whatever I think of that . . . of *Colin*, you know I have nothing but high regard for Thurman. He will want you on the team, regardless. I am certain of it, virtually certain. Look at it this way. If you keep one woman from committing suicide, you have earned your place. If you keep two, you are far ahead in the equation in terms of morality. I'm certain that's why Thurman never even brought it up. He saw this logic. You are an obvious exception to the normal protocols."

Eve was still staring at the aquarium. "But if I tell him and I'm disqualified, that keeps you from going too. I need to know if you really want to do this. I don't think I could cover up my condition for myself, but I would do it for you."

Colfax frowned. "That hardly strikes me as an appropriate decision-making strategy, Eve, especially for an ethicist. You are telling me you will go on my behalf, but not on your own. In framing it that way, you are avoiding taking full responsibility for your own decision. That seems neither honest nor appropriate."

Eve's cheeks flushed. "Are you saying no? You don't want to go?"

"I am saying we need to be brutally honest about this. You want to go, with or without functioning ovaries and with or without me. That is your hundred percent. And if I say yes, that will be my hundred percent. I do not wish to feel pressurized to go just to make it possible for you to go. I want no part in an emotional hostage situation. So, I want to hear you say that you will make this last voyage with or without me, that it will be your choice independent from mine, and that you desire this future enough that you will not sabotage your chances by bringing up a medical condition that Thurman failed to flag, which is *his* job to do, not yours. If you cannot say that, then I cannot say yes either. My own moral framework forbids it. Besides, I am no tottering, drooling dotard who needs senior day care. At least not yet."

Colfax folded his arms, awaiting her reply.

Eve started nodding, slowly. "OK. OK. I'm saying yes. With or without you. This is what I am willing to give my whole life to. This is where I'm needed most, as long as the reproductive issue doesn't present itself between now and launch."

"Well then." Colfax nodded. "We have that settled."

"And what about you, Dad?"

Just then, a few noisy couples came in and sat at tables too close for Colfax and Eve to feel comfortable talking further about the voyage, so they finished eating and chatted for a few minutes, letting Eve's decision sink in by not talking about it. Colfax praised the quality of the food, keeping Eve's question about his decision at bay.

Ms. Khung arrived with a bowl of mango sticky rice and two spoons. "I know it is your favorite," she said to Eve. "It is on the house for my very best customer. You can share. See? Two spoons."

"How could I leave this?" Colfax said, his mouth full of sticky sweetness. "*This* is the meaning of life!"

They finished their meal and rose to leave. Colfax turned on his com bracelet to pay at the scanner, trying not to show the CCTV how much he loathed the perky "God bless America!" bot. They stepped outside, and Eve turned to face him on the sidewalk.

"So, what's your decision?" she asked, her breath visible in the cold. "Stick with your sticky rice or go with your daughter?"

Colfax appeared to ignore her. He punched a few buttons on his bracelet. He heard Thurman's voice in his implant. "Thurman," he said, "I am here with Eve. We have reached a decision. Yes, certainly. Just a moment."

Colfax took Eve by the elbow and led her around a corner. He quickly scanned for CCTV cameras and said, "Eve, Thurman would like you to patch in through your implant." He touched his bracelet, and Eve did the same.

"Good evening, sir," she said.

"Well, let's have it then," Thurman croaked. "Good news, I trust."

"We have discussed the matter thoroughly," Colfax said quietly, almost reverently. "You have determined that Eve is absolutely vital to the project, *absolutely vital*, correct?"

"For reasons you now better understand, undeniably so," Thurman replied. "I need her. We need her."

"Yes. I concur. She *must* be part of this last voyage. So, Eve has agreed to go whether or not I do so."

"That is good news indeed, a real relief," Thurman said. "What does this mean for you, old friend?"

"I also have agreed to respond affirmatively to your proposal, assuming my presence is still desired. An unqualified yes from both of us."

"Good, then," Thurman growled. "I just arrived in . . . this place, and it's godawful late, or early, in this time zone, so I need some sleep before daybreak. After some meetings here, I'll be off to . . . to another location later today. You'll understand if I bid you good morning. And welcome aboard. I will see you both soon. My staff will contact you in several hours with the next steps. Until then, don't do anything that attracts attention." The call clicked off.

"So, it's done," Eve said. She took a deep breath and sighed. "It's done."

"You do not sound happy," Thurman replied.

"I should be happy, and I am, but . . . I feel terrible about . . ." Eve said, looking away.

"Aristotle said that whether you speak the truth or intentionally lie is a moral matter. How much of the truth you tell any given person in any given situation is not a moral matter, but a matter of practical wisdom, or *phronesis* in Greek," Colfax said.

"You have not prevaricated, so no regrets are necessary. Or permitted."

Eve nodded. "OK," she said. "No regrets. But I'm still . . ."

"No buts either," Colfax replied firmly.

Eve took another deep breath and exhaled slowly. This time, her sigh sounded less like anxiety and more like resolution.

Colfax and Eve walked slowly back toward her apartment arm in arm, talking just loud enough to be heard. Eve explained how Macopro staff would take care of all their final arrangements. "We'll simply become two more of *the disappeared*, something people are getting way too used to these days, between the government and the oligarchs and the thugs that work for them both."

When they reached Colfax's car, Eve kissed him on the cheek. "We won't need to say goodbye," she whispered.

Colfax turned and stroked the roof of his car. "Ah, but this sublime vehicle. I will hate to say goodbye to *this*," he said. He dropped into the driver's seat, voice activated the auto-drive, and as the car carried him home, he felt strangely free, strangely young, strangely alive.

How much can change in a single day, he mused. He looked in the rearview mirror and saw Eve standing on the sidewalk beneath a streetlight, watching his red taillights disappear into the darkness.

8
Clean and New

It was December 2, 2056. Not long into his third session in the Gauntlet, Colfax Innis vomited in his excursion suit.

One disgusting pink stain ran like a squashed worm across his visor and another amoeba-shaped blob of warm gastric liquid dribbled down his cheek from just below his left eye. A much larger smear ran down his chin, through his goatee, down his neck, and into his undershirt. There was no way for him to clean up until he unsuited. The bouquet in the suit evoked scrambled eggs and Pink Bismuth, recalling the double dose of the latter he took just after eating the former, in hopes that doing so would help him avoid replicating his experience the day before, when he vomited, experienced syncope, urinated, and shat himself. Twice, in fact: once in the morning and once in the afternoon.

"No wonder they called this infernal, insufferable torture apparatus the Gauntlet," he muttered.

Macopro engineers had designed the Gauntlet to help crew members prepare for the rigors of multiple Gs during takeoff and landing, and to expose their bodies to the sensations of high and zero gravity during the voyage. Many agreed with Colfax that the line between help and homicide was very thin.

"Being sixty-three is more arduous than the young can fathom," he mumbled to Thurman, who was trying to suppress a smile as one of the attendants helped his old friend unsuit. "The utter discomfiture of senescence is appallingly grotesque. And profoundly humiliating. Sorry to soil your damn suit. Again."

"Not to worry. They're washable. I recall you hugging the toilet more than a few times back in college," Thurman said, now visibly cracking a grin. "It's nothing I haven't seen before. And it's absolutely normal. They say on your fourteenth Gauntlet session you turn the corner. It has to do with neural pathways, they tell me. So, the humiliation bears fruit. There's no known shortcut to new neural pathways."

With the attendant's help, Colfax wrenched off his helmet, and Thurman handed him a white towel.

"Three complete, eleven remaining," Colfax replied, wiping his face and neck.

"Bodies," Thurman replied. "They have a mind of their own. We'll schedule you for two more sessions this afternoon and two tonight. We'll have you habituated by the end of the week, Innis."

"If I survive," Colfax replied. He unsuited and stood in his underwear in front of six or seven attendants in lab coats, all young Icelandic women. "All shame is gone. At least my undergarments are unsullied after this episode," he said, bowing to his audience.

The attendants laughed and clapped. Thurman pointed to the side of his own face, and Colfax wiped the towel on the corresponding spot on his own face. *Curious how that works*, he thought.

"When you're showered up, please come to my office," Thurman said. "I have some people I want you to meet. You'll be with them for the rest of your life. So . . . use a lot of soap. And mouthwash. And please wear some pants. And if you can, be charming, but not pretentious. Mute your show-off vocabulary, OK? I want them to like you. Or at least understand you."

Colfax bowed once more, this time to Thurman. "Understood. Your longanimity has reached its terminus. If my speech appears *sensu lato* bedizened or daedalian, whether or not I do so with prepense, you will require me to absquatulate, correct?"

Thurman shook his head and smiled. Colfax sensed that behind the smile, feelings of a less sanguine nature remained concealed.

A half-hour later, Colfax walked up the hall toward Thurman's office, freshly showered, fully clothed, with minty breath, and vowing not to say *nimiety*. It was early afternoon, but as he looked out through the window of Macopro's headquarters in Iceland, the hour felt much later due to the latitude. Thurman was standing outside the door, looking at his com bracelet.

"Innis, I sincerely hope you're feeling and smelling better. I want you to meet your fellow crew members. Four of them, along with Eve, are inside, and then you'll meet the final four when they arrive, hopefully in the next hour or so."

"Only ten of us?" Colfax asked, tallying the numbers in his mind. "I thought the normal crew size was over twice that."

"This last voyage is unique in many ways, as you are about to learn," Thurman said, opening the door. "Please come in."

Three unfamiliar women and a man were seated on orange couches in the brightly lit room. They immediately stood, joining Eve who was already standing, pouring herself a cup of coffee, her back toward her father. He hadn't seen much of his daughter lately. She had been working closely with Thurman to orient the final members of the crew and transport them to Iceland.

Before Colfax was all the way through the door, Dei-Lin Wu approached him, called him *sir*, grasped his hand, pumped it once with some force, and let it go decisively. She introduced herself and summarized her professional resume: she did six years active duty in the Air Force, then got a BS and MS in botany and agronomy with specialties in plant propagation and plant pathology. She had just graduated, having worked in an aquaponics lab for three years, as part of her studies. "I traded the life of a soldier for the life of a gardener," she said, still sounding like a soldier.

She was slightly below average height, with the lean physique of a runner. Her hair was straight and black, and fell just past her shoulders. Her smile looked friendly but disciplined. When Thurman told Colfax that Dei-Lin was from L.A., he was not surprised: she wore a tough urban expression on her face, as if to say, "Don't even think of trying to bullshit me."

"It's good to finally meet you," she said as she stepped back, with a slight bow of the head, formal but in no way deferential. She reminded Colfax of a red-winged blackbird, bold, clever, maybe mischievous, fast and sure of herself.

Thurman explained that Dei-Lin was not only the crew's master botanist and plant pathologist, but she would also serve as co-pilot. She had never been to space, but was Macopro's top scorer ever in all the A.I. flight simulators.

"With a small crew, a lot of us have to do double duty," she said. "My time in the Air Force plus all those hours I spent playing video games as a kid actually paid off."

"Quite a voyage for your premier unsimulated test flight," Colfax replied. By the look in her eye, he realized she was not certain whether he was joking or genuinely anxious about her inexperience. "I can tell we shall be in the best of hands," he quickly added.

The muscular young man standing next to Dei-Lin smiled and interrupted. Colfax couldn't place the accent – maybe Caribbean or West African? "Something you should know about Dei-Lin," he said. "She is a devotee of Trashno. If you see her head bobbing or her body making strange, convulsive movements, just know that's what's playing in her implants."

"Trashno? This is a term that has thus far eluded me," Colfax replied.

The man laughed. "It was big about ten years ago, although it still has its loyal fans. The only instruments are found objects, like plastic buckets or trashcan lids or pieces of metal pipe. And the voices are . . ."

Dei-Lin finished his sentence. "What he's trying to say is that there's a lot of screaming." She offered a shrug and a smile. "The name is a combination of *trash* and *noise*. Trashno music is an acquired taste. It's an L.A. thing. Big on rhythm, short on melody. I find it soothing."

"Give me an Afrobeat any day," the man replied. "I find it energizing."

Thurman steered the conversation back to introductions. "This gentleman is Ikemba Kalu, our pilot. He trained with the Nigerian Defense Force prior to joining Macopro just over three years ago. We have kept him very busy since he joined us." Ikemba took Colfax's hand in both of his hands, and seemed to vibrate as Thurman introduced him, as if his body constantly needed to shed excess energy. Gregarious and warm, Ikemba met Colfax's gaze with a broad and playful smile. He seemed to be looking for some sort of approval, Colfax felt, so different from Dei-Lin with her cool and austere confidence.

"He's had quite a journey," Thurman continued, "from a tough neighborhood of Lagos called Makoko to a decorated career as a fighter pilot, and now piloting a spacecraft to Mars."

"Ah, Makoko," Ikemba said with a wink. "Some call it the world's most notorious slum, but I call it an urban commune where we have so little that we share everything. From Makoko to Macopro to Mars!" His hair was close-cropped on the sides with twisted curls on top. His short beard was fuller on the chin. Thurman explained that Ikemba was the only crew member with space experience, already having piloted several trips to the orbiting resource hub that was so crucial to Macopro's strategy.

"He can fly anything and fix anything," Thurman said, "and there's no one anywhere I would rather have beside me in a crisis, because he is both brave and resourceful."

Ikemba told Colfax, with another wink, that he would be glad to have a father figure on the trip, then quickly corrected himself to say that Colfax would be more like a wiser older brother to keep him out of trouble. Colfax noted to himself who the crew's politician would be. He thought of the Abyssinian roller, a colorful bird he had seen often in Nigeria, with its flashy personality, perky audacity, and fierce yet graceful speed.

Thurman next introduced a woman of medium frame, angular, muscular, her hair pulled back in a loose ponytail, with big glasses, the kind that were far more common in the last century before lens implants and retinal remodeling became commonplace. "Dr. Soraya Rasul comes to us from Luton, England, just outside of London," Thurman said.

As Colfax reached out to shake her hand, Thurman continued, "As a biologist, she specialized in invertebrate biology with a particular specialty in entomology. She is an expert in the global pollinator extinction crisis and the great insect die-off. That's what's landed her on our radar. She will serve as captain of this crew."

Her dark eyes seemed mysterious to Colfax, warm yet serious, and they spoke to him of fatigue or loneliness, or both. He guessed she was at least thirty-five, on the older side for Macopro. She wore no makeup or jewelry except for two tear-shaped pendants of striking azure stones.

"I read your book, Dr. Innis," she said in an accent that felt half-British, "and I have long admired your accomplishments in environmental policy before . . . well, be that as it may, I never thought I would get to meet you. And now, I have the great privilege of working with you as a member of my crew." Only then did she let go of Colfax's hand, but still held his gaze. Her warmth had a certain power: invisible, magnetic.

"A month ago, I never expected to depart for Mars as a member of this illustrious crew under your intrepid leadership," he said with a slight nod. They exchanged a few more pleasantries, and just as Thurman took Colfax's arm to steer him toward the next crew member, Colfax turned back toward Soraya. "May I say, those earrings are stunning. I have never seen stones quite like them before. Are they—"

"They're lapis lazuli from Afghanistan, a family heirloom from my father's side," she said. That simple fact told Colfax a lot about her story, and he made a mental note to ask her more about it in the future. He associated her with a demoiselle crane with her deep moist eyes: regal, self-possessed, understated in beauty.

Finally, Thurman introduced Dr. Gabriela Mercedes Coroy, her long black hair in a single braid across her left shoulder, her skin dark, her lips full, wearing a multicolor blouse that reminded Colfax of designs he had seen in Central America. Colfax noticed that the left side of her face was slightly scarred and her left ear slightly disfigured. She was from Guatemala, Thurman explained, and would serve as Soraya's first mate, as well as crew medic. "She earned her BS in biology at eighteen, her MS in amphibian ecology at twenty, and a PhD in genetic engineering at twenty-two, all three accelerated degrees from Harvard as part of a single scholarship. She is obviously a real slacker," Thurman added with a grin.

Her name sounded familiar, and then Colfax recalled why. "Do I remember correctly – that you authored that breakthrough article in *Nature* on epigenetic adaptation among corals in warming ambient ocean temperatures and falling pH levels?" he asked. "I footnoted that research in my book. A rare sign of hope these days. I admire what you have accomplished, although it remains truly tragic how the world's coral reefs are . . ."

Gabriela interrupted: "My most famous article was not about coral, and it was not in a scholarly journal. It was about the release of methane in shallow Arctic seas and it went viral online. You may have heard . . ."

"You?" Colfax exclaimed. "You wrote that article? I have forgotten its clever, though somewhat crude, name."

"*When the Earth Farts, It's No Joke*," Gabriela replied, taking a bow. "It succeeded in getting attention, but sadly, it did not succeed in getting governments to take action."

"Believe me, Gabriela, I empathize," Colfax replied. "My entire career has been characterized by a rapid careening from one failure to the next. The only constant has been being ignored."

"Dr. Innis, when you mention my research, it reminds me of a funny story. Would you mind if I tell it to you?"

Colfax was not a fan of funny stories and jokes. But he remembered how Thurman urged him to be friendly. He opened his eyes as if surprised and smiled, convincingly, he hoped.

"OK. Well, during my coral research, I was snorkeling along a coral reef one day and I saw something really colorful but really scary waving at least a hundred arms in the current, like this . . . I had never seen anything like it before and wondered if it was a friend or . . . anemone."

She waited for Colfax to laugh, but he didn't. So, she started laughing so enthusiastically that after a second, everyone else, including Colfax, joined in. He felt that if she was having so much fun laughing at the story, he should join her in at least a chuckle.

She seemed to Colfax to be a contradiction: obviously brilliant but also funny in a low-brow sort of way, extremely confident yet . . . was it shyness that hid behind her confidence? Or was it self-doubt? Colfax thought of the endangered wood thrush, that haunting singer of deep forests whose unique, liquid melody he heard only once about twenty years earlier, and still remembered. There were rumors that they had gone extinct in recent years, but Colfax held out hope that at least a few survived somewhere in remote patches of forest in Guatemala during the winter and northern Pennsylvania during the summer.

Now Thurman spoke about Colfax to the others. As he spoke, he turned his head slowly, left to right, owl-like, Colfax thought. "You already know a lot about our senior crew member, Colfax Innis," Thurman said in his resonant bass voice. "You briefly met his daughter last week, before I rushed her away to help us with our final recruits, and now you finally get to meet him. Dr. Innis headed the American EPA before American politicult – shall we say, drowned it in a bathtub? – a few years ago. His specialty on Mars will be ecology. A little-known fact: Dr. Innis is a dedicated birder who knows the Latin genus and species names for every bird on Earth and carries binoculars wherever he goes. Did you bring them here to Iceland? Of course you did." He smiled with a tilt of his head. "Another little-known fact: he and I went to Vanderbilt together, where we tested and occasionally exceeded our capacity for the consumption of hop-based beverages and other herbal remedies. One last fact, which is more of a warning: if he is cross with you, he will deftly combine polysyllabic Latinate insults with Anglo-Saxon expletives. Those of us who know and love him have learned to take his intelligence seriously, but not his habitual pedantry or occasional outbursts of profanity."

This introduction drew some smiles, comments, and questions. Thurman seemed comfortable in his role as master of ceremonies and Colfax felt a rush of unexpected pleasure that this great man, a figure of historic proportions, really, was happy to be known as his friend of considerable long-standing.

Thurman looked down at his bracelet. "Colfax has an hour before his next Gauntlet session on the ground floor. Soraya, will you and your team give him a virtual tour of the LVRV? Use the holographic projector in the second-floor control center. And please do not offer him anything to eat. He spent yesterday afternoon and the whole morning in the Gauntlet, making up for lost time. He's still eleven sessions short of fourteen."

As the crew turned to leave, Thurman said, "Eve, I need your help with something. Please stay."

As Colfax left with his flock of new colleagues, he caught Eve's eye and she gave him a smile and a nod, pert and bright like a song sparrow, he thought. He felt a wave of gratitude for her as the door closed behind him: *If not for Eve, I would still be shipwrecked in Seattle, disconsolate in fog and feeling utterly alone.*

9
Stromatolites

Colfax and his four companions boarded an elevator, and before the doors had closed, Ikemba began telling Colfax stories about his first Gauntlet experiences several years earlier. Then Dei-Lin followed with her more recent experiences, each involving bodily discharges of various types that would normally be embarrassing to talk about. By the time they left the elevator, Colfax understood that these four had been at the Iceland facility for several weeks already and were completely at ease with one other. He was not sure where and how he would fit in. Most groups he had ever been a part of, he was also in charge of.

When the elevator door opened, Colfax stepped across the hallway and looked down through a large window at the front entrance of the office building he had entered through the back. There was no sign on the exterior. In fact, the gray 1970s-style structure was as nondescript as a six-story building could be, even though it was just across the street from the Icelandic prime minister's office. Apart from the security screening at the entrance, they could have been in an accounting office or medical center, Colfax thought.

They reached the midpoint of a long, featureless hallway and stopped at an unmarked door with an electric keypad instead of a handle.

"I am still somewhat confounded about the diminutive size of our crew," Colfax said.

"This launch is different in many ways," Soraya replied, her hand poised just above the keypad. "We should continue this conversation inside."

She tapped the keypad, the door clicked and opened, and the five recruits filed into a room as impressive on the inside as it was unexceptional on the outside. Colfax sensed that the others had been inside before, but even they seemed impressed by the array of screens and CCTV feeds that covered the walls, not to mention three large holo-tables. They arranged themselves around one of the holo-tables. Only Soraya remained standing.

Soraya leaned over the table, two straight arms perched on ten fingers, the illuminated surface lighting her face from below. "So, that's the first thing you need to know, Dr. Innis, about this last voyage. It's different. Different crew size, different payload, different mission."

She continued. "Our previous launches have carried twenty-one to twenty-four crew members, along with large payloads of equipment and a limited cargo of plants and animals needed for agriculture. But on this final voyage, the proportions are different. Our human crew and equipment payload have been dramatically reduced so we can greatly expand our non-food flora and fauna. In addition to the live specimens, we are carrying one of the largest seed and spore banks ever assembled, the result of hard work by Thurman and Dei-Lin."

Soraya reached to her right and put her hand on Gabriela's forearm. "We are also carrying an equally important gene bank that Gabriela assembled for her previous employer, long before she knew how precious it would be for this last voyage. It's the largest portable repository of DNA ever collected – human, plant, animal, and eukaryotic. It represents four billion years of evolution on this wet blue planet. Her repository includes a massive microbiome and fungal bank drawn from Earth's forests, savannas, tundra, and deserts, as well as from the deep crust and mantle. These biome banks will be essential in helping us establish beneficial bacterial and mycorrhizal communities in all our greenhouses. These repositories are, I would say without any hesitation, the most precious non-human cargo in the history of the universe. Together with the living specimens we will transport, these banks will be essential to the long-term evolution of life on the dry red planet where we will all spend the rest of our lives."

Colfax replied, "I am . . . speechless, a rare experience for me. The expansive extent of your endeavor surpasses anything I might have imagined."

Dei-Lin, seated directly across from Colfax, spoke up. "Well, it's our shared endeavor now, Dr. Innis, yourself included. I'm sure you know about the *situation* at Mars Base. One of our working theories is that human beings evolved as part of vibrant ecosystems on Earth. We suspect that if people are extracted for a long period from a living system, depression results. Gabriela calls it ecological loneliness. The original Macopro plan involved rather sterile living and working spaces, entirely separated from the agricultural greenhouses. Over the last year, they've already been modifying that plan, trying to integrate living things into all spaces. Our living cargo will boost that process. There are two greenhouses now, and they are at this moment in the process of converting them from agricultural monoculture to diverse permaculture. But we are going to recommend that the colony creates, literally, hundreds more greenhouses over the coming years, and ultimately thousands. We realize we need to get into the larger life and ecosystem business, not just the human survival business, if we want this project to succeed. How do you say it, Gabriela?"

"We have to center the web of life and decenter our species," Gabriela said, on cue.

Colfax nodded. "I am drawn to this scientific approach to dealing with suicidal depression far more than . . . alternatives," he said, realizing too late that he had slighted his daughter's work.

He noticed that Soraya's eyes seemed to narrow for a brief second, but whatever bothered her, she decided to let it pass. "We have used several criteria in selecting living species to bring with us. Many will serve as a food item for other species, and many will eat other species, helping us sustain ecological balances. Many species will enhance habitats or create microhabitats. In general, we're looking for species that will contribute to holistic ecosystemic well-being rather than . . ."

"Set the world on fire," Colfax completed her sentence, "as ours is doing."

"We have a lot to learn from our fellow species," Soraya said, smiling. "Thurman often speaks of the *beautiful logic of life*."

Gabriela spoke. "Take worms, for example. We'll have several large worm, arthropod, and isopod colonies on this voyage. They'll serve as food items for reptiles, amphibians, and fish, of course. The little critters will also create compost for soil out of our waste products. And over time, they will create the bioactive soil communities that will form the substrate – very literally – for all future land life on Mars. They're not glamorous, but they're absolutely necessary, and they contribute so much to the larger ecosystems they're part of. I mean, it's only recently that we've begun to appreciate the amazing evolutionary community of a mature soil system. Worms and fungi look like superheroes in that story—"

Dei-Lin interrupted Gabriela: "Dr. Innis, wait until we tell you about our special collection of tundra and krummholz lichens, mosses, plants, and shrubs. We hope to establish a greenhouse where they can grow with as little artificial climate control as possible."

Now Soraya interrupted Dei-Lin: "Dei-Lin, we're going to have a long voyage ahead of us for you and Gabriela to inform Dr. Innis and the rest of us about the wonders of mature soil systems and tundra and krummholz ecosystems. I imagine we have a lot to learn."

Gabriela and Dei-Lin smiled at each other. "You do!" they said in unison, with a laugh. "Gabriela and I will be happy to teach you everything we know," Dei-Lin added.

Soraya continued: "As I was saying, we're also choosing robust and adaptable species that we believe can survive the nine-month voyage in weightlessness, and then thrive, reproduce, and coexist in the evolving low-gravity microhabitats that we and they will co-create in the coming centuries."

Colfax responded, "I can only imagine how challenging it has been to meet that adaptability criterion."

"Yes. The issue of weightlessness presents a wide range of difficulties for the voyage, from waste management to stress management to nutritional management and exercise. Then, after surviving the voyage, our menagerie will need to adjust to the environments we create on Mars. We imagine it will take a long time to achieve anything like homeostatic ecological balance – including *mature soil systems* – in our greenhouses. The old Biosphere 2 experiments of the last century made it clear how difficult that is. You, obviously, will contribute greatly in this area, Dr. Innis."

Colfax offered a modest bow of the head to acknowledge the compliment. "I have already been reviewing those experiments," he said, "crude as they were. I was more concerned about the psychological than the biological challenges. The phrase *irrational antagonism syndrome* sticks with me from the Biosphere saga."

"No doubt," Soraya continued. "Highly relevant to our . . . current situation. Your daughter Eve is our expert on that subject. Again, we'll all have plenty of time on the voyage to explore this with her, and you. Back to our orientation. Symbiotic survival value and adaptability are our first two criteria. Third, we have selected species from as many different orders, families, and genera as possible, so that eventually we can derive additional species from them, using genetic resources from Gabriela's gene bank and employing a range of genetic engineering and cellular electronics techniques, many that exist already and others that we hope to perfect on Mars in the coming years when we aren't working under . . . Earth's political oversight. Finally, we have chosen animals that we believe will enhance human thriving through companionship, aesthetics, and interest. As Dei-Lin and Gabriela said, we believe this enhancement will play a role in addressing the deficits experienced by the colony in recent years."

"Dr. Innis, you mentioned my research on corals," Gabriela interjected. Colfax wondered if she was setting him up for another joke. "On this voyage we will bring the first salt-water creatures to Mars. We plan to set up a large habitat as soon as possible in one of the greenhouses: fish, corals, gastropods, arthropods, even some cephalopods and a colony of siboglinid tube worms, along with a variety of marine algae. As I'm sure you know, way back in the 20s, NASA's *Curiosity* rover found outgassed sulfur deposits on Mars' surface, which pointed us to immense frozen subterranean saline lakes beneath the planet's surface. We are already mining that water, and we anticipate using it to create large-scale aquatic habitats as soon as possible."

Colfax nodded. "Salt-water algae species played an essential role in oxygenating Earth's early atmosphere, so you anticipate they will do the same on Mars, I assume."

"Exactly, that's our hope," Gabriela replied. "We have assembled a wide array of cold-water phytoplankton, along with a variety of cyanobacteria. We even have some living stromatolites we collected from Lake Thetis in Western Australia. We need a wide array of genetic material to work with, in hopes that we can modify them as needed through selective cultivation, boosted breeding, and genetic enhancement." She then gave Colfax a mischievous smile. "Speaking of genes, Dr. Innis, I'd like to tell you about a gene I once worked with."

This time he gave no signal of encouragement to proceed, but she did anyway.

"Oh, sorry. I can't tell you, because it's been edited." She laughed, and then interrupted her laughter. "I actually have a lot of jokes about genes, but I can never figure out which one to naturally select." Colfax shook his head and the others groaned. Without missing a beat, she added, "I know why bird lovers like you find it hard to laugh at my jokes, Dr. Innis. It's because you have seen so many egrets."

Everyone groaned again, as expected, and Gabriela smiled and winked at Colfax. Colfax was unsure about her. Was she a desperate attention seeker with histrionic personality disorder? Or was she more intentional in her comedic interventions? He hoped it was the latter but feared it was the former.

Gabriela now turned to Soraya, "On a more serious note, Soraya, I just realized that we haven't told Dr. Innis the regrettable news that we have made no provision for birds on this voyage." She turned back to Colfax. "Dr. Innis, apart from the chickens, ducks, and quail that are already part of Mars-based agriculture in our greenhouses, we have not acquired other bird species. We do have DNA samples of corvids, raptors, alcids, passerines, and many other genera, of course. As you know, here on Earth, there has been some success in fertilizing domestic bird eggs with wild germ cells. I hope to replicate these experiments on Mars. But now that you are with us, perhaps you will convince us that some living specimens should be included at the last minute. It would be such an asset to bring songbirds, as Soraya said, to *enhance human thriving*, at least that's my opinion. I hope I am not overstepping bounds, Soraya?"

"Our biomass limits are strict, and our time to acquire new species and transport them to our launch site is terribly limited," Soraya answered, "and that's without taking into account the issue of quarantine. But we have five weeks until launch, not to mention Macopro's bountiful array of resources, so within those parameters, as Thurman always says, what is possible is possible, especially on this last voyage. It would be a shame for us to have one of Earth's great ornithologists but only a few living birds for him to work with. The Center for Biological Diversity in St. Louis keeps a wide array of captive-raised specimens, and Ekaterina is on their board of directors, so I suspect they would cooperate if asked. Of course, confidentiality will be essential. Gabriela, would you assist Dr. Innis with this as soon as possible?"

Gabriela nodded with a wide smile to Soraya. "It would be my pleasure. I would be egg-cited to assist." Colfax looked down and shook his head, trying to hide his smile. He still wasn't sure about this bright young woman, but of this he was sure: Gabriela Mercedes Coroy was a force to be reckoned with.

Dei-Lin spoke next. "One of our toughest constraints for plant species is the 270-day voyage. For deciduous temperate tree species, this means that we need to simulate seasons for any seedlings we bring, or else bring seeds only. Then, on arrival, we will have the additional challenge of adapting to Mars gravity and photoperiods. That's your specialty, Ikemba. Care to chime in?"

"I thought you'd never ask. Dr. Innis, a Martian day is almost identical in length to an Earth day. But a year is six hundred and eighty-seven Earth days. Big difference. You also need to know that Mars is on a tilt almost identical to Earth's. That means there are seasons. But Mars Base is just south of the equator in the huge Valles Marineris rift, so seasonal effects from tilt will be minimal. The biggest issue is that Mars is so much farther from the sun that it only receives about half of the strength of sunlight as we do here. On top of that, Mars has a more elliptical orbit than Earth, and at its farthest from the sun – which we call the aphelion, the sunlight it receives has about half the strength it does at the perihelion, the closest point. Much of our light will be artificial, of course, but we must anticipate adaptation of our stocks over time to natural intensity and photoperiod, and we expect that photo-adaptability will be a critical challenge for many plants, and animals too."

"Soraya and I have been calculating the carrying capacities of our greenhouses on Mars in relation to reptiles, amphibians, fish, insects, and other invertebrates," Gabriela added.

"I have to keep reminding Gabriela that my insects and other arthropods have value apart from being prey items for her frogs, toads, and salamanders," Soraya joked, "and although she's always smiling, she is a tough negotiator."

Gabriela replied, "Really, your insects are so important . . . for pollination, for their interest and beauty, and yes, also because so many other species depend on them. One of our greatest challenges has been selecting mammals that won't eat everything that everyone else works so hard to grow. We've chosen rabbits, hedgehogs, and prairie dogs to live free in the greenhouses on Mars Base, along with some other small mammals that will be kept in cages. And we will bring our first small dogs, much to the delight of the Mars Base residents. As our first ecologist, Dr. Innis, you can be our referee and assure that everything stays in a sustainable, harmonious balance."

Colfax smiled and said, "Friends, I know my visage is relatively grizzled and superannuated. But I notice you employ first names for one other and forego the honorifics. Please do the same for me. You may use my first name from this point forward. Agreed?"

"Gladly, *Dr. Colfax, sir*," Gabriela said. She smiled at Colfax and made eye contact as her colleagues chuckled. Her smile seemed to him to be unironic, uncomplicated. The word *pure* came to mind. In that moment, he decided he trusted her. At least for now.

"Shall we proceed with the Launch Voyage Resource Vehicle simulation tour?" Soraya asked, and then tapped a code onto the surface of the holo-table. Immediately, a hologram of the LVRV appeared above the table, slowly rotating. To Colfax, the vessel's exterior resembled a portly aircraft, slightly flattened, without wings. He noted its spatulate shape, wider at the rear than at the front, along with the dorsal ridge that ran from the midpoint of the fuselage to its tall vertical stabilizer. The vessel was white except for the Macopro logo on either side of the stabilizer: a blue and red dragonfly whose two pairs of wings were infinity signs, the forward pair yellow and the rear pair green. That same logo was embroidered on the crew's shirts.

"There she is, Colfax," Ikemba said. "I'm no expert in plants or stromatolites, whatever they are. But LVRVs are my specialty. Isn't she beautiful? The most advanced LVRV model ever. She gets us into space – which is the *launch* part of her name, and then carries us on the whole *voyage*. And then after we land, every part of her will become a *resource* for Mars Base going forward. Not a molecule will be wasted. You're looking at one of the greatest feats of engineering in human history. I love her already, even though I haven't actually met her in person yet!"

"I am curious about the corporate logo," Colfax asked.

"Ah, that will make sense when Soraya simulates deployment of the solar array," Ikemba said. "Watch."

Soraya touched the holo-table again. Colfax couldn't help but smile as a section of the dorsal ridge opened and four racks of solar panels deployed from the opening. "Wings. Of course. Both elegant and functional. Impressive indeed," he said.

Soraya pressed a few more buttons and the exterior skin of the LVRV disappeared, revealing a simulation of the interior. It was pristine. It reminded him of his McLaren Gen II vehicle: as beautiful as it was functional. All Colfax could think about was how he didn't want to regurgitate in a Launch Voyage Resource Vehicle, under any circumstances, ever.

10
Evacuation Plan

When the virtual tour of the LVRV was complete, Soraya turned to Colfax. "Colfax, while you were enjoying your Gauntlet ride earlier, we were discussing a name for the LVRV. Because of the nature of our mission, your daughter suggested we name it the Ark, recalling the mythical biblical story. It seems appropriate because of our biotic cargo, especially the gene bank and the seed and spore bank."

Colfax tried to cover his distaste for a name with such religious connotations, especially when Soraya seemed enthusiastic about it. Influenced by Gabriela, he offered a joke. "I hope that choice does not mean you will nickname me Noah, as the senior crew member. In the legend, I believe he was five hundred years old or thereabouts."

Soraya replied, "Actually, Eve was concerned that you might disapprove of this name."

"Well," Colfax answered, "I do have another suggestion: *The Josefina*. Eve told me the story of Josefina Vargas and the role she played in making Macopro possible. What do you think?"

"The porn-star billionaire?" Dei-Lin asked.

"Is working in the adult entertainment industry worse than building a boat, shutting the door, and letting the rest of the world perish outside?" Colfax replied. He immediately realized that his overly clever answer had just indicted all of them along with Noah, so he quickly backtracked. "I jest. I can live with the Ark. And within it. I shall leave further attempts at humor to Gabriela."

Then Soraya reached over the holo-table as if to shake his right hand, but instead took his left wrist. "We have a gift for you, Colfax." She nodded to Dei-Lin.

Dei-Lin took a small box out of her jacket pocket. She opened it, revealing a new com bracelet.

Eve and Colfax had given their personal com bracelets to Macopro operatives just before leaving Seattle. So that the digital tracking bots would not detect Eve and Colfax's absence, those operatives would use them each day until well after the launch date as if Eve and Colfax were going where they normally go, shopping where they normally shop, and so on.

At this moment, all that was visible on Colfax's left wrist was a pale stripe where his old bracelet had been for decades. Dei-Lin reached across the table and placed the new bracelet on that pale stripe as Soraya spoke.

"You can't buy anything with this, and you can't call anyone with it either, except for us," Dei-Lin said, smiling. "It won't even access a quantum network until after launch. But putting on this bracelet now symbolizes your new identity as a member of this crew and as a future founding member of Martian society. Welcome to the crew of the Ark, Doct . . . I mean, Colfax Innis."

She snapped the bracelet in place, his crew mates stood and clapped, and Colfax felt something hard to capture in words.

"Well. I feel like a new man, indeed," he said. "Or a new Martian." He held up his wrist for his new friends to see.

More laughter, more clapping, hugs, and joking followed. This intense rush of joy reminded him that he hadn't felt this happy since . . . since he couldn't remember when.

Suddenly he felt as if everyone's voices and smiling faces faded into a fog of white noise. His perception seemed to shift into slow motion. He felt more disoriented than dizzy . . . a mix of euphoria and longing, and then a pang of sadness washed over him like a cold wave. *It is my instinct to share this moment with someone I love*, he thought. *Like Ann. Or Hailey. I wonder if there will ever be another person who fills that place. Especially because I will be twenty years older than anyone else on Mars.*

So, a bittersweet loneliness mingled with his joy, until the disorientation gradually passed, and he felt himself opening his heart fully to these young people, their smiles, their intriguing personalities, their vigor and brilliance and youth.

"Look!" Gabriela said, pointing to his face. "He's leaking a bodily fluid!"

She was right. A tear ran down Colfax's left cheek. "You four are as humiliating as the Gauntlet," he said, and everyone laughed, everyone except Soraya. Colfax reached his right hand up to wipe the tear away, but Soraya gently intercepted and took his hand in hers.

"Ah, this isn't a problem to be embarrassed about, Colfax," she said. "Your tear is a gift to our team. These are emotional days for us all. It is important that we are here for one another. None of us can imagine the challenges that we will face, but we must face them as a team."

"Together," Colfax said, his voice cracking a bit.

Heads nodded. Soraya's eyes brimmed, too, Colfax noticed.

"Let's get some lunch," Ikemba said.

Dei-Lin interjected, "Except for anyone who has a Gauntlet session this afternoon." She didn't even crack a smile as she placed one hand over her mouth and the other over her abdomen. Even Colfax chuckled.

At that moment, three things happened almost simultaneously. First, a blue light began flashing on their com bracelets and an alarm ping sounded in their implants. Then a split second later, they heard the faint sound of leather shoes slapping against the floor outside the control room where they were seated. The door clicked open and Thurman's face appeared: tense, alarmed. "A terrorist group has attacked our facility in Kenya, and we may soon be under attack here. I need all of you to evacuate. Fast. Soraya, you know the protocol. Please lead the way."

Being new at the facility, Colfax knew nothing about the evacuation plan. But the others seemed to know exactly what to do.

He followed them out of the control room, down the hallway in the opposite direction from the elevator, through a glass door, and down one flight of stairs, two, three.

Colfax was breathing heavily, from the exercise or anxiety or both. At the bottom of the stairwell, they came to a single locked door with a keypad. Soraya punched in a code and the door clicked open, not into a hallway, but into another stairwell, this one narrow, circular, reminding Colfax of a missile silo, lit only by a single light fixture above them. Below, a deep shaft faded into shadows, metal stairs spiraling down, a strand of DNA. Thurman led the way and the crew descended in single file, flowing like water spiraling down a sink. No one spoke. The sound of shoes scuffing against metal echoed downward and upward. Colfax couldn't help counting stairs but lost count after seventy, eighty, ninety. His thighs were burning, and he felt his pulse pounding in his neck.

At the bottom of the stairwell was another keypad. Soraya punched the code, and the door opened to a dark room with rock walls. Everyone but Colfax turned on their wristbeams – a function of their bracelets that he had no idea how to operate. The wristbeams lit up a nondescript white van that filled most of the space. Ikemba climbed into the driver's seat and the rest of the team streamed into the van. The van began creeping slowly through an unlit tunnel, barely wide enough for the vehicle. No one said a word, although a flood of questions churned in Colfax's mind. *How deep underground must we be? Is this an old lava tunnel? Is that why I am sweating – because we have descended into the inferno?*

Gradually the tunnel began to ascend. Curves gave way to a long straight stretch. After ten minutes of heading straight on, the tunnel took a sharp left turn. A series of doors opened automatically and the van entered a garage on ground level. When the door opened, Colfax was surprised to emerge into a residential neighborhood. Thurman was working his bracelet, trying – unsuccessfully – to make a call.

"What now?" Dei-Lin asked from the back seat.

"We drive," Thurman replied from the front seat, punching buttons on his bracelet.

Suddenly Colfax shouted: "Just a minute! Where is Eve?"

"I don't know," Thurman said. "I don't know. That's what I'm trying to find out. But I'm not getting an answer."

Colfax clenched his fists, clenched his toes in his shoes, squeezed his eyes shut, trying to suppress his panic, trying to keep a certain memory at bay, a memory that resurfaced from time to time like a recurring nightmare, the memory of a softball game when seven-year-old Eve disappeared and he couldn't find her. It was the worst twenty minutes of his life. Running from car to car in the parking lot, asking perfect strangers if they'd seen a little blonde girl with big blue eyes and a blue baseball cap, then calling the police, then frantically calling Ann, then Ann arriving. The feeling of failure, a father's failure to protect.

Then another set of memories came, unbidden but unstoppable, of Ann suffering night after night, insomnia, nausea, insane itching as her liver began to fail, the same feeling of failure to protect, this time a husband's failure to protect. He tried to speed the stories forward, to the scene where a police officer carried Eve to him and Ann after finding her playing in a nearby creek with a schoolmate with whom she had wandered off, bored with the game, oblivious to all the commotion, crying not for being lost, but because she was afraid of the police and their big German shepherd. He tried to fast forward to Ann's kind words to him near the very end, her forgiveness, her gratitude, her gentle goodbye. But he couldn't stay in memories of comfort. He kept slipping back. *Failure to protect* blared like a buzzer in the center of his brain.

"Stay calm, everyone," Thurman said. "Our staff is well-trained and we should meet up with the others at our rendezvous point in . . ." – he looked at his bracelet – "about twenty minutes."

Colfax noticed Thurman's use of the word *should. Oh, epitome of shit*, he thought. He began sweating profusely. He felt the urge to regurgitate sliming his throat. He cursed his body for rebelling against the control of his mind. To be nauseous and in the middle seat of a van . . . *not my conceptualization of a salubrious experience.*

There was a hand on his shoulder. "Are you OK?"

His eyes were still clenched shut, but the British accent identified Soraya as the source of the almost-whispering voice from the seat behind him.

"Of course not. I am completely nonplussed. About Eve. And the others. And us."

"Colfax, she'll be OK. Trust me."

He didn't, and, in fact, he felt a flash of resentment against her for asking him to do so.

For what seemed like longer than twenty minutes, they drove. A few people whispered among themselves. But Colfax remained silent, trying not to vomit. He started feeling short of breath and his heartbeat began to pound in his skull so incessantly that he wondered if he might burst a blood vessel, which made him only more afraid. *This is worse than the Gauntlet*, he thought. *Forget Mars. Forget space. I cannot even stand danger on Earth. I am nothing but a contemptible poltroon. I am suited to academic and bureaucratic life, not this chaos and danger.*

He concentrated on slowing his respiration and trying not to think of regurgitation, because if he even thought of it for more than an instant, he knew his body would translate the thought into reality.

Thurman turned from the front seat to make eye contact with Colfax. "Innis," he growled. Colfax opened his eyes. "Here's what I know. Eve went out to the front entrance to meet our final four crew members, who were accompanied by my colleague Ekaterina Deripaska. Before they came upstairs to my office, I received notice of the Kenya attack. I immediately sent Silva

Sturludottir, my top assistant here in Iceland, to find them. Then I came to find you all. Frankly, I expected to hear from them by now. Silva has received instructions through her bracelet to meet us at our rendezvous point, but she has not replied. That's all I know."

"How destructive were the explosions in Kenya?" Colfax asked, his voice just above a whisper.

"I know nothing more than you now know," Thurman growled. "But attacks like these are often coordinated. That's why we got you out of there so quickly. If they had targeted Iceland first, we might not be . . ."

Ikemba seemed to be driving randomly, turning through residential neighborhoods, pulling in and out of shopping centers. He glanced frequently in the rearview mirror. Eventually he pulled into a small parking lot and drove behind a bland warehouse. Just as he pulled into a parking spot, another van screeched to a stop beside them. It was white, but its windows were tinted and looked black, opaque. *A friend or an enemy?* Colfax wondered, and he couldn't help but remember Gabriela's coral reef joke. It wasn't funny now. Not at all.

He put his hand over his mouth, trying not to puke, and clenched his eyes, expecting machine-gun fire. Instead, a fist started banging on the window and he heard tense voices shouting.

11
White Vans

"Dad?" It was Eve's voice. "Dad!"

She had jumped out of the van with the tinted windows and was peering through the side window of the van in which her father sat with his arms folded and eyes clenched.

Thurman opened the door, stood, and spoke. "Your father is here. He's safe. And so are we all. And with you? How many?"

"Five, including Silva."

Something about that math didn't seem right to Colfax, even in his daze.

Ikemba interrupted. "Out, everyone. We can talk inside."

Colfax got out and Eve grabbed his arm and walked quickly with him into the building.

The sign above the door read, "Pípulagnir." *Sounds like pipes, perhaps a plumber?* Colfax wondered. They passed through a reception area and entered a large room that looked like a waiting room . . . scattered couches, a coffee pot, a door on the far wall with a toilet icon under the word "Silarni."

Once in the room, Eve embraced her father. "I was so worried about you," she said.

"And I about you, Eve," Colfax said, squeezing her harder.

Thurman turned to an older woman with short-cropped gray hair. "You are certain you weren't followed?"

"Certain as I can be," she replied. Her accent identified her as the Ukrainian woman Eve had told him about, Ekaterina Deripaska, Thurman's partner. "The Kenyan facility is in flames, in ruins. It was a fucking truck bomb. *Dermo!* You know what this means."

"It means that someone knows about the last voyage," Thurman replied.

Eve pulled her father into a corner and sat with him on a couch. "Here's what happened, Dad. When you left for your briefing, Thurman asked me to go to the front entrance to welcome the last four crew members," Eve whispered. "They arrived with Ekaterina in a nondescript white van, the kind you see everywhere here in Iceland, the kind you were just in and so were we. I was greeting the four crew on the sidewalk when another white van pulled up and several men got out. They surrounded us and . . . I remember one of them spraying something in my face and I felt dizzy. I remember falling and being caught, and the next thing I knew, my hands and feet were in zip ties and I was lying in the back of their van with duct tape over my mouth. Two of the new crew members, Nikau and Refa, were on either side of me, and Ekaterina was lying across our legs. Two more, Manindra Murty and Sangamitra Srinivasa were piled on top of each other near our heads."

"Your lips are bleeding. Are you hurt elsewhere?" Colfax asked, grabbing her wrists. They were raw from the zip ties, bruised, scraped, and swollen.

"I don't think so, but my adrenaline is still running so high, I could have lost my right arm and wouldn't feel it yet," she said. "Anyway, I was groggy and drifted in and out of consciousness for a while. Then, I woke up as the van was pulling off the paved road onto the gravel and slush. The back doors opened, and two men hauled four of us out and threw us into the slush. The next thing I knew, Silva was there, cutting our zip ties."

"What happened to the other two?" Colfax asked

"Murty and Srinivasa – the kidnappers drove off with them. Murty is a robotics expert and Srinivasa is a computer systems artisan. That's . . ."

"Why did the kidnappers discard the four of you at the side of the road?" Colfax asked. "And why did they retain the robotics and computer experts?"

"Maybe the four of us weren't the people they were looking for?" Eve replied. "Maybe the two of them were."

"How did Silva find you?" Colfax asked next.

"She explained that as we were driving back here. It turns out that Silva came out of the building just as the kidnappers were pulling us into their van. She was going to tell us about the attack on the Kenyan facility and get us to a safe place. She thought fast and commandeered the van that brought Kat – that's Ekaterina – and the new crew, and she managed to follow the kidnappers from enough of a distance that they weren't suspicious. When she saw them pull off the road, she pulled off too. When they left, she came and picked us up. She was afraid we'd be four corpses when she found us. Nikau – that's Nikau over there – was still unconscious, so it took all four of us women to lift Nikau into the van. That's why Nikau's pants are wet . . . we accidentally dropped Nikau in a puddle of melting slush. Silva drove us around for a while as she made her way to this rendezvous point. Nikau woke up on the way and was shivering so hard that Silva had to turn up the heat all the way. So here we are, thanks to Silva. Wait, where is Silva?"

"She must have departed," Colfax said.

"She saved our lives," Eve said. "I'm sure she's trying to find Srinivasa and Murty. I hope they're safe."

Colfax put his arm around Eve, pulled her close, and kissed her on the forehead.

Thurman called for everyone's attention. The group gathered in a circle, some standing, some sitting. Eve and Kat recounted their story to everyone. Then Thurman said, "Silva has left to try to locate our final two crew members, Manindra Murty and Sangamitra Srinivasa. I know we're all terribly concerned about their whereabouts and well-being." He paused for a moment and rubbed his brow before continuing. "I wish we were in better circumstances to make these final introductions, but here we are, and we don't have time to waste, especially now. I know that some of you need first aid and some fresh clothing. I have people working on that for you.

"So let me introduce you . . . first, to Nikau Ruka. Some of you may have heard of Nikau. Nikau's band, The Beast in the Jungle, had a number of hit songs back in the early 40s. The *New York Times* called Nikau *the pied piper of generation dread* because Nikau wrote songs of lament for the Earth and songs of rage against what they always called *the suicidal system of plutocracy, gerontocracy, patriarchy, and oligarchy*. Nikau's fans didn't call the band's live performances concerts. They called them *Wakes*. Multiple meanings there, no doubt. What is less known is that after a successful decade recording and touring, Nikau studied psychology and worked quietly as a music and art therapist with orphaned and traumatized children for the last eight years. Nikau's parents were born in New Zealand, but Nikau comes to us from Juneau, Alaska, although they were raised . . ." Thurman paused, apparently forgetting where Nikau was raised.

"I grew up in the Bay Area," Nikau offered, managing a smile.

"You've been through a harrowing experience in the last few hours. Are you OK? I know we have someone bringing dry clothes for you," Thurman said.

Nikau gave a thumbs-up and a smile, wide but strained, and Colfax noticed elaborate manta ray tattoos on both of Nikau's thick forearms. "I'm in one piece. I'm glad to be alive and in your company. For those of you who are wondering, I identify as *takatāpui* or *tāhine*, our words in Māori for the third gender." Colfax recalled religious fundamentalists protesting outside Nikau's concerts, carrying "Ban Gender Ideology" signs. Those protests had the opposite of their intended effect, boosting The Beast in the Jungle's popularity among young people around the world. Nikau's long, wavy black hair was streaked with a few strands of gray. *Nikau is probably the closest to me in age of anyone on the crew*, Colfax thought.

"*He waka eke noa*," Nikau said. Without being asked or even knowing what they were saying, the others echoed back the Māori words: "*He waka eke noa*."

"We're all in this together," Nikau translated, and the others repeated the translation too, as if Nikau were a priest or shaman.

Extraordinary charisma, Colfax thought. *Simultaneously commanding and . . . gentle, like a swan, perhaps . . . a New Zealand kakīānau swan.*

Thurman continued, nodding toward the young woman who was seated next to Nikau. "Refa Barghouthi is from Palestine, via the Bronx. She is – or until recently was – a college student, studying music. She is a multi-talented musical prodigy and has also been, since she was fourteen, a published poet. Refa is the youngest person ever recruited for a Macopro crew. She and Nikau have already proven their courage and resilience in what they've endured today. Welcome, Refa, welcome to both of you. I'm sorry you've had to endure this terrifying experience."

Refa smiled, a little more defiant than afraid in Colfax's reckoning, but said nothing beyond, "Glad to be here. And, as Nikau said, in one piece and in your company. I'm just worried about the other two."

As tears pooled in her eyes, Colfax noticed a scrape on the side of Refa's face, and like Eve, her lips had dried blood on them. *From the duct tape*, Colfax surmised. *She is tough but brilliant, like a corvid . . . ah, yes, the hooded crow, of course*, he thought, remembering his many encounters with them across Europe and the Middle East.

Thurman encouraged the group to welcome the new crew members, then excused himself with Ekaterina and Soraya to speak privately in an adjoining room.

Refa came over and sat down near Eve and Colfax. Ikemba, Gabriela, and Dei-Lin gathered around Nikau.

Colfax suspected that Refa would rather not talk further about the abduction. To change the subject, he told Refa that he had done ornithological surveys in the West Bank and Gaza back in the 30s. Refa immediately asked him if he ever saw the Palestinian sunbird. "Ah, *Cinnyris osea*," he replied. "I remember watching one feeding on a cluster of cactus flowers with its decurved bill. What a treasure. The iridescent blue, green, and indigo. Unforgettable."

Refa smiled faintly, and soon she was telling a bit of her story: "My father's ancestors were from the ancient city of Taybeh. His family identified as Christian, but he was raised without religion. When Taybeh was annexed into Israel in 1967, my dad's ancestors were displaced to a refugee camp. My dad, his father, and his grandfather were all born in that camp. Three generations waiting for a resolution that never came.

"He was radicalized when he was fourteen, after the Hamas attacks on Israel in '23 and the horrific violence of the following years. For him, being radicalized meant he became a nonviolent political organizer working for Palestinian human rights. In his activism work, he met an Israeli activist who was also working for Palestinian equality, and the two of them fell in love and got married in '32. Israeli laws had been changed, so that if a citizen married a noncitizen, the citizen lost their citizenship. That meant that my mom became a refugee herself. I was born in '38, in the same camp as my great-grandfather. I guess you could say I come from an . . . interesting family," she concluded. "The refugee camp was poor, but everyone took great pride in keeping our culture alive, and that's where I became interested in music. My first instruments were the oud, ney, and santur."

Colfax nodded, but he had no idea what those instruments were.

"My dad was killed by a truck bomb in '51 when I was thirteen, and I guess you could say that radicalized me. I got arrested shortly after that for throwing rocks and gesturing at a CCTV camera during a protest. I showed them an illegal finger," she said, "them being the Israel Defence Force.

"My mother used some of her connections and was able to bribe someone to get me released. But eleven days after I was released, my mom was shot by the IDF and killed. My wage-earning relatives had escaped Palestine by then, and my younger brother had nobody but me. It turns out we had an uncle in New York and he took us in. He appreciated my musical talent and made sure I got lessons from the best teachers he could afford. In New York I picked up violin, cello, guitar, and piano. Then my little brother was shot by a police officer in New York."

"How old are you?" Colfax asked.

"Almost nineteen," she said, then added, "And yeah, I know that's a lot of death in one short life. Trouble seems to follow me, as recently as today. Let's hope it doesn't follow me to Mars, right?"

"I first heard of Refa through her poetry, Dad," Eve said. "That was three years ago. Then I heard some of her music. Then I saw a vid of her telling her story. I was so impressed with her. As soon as Thurman began recruiting me, I recommended that he consider her. I was so thrilled when Thurman selected her as a potential crew member and she said yes."

To Colfax, Refa seemed vigilant, her corvid eyes scanning the room for danger or opportunity, never at rest. He tried to reassure her. "We shall be safely out of here soon," he said, immediately realizing that he, like Soraya earlier, was utterly unable to deliver on that promise and Refa was smart enough to know that. So, he added, rather awkwardly, "I hope."

Thurman, Soraya, and Ekaterina returned and Thurman spoke, his voice decisive. "Friends, it isn't safe for us to go back to the facility. Not now or ever. The fact that there was an abduction attempt here in Iceland and an attack in Kenya means that whoever is after us knows too much about us. And this is our dilemma: we launch in five weeks, and most of you need a great deal more preparation before launch. We have much to do in the next thirty-odd days. If we cannot get prepared in time, we will have to wait twenty-six months for our next window. And I don't think we have that long. Our staff is already working on options for where we go next. So, we will have a brief wait here—"

Dei-Lin interrupted. "Just a minute. Is this some sort of test? I mean, is this some kind of team-building experiment, some final cut based on how we respond? Because—"

Thurman didn't let her finish. "I assure you, Dei-Lin, that is not how we operate. This is all too real."

"I wouldn't appreciate being manipulated," she replied.

"Nor would I." Thurman seemed not to be offended by her question. "My only concern, as I said, is that we have very little margin in terms of time before launch."

Nikau raised their hand. "Couldn't we just delay our launch – like even a month or two?"

"I wish it were that simple, Nikau," Thurman replied, "but getting to Mars is far more complicated than most people realize. It's not like driving from New York to Los Angeles." Thurman turned to Ikemba. "Ikemba, could you take a minute and explain our trajectory, because some of our new recruits haven't yet watched the training vids that explain the HTO."

Ikemba leaned forward on his chair and began to draw a large oval in the air as he spoke: "OK, my friends. You can think of Earth and Mars like two racing cars on this huge elliptical track, with the sun right here, in the center. We travel a lot faster on the inside track and we lap Mars every two Earth years. At our closest possible point, which is called our periapsis, when we're catching up to Mars, so to speak, we're about fifty-five million kilometers apart. But at our farthest point, when we're at this end of the track and Mars is far away at the opposite end over there, we're seven times farther away, about four hundred million kilometers apart. So, we work in very limited launch windows, because we're trying to intercept Mars when we're as close as possible."

Nikau interjected: "So you're saying our trip will be fifty-five million kilometers if we leave January eighth?"

"Ah, Nikau, my friend, if only," Ikemba answered. "Remember, you can't aim your vessel at the point where Mars is now; Mars is always moving, so you have to set your course to where Mars will be when you get there. To add one final level of complexity, we use the sun for a slingshot effect, using solar gravity to speed us up, so we take a curved path called the Hohmann Transfer Orbit: the HTO. Using the HTO, our 140-million-kilometer flight plan will maximize fuel efficiency and minimize flight time. Is that clear now?"

Nikau replied, "Do you want me to be honest, or to say yes? I'll just say I'm getting clearer on how much I have to learn."

"OK. Try this," Ikemba said, determined to help Nikau see what he himself saw so clearly. He marked out a circle in the air with his hands. "If you think in terms of a clock, when we take off, Earth will be here, at about seven on the clock face, and Mars will be out here, at about six. They'll be moving like this, with Earth moving a little faster on its inside track. When we reach Mars, it will be at the one o'clock position, and Earth will have moved to about half past eleven."

"That helps a lot," Nikau said. "It's a good thing you're our pilot, Ikemba. I'd probably take us to Mercury by mistake and we'd all burn up."

Gabriela couldn't resist. "Nikau, that reminds me of a little-known fact about Mercury. Would you like me to tell you?"

Nikau looked confused for a second, but then smiled and nodded, detecting a possible joke.

Gabriela replied, "Mercury is the smartest of all the planets. That's because it has the most degrees . . ." But before anyone could respond with a groan or a laugh, she continued: "And you might be interested to know what happens on Mercury to naughty light rays." Again, she didn't wait for a response. "They're sent to prism, but don't worry, they only get a light sentence."

"It may be a bit too soon for humor," Thurman said as a few people really did groan.

"Not for me," Nikau replied. "Gabriela reminds me of my sister. She was always able to make me smile."

Thurman shook his head. "As I was saying, our launch window is only two months long. It opened November eighth and ends January eighth. As Ikemba has explained, it can't be stretched. Besides, all our supplies have been loaded in at the space station, thanks to Ikemba and his fellow pilots. The robot crew there stands at the ready. Here on Earth, Soraya, Dei-Lin, and Gabriela have been working tirelessly for several months readying a menagerie of plants and animals for the voyage. It's a monumental challenge and we can't simply keep them in storage indefinitely. So, January eighth is, very literally, our last chance, given our delicate payload and fuel. That's why I said that on January ninth, the window is closed for at least another twenty-six months. There is no wriggle room."

Dei-Lin interjected. "I'm sorry, people, maybe I'm missing something. If terrorists or oligarchs – or whoever – are able to execute coordinated attacks on our public facility in Kenya and on our so-called secret facility in Iceland, what makes us think we can launch safely from either place?"

Colfax noticed as Thurman caught Soraya's eye. He nodded almost imperceptibly. She spoke.

"Our launch location remains undetected, as far as we know. That is all that should be said at this point. Even among us in this room, only Thurman and Kat know our launch site options. Even Ikemba and I don't know yet. Neither do Murty and Srinivasa."

Dei-Lin still wasn't satisfied. "OK. I get the need for secrecy. I'm not trying to be negative, just realistic. Because, obviously, somebody already fracked up. I hope you don't have a rat."

Ekaterina snapped back. "You can be sure that senior Macopro staff around the world are honest, loyal, and hard at work on contingency plans. There are no leaks."

"Who would do this to us?" Refa asked. "And why?"

"Long ago, Macopro fell out of favor with certain of the iron quadrangles," Ekaterina explained. Colfax recognized the term. It referred to a shadowy four-way alliance between oligarchs, corrupt politicians, organized crime syndicates, and religious leaders. "We refused to comply with some of their . . . shall we say, requests. Attacks against uncooperative corporations like ours are not uncommon, and they are often followed by threats of increasing magnitude if we refuse to, shall we say, share some of our assets, or won't assist in some of their ventures."

"So," Dei-Lin replied, "it's typical street gang or mafia tactics: oligarchs pressure each other to join them in money laundering or human trafficking or other criminal activities, and if anyone refuses, they are punished."

Ekaterina replied, "Exactly. Corporations who don't play their game or make the requested *contributions* . . . tend to suffer an extraordinary string of *nevezeniye* or bad luck: firebombings, assassinations, kidnappings, planned 'accidental' deaths, massive computer hacking, being framed for crimes they had nothing to do with, that sort of thing. Most eventually play along and ultimately consider all this mutual intimidation and mutual protection a necessary part of doing business."

She paused, then added, "The *Excelsius* disaster was one such act of sabotage by one of those corporations with whom we refused to cooperate. The oligarchs have little regard for human life, and even less regard for morality or legality. When they want information, they will employ the most inhuman forms of torture to get it, and in the end, they always kill those they torture so the story of their crimes can never be told. Their only moral imperative is to get what they want when they want it, and they measure value in money alone, money that brings them power."

Everyone fell silent for a few moments. Then Gabriela stood up and began speaking as she walked around the room. "Excuse me. I wonder if we are missing something here. It seems to me that the most precious asset on Earth right now is not Americredits, euros, crypto, or whatever currency you want to operate in. And it's not political power, or property, or even intellectual property, but rather – it is access to the colony on Mars and the means to get there. If that's the case, might some of your oligarch opponents now be waking up to the catastrophe that faces them? And might their real goal be not merely to intimidate you into paying them off with assets of questionable long-term value, but rather to kill us or capture us, so that they might take our place on the last voyage, and escape to Mars themselves?"

Colfax looked at her, impressed, and made a mental note that this cheerful jokester could be deadly serious when the occasion called for it.

Colfax saw a number of sideways glances as the possibility that this might be the truth sank in. He looked at Ikemba, realizing that a pilot may be their real target. Ikemba's jaws were clenching and unclenching. *He sees what I see*, Colfax thought.

Dei-Lin saw it too: "So I would think they at least need a trained pilot like Ikemba, along with an LVRV."

"Which might explain the simultaneous attacks," Gabriela added. "They would be looking for a skeleton crew, and especially a pilot, in one place or the other."

"Which would also explain why they kept Dr. Murty and Dr. Srinivasa," Refa said. "They have technical expertise. And it also explains our being dumped like trash at the side of the road. They were hoping for a pilot, but we were just a kid musician, a rock star, a theologian and . . ."

Ekaterina added, "And a *staraya zhenshchina*, an old woman."

"Thank God they didn't realize who you were, Kat," Eve said. "And less of the *old*, OK? Imagine the information they could have tried to extract from you."

Kat nodded. "And we know they aren't shy about using any means necessary to get what they want. They're oligarchs, after all. First, they deregulated the economy, and then they deregulated morality."

Colfax looked across the room. He saw Thurman make eye contact with Ekaterina, who said, "*Resheno*."

"Yes. It is decided." Thurman stood up, and the rest scrambled to their feet as well. "We need to get out of Iceland as soon as possible."

12
Floating

Colfax was floating, his face to the blue sky, a few white clouds suspended above him. The salty water was warm, maybe thirty-two degrees Celsius. The waves were gentle. *Christmas Eve . . . our last day on Earth. We get to spend it in the most beautiful place I have seen*, Colfax thought, rocking gently.

Before arriving three weeks earlier, Colfax had heard of Kiribati but couldn't have found it on a map. The tiny nation of thirty-some atolls and reef islands in the Pacific straddled both the equator and the 180th meridian, which meant it – uniquely in the world – occupied all four hemispheres. It was about two thousand kilometers south of Hawaii and just east of the International Date Line. About half of its hundred thousand inhabitants lived on the island of Tarawa. The crew of the Ark was on a tiny atoll seventeen kilometers south of Tarawa and a few kilometers east.

After the attacks in Kenya and Iceland, the crew of eight, accompanied by Thurman and Ekaterina, flew in a Macopro jet from Keflavik to Luxembourg, and then, on a series of private jets without the Macopro logo, to Delhi, then to Hong Kong, and then to this small private island the crew referred to as Gilligan's Island. As to who Gilligan was, Colfax had no idea. He asked Eve, but she didn't know either.

Dr. Murty and Dr. Srinivasa had not yet been located. Over breakfast that morning, Colfax had asked Kat about them. "Silva is on it from morning to night," Kat said. "If they can be found, she will find them. Murty was going to repurpose the robot fleet for the next phase of greenhouse development and start a robotics training program to disseminate her expertise. Srinivasa's role was to develop a computer lab and teach residents how to repair and adapt all the computers from the first twelve LVRVs, and also how to make computer components from salvaged equipment and from native Martian materials. Without the two of them, others will need to educate themselves and fill those gaps. Of course, without the robots, labor can be done the old-fashioned way: with muscles and shovels. And without the computers, well . . . we survived without them for a quarter of a million years. I suppose we can do so again. But I'd rather not."

Kat gave Colfax a basic history lesson regarding all things Macopro and Kiribati. Thurman had acquired Gilligan's Island in the late 40s and developed it as a secondary and secret launch site for Macopro. Nobody, including the Kiribati president and her cabinet, had any idea of who this new island-owner was or what he had been up to since his purchase. They, like literally all heads of state, were used to making secret deals with unidentified oligarchs through intermediaries well acquainted with the power of generosity. Colfax imagined that Thurman would have been more generous than most in rewarding Madame President for her paucity of curiosity and her nimiety of secrecy.

Back in the 2030s, Kat and Thurman had chosen Kenya as Macopro's main launch site for several reasons. The U.S. was out of consideration because its economy was too unstable, its government too corrupt, and the white supremacist militia of the Christian Unity Party were threatening civil war. A charismatic prophet named Bickle Johnson claimed "divine right" to southern and midwestern states, along with inland California and Oregon, and announced plans – God's plans – to forge them into a new confederacy of states called Heartland, with its capital city in Fort Worth, Texas. The Christian Unity Party's militia were constantly agitating in other states as well, staging marches and not-too-covertly bombing universities, churches, mosques, and synagogues they deemed "leftist," all the while extolling the virtues of *Family, Faith, and Freedom*. That meant that locations in Florida, Texas, and California were out of the question, all the more so because American infrastructure had hardly been updated since the last century and American schools had fallen far behind global standards.

In contrast, Kenya's close economic relationship with superpower China gave it financial strength and protected it from Russian American crime families, leaving its government relatively stable, a rarity in recent decades. With China's help, Kenya had annexed the rest of East Africa and the Congo in the 30s, yielding the world's highest concentration of mineral wealth and enabling Kenya to create the world's second-best educational system. As a result, the Sino-African Alliance offered a highly skilled workforce to build Macopro's considerable infrastructure, including its reusable rockets and robotics.

Since Macopro's many offices around the world kept a low profile, when people thought of Macopro, they immediately thought of Kenya.

Nobody thought of Kiribati, which made it ideal as a secret launch site for the last voyage. Here Thurman developed a unique launch strategy, as yet untried, but that was about to change.

In 2049, construction began on a massive hangar and a long runway, not unheard of for an oligarch with a collection of private jets. Then Thurman extended the runway, requiring the construction of a wide causeway down into the shallow sea. Doing so, Colfax imagined, broke any number of environmental laws, but nobody seemed to have noticed, and even if they had, nobody would have cared, since Kiribati's future was already bleak due to sea level rise. In fact, many of the smaller islands had already been depopulated and many had disappeared under the waves.

Next, Thurman bought an old Airbus A380 from the United Arab Emirates, built by the U.S. back in the early 2040s. It was an antique now, especially since drones had replaced most manned military aircraft, but it was still serviceable and easily upgradable. Thurman had it flown to Gilligan's Island, where he installed state-of-the-art engines for increased altitude and carrying capacity. Then he had the A380 modified to carry a winged spacecraft on its back, much like the old Boeing 747s that carried the Space Shuttles back in the late twentieth century. At launch, the upgraded A380 would carry the Ark to 48,000 feet. At that altitude, the spacecraft would separate from the A380 and its rockets would fire, not for a vertical ascent, but for a sharply angled rise out of the upper atmosphere and into space. After docking with an unmanned space station to stock up on supplies aided by the station's robot crew, the long voyage would begin. After about 270 days, the Ark would land on Mars like a traditional landing module, using a series of massive parachutes.

In light of the recent attacks in Kenya and Iceland, Thurman and Ekaterina decided to move the flight from the end of the launch window to the middle, which meant a launch the next day, Christmas, two weeks earlier than planned. The rush, they felt, was prudent, and the holiday would reduce surveillance at least very slightly.

So, Colfax floated in a sandy lagoon of warm, clear Pacific water, savoring his last day on Earth.

Meanwhile, his fellow crew were lounging on the beach. Ikemba and Nikau were kicking a soccer ball. Eve, Refa, and Gabriela were talking and laughing at the water's edge. Dei-Lin and Soraya were sharing a drink in the shade of a coconut palm.

Eve had encouraged everyone to be "fully in the moment" and to try not to think about the future or the past. Colfax felt only partially successful at that. But every few minutes, for a few blissful instants of timelessness, he was simply there, floating, trusting the water, enjoying the gentle waves, open to the sky and the warm light that bathed his face, temporarily forgetting the loneliness that was his almost constant companion.

He heard someone swim up to him, but he didn't move. "You look happy." It was Soraya's voice.

He smiled but kept his eyes closed. "Exceptionally."

Soraya turned on her back and joined him, relying on the salt water to hold her up. After a few minutes of gently rocking on the waves, she said, "I know we're supposed to be in the moment, but I would like to ask you a question that is very much not in the moment."

Colfax dropped his feet to tread water and face her, and she did the same, facing him, a concerned expression on her face. "Are you satisfied with your allotment of birds?" she asked.

"It seems a little late to be asking that," he replied. "There is nothing more that can be done."

"Yes, that's true. But I am not asking so anything can be done. I am asking because I care about you, Colfax. I know how much it has meant to me to choose my allotment of arthropods, and I know how Gabriela agonized over her allotment of amphibians, just as Dei-Lin did with her fungi and algae and plants. It feels like . . . holy work, holy and at the same time, sad work, tragic for those species that are being left behind. And so I can only imagine that you must feel torn. We allowed you such a small allotment of species, and so little time to procure them."

"I was a late addition to the team, and I understand that others had to make some space and biomass adjustments for me to include some new additions. So, I am grateful for the species we have managed to secure so quickly. And like you, Soraya, I feel that this process, rushed as it has been, is very . . . meaningful. I suppose there is some small consolation knowing that we are bringing Gabriela's gene bank for future use. We can only hope that greenhouse construction will proceed quickly and that future generations will discover how to more fully employ the bank's potential, long after we have passed on. Then, one can hope, they will develop species on Mars that we could not bring with us, and perhaps they will engineer new species altogether, the first Martian endemics."

"You must have some regrets," Soraya said.

"Thousands. Literally. There are ten thousand species of birds on Earth – or at least there used to be, and each one is – or was – a delight. But I shall be grateful for the simple pleasures of mockingbirds and several finches from North America, common blackbirds from Europe, ground doves from Asia, and three species of parrots, one from Africa, one from Latin America, and one from Australia. They are adaptable species with varied diets, and I think they will handle the voyage well. Thank you, Soraya, for your help in making this possible."

"It was Gabriela's idea. I only wish it could have been thousands more," she said, her warmth utterly sincere. "I know you were hoping for wood thrushes."

"Mockingbirds and blackbirds are cousins to the wood thrush," Colfax said. "And nobody even knows if wood thrushes still exist. It was generous of Thurman to send some researchers to try to find some in Venezuela on such short notice. Quite a surprise that they came back with some baby Galapagos tortoises."

Soraya laughed. "You probably heard that they bought them from a drug runner who owned a huge menagerie in the Venezuelan jungle. Only Thurman could pull that off in three weeks."

"Only Thurman could waive the normal quarantine rules too," Colfax added. "I suppose he trusts Gabriela's workarounds."

A magnificent frigate passed overhead, gliding on angular wings, steering with its forked tail. Colfax couldn't help but notice. He pointed it out to Soraya.

"Is it true that they can fly for weeks without landing?" she asked. "I remember hearing that somewhere."

"Not weeks, but at least ten days," Colfax replied. "They catch short, intense naps on the wing, one hemisphere of their brains alert at a time, the other one resting," he said. "What a feat of evolution. I shall miss them. I shall miss them all."

Soraya was silent, sharing Colfax's mixed emotions. "I can't imagine what the animal containment area will be like on our voyage. Do you think the birds will sing on Deck 4? I know the crickets will chirp, because crickets have been included on space voyages for decades now, and they've proven very adaptable. Good dietary protein source too."

"I doubt the birds will sing. Singing normally relates to breeding behavior and territory defense, and there will be none of either during the voyage. But surprises occur. Some of our finches may sing. And perhaps some of the doves. I have little doubt that the parrots will screech. I imagine we can teach them some simple words. They are still young."

"I was worried we had cheated you," Soraya said, "but now I feel better." She leaned back into a floating position. Colfax did as well.

They were quiet for a few minutes, slipping into the moment and out again.

"It is my turn this time," Colfax said, "to take you out of the moment." They both returned to a vertical posture in the warm sea water.

"I do not normally think of an entomologist as a leader, and especially not as gifted a leader as you. How did you . . . how did you, a bug scientist, become the amazing and wonderful *Captain* Soraya Rasul?"

"Ah, we entomologists are used to being stereotyped. Boring, nerdy, odd, that sort of thing. But you have to understand that, for me, entomology was a matter of the heart from the very beginning. We moved from the U.K. to the U.S. when I was in middle school, to the state of Maryland. I was enthralled with butterflies. The Baltimore checkerspot was my spark species. I actually saw three before they were lost. And I also saw a few of the then rare and now extinct-in-the-wild monarchs. Then I became fascinated with cicadas and their metamorphic cycles of prime numbers. Then grasshoppers. Then crickets. I started with the species that were beautiful and easy to love. That helped me extend my curiosity to those species that were harder to love. Like mosquitos and ants, bees and wasps . . . I learned that behind every obnoxious quality there are amazing stories of survival, adaptation, and evolution."

"I hope *they* will not be part of our biomass budget," Colfax said.

"No mosquitos, but several callibaetis species. And we have a lot of bee and other pollinator species. Pollination is well worth an occasional sting, but the truth is that most pollinators are completely benign."

They stared toward the shore.

"It's worth saving what we can, isn't it, Colfax? What we love, we see value in, and what we value, we protect and save."

"So much has already been lost, even in the last forty years. It is dreadful, appalling," he replied. "Unconscionable."

"Ah, yes, but if not for this mission . . ." Soraya tried to turn toward hope.

"If only we had been able to institute the changes we needed thirty years ago, sixty years ago," Colfax replied. "If only my father's religion had . . . alas. There is nothing to be gained by hypothetical conjecture."

"There will be two hundred or so of us who will have the chance – and the challenge – to begin again," Soraya insisted.

Two hundred out of nearly ten billion, Colfax thought. "Not a stellar success rate," he said aloud. "And barely sustainable in terms of genetic diversity."

"But not a total loss, either," Soraya countered, and then added, "As you well know, explosions of evolutionary diversity have often followed mass extinction events. And some geneticists say that nearly all living humans are descendants of a post-catastrophe relictual population of about two hundred, just like us."

"You impress me, Captain," Colfax said, making eye contact. "You have a brilliant mind, but also a . . . generous and hopeful heart. I envy you because I lack that . . . internal gyroscopic buoyancy. How did you acquire it, or did it come naturally?"

"Colfax, you remember where I'm from," Soraya replied. "My ancestors were Tajiks, from the Afghan aristocracy. Over the last century, we watched our fortunes evaporate as our nation was exploited by the British, the Russians, the Americans, and the Chinese, and most of all, by our own fundamentalist religious parties. That is something you and I share . . . a deep aversion to fundamentalist religion in all its forms. Most of my relatives fled to the U.K. as refugees. Then many of us came to the U.S. as immigrants. We survived, but every day, we feel grief for all that was lost as our beloved homeland descended down into a century-long trail of civil war and theocracy. So really, my only choices were despair and cynicism or . . . the opposite."

Colfax leaned back to a floating position. "I am more gratified than ever that you are our leader, Soraya. You have my deepest respect. I am glad that you have escaped the cynical gravitation that pulls me perpetually downward."

She leaned back beside him, an arm's length away. "I am glad for your friendship, Colfax Innis. We will need to depend on each other because many challenges are ahead. But for now . . . for now we float. In the moment."

And for ten minutes or so, they did.

Colfax broke the silence and went vertical. "Soraya, what will happen to Thurman and Ekaterina . . . after we have launched?"

"I've been worrying about the same thing," she said, also dropping her feet toward the white coral sand below.

"Why are they not joining us?" Colfax asked.

"The weight budget, I suppose. Thurman always talks about the weight budget."

"But without Murty and Srinivasa . . . should that not be enough to compensate for their biomass?"

She paused, then Colfax saw something in her eyes he hadn't really seen before. "Have you mentioned this idea to Thurman?"

"No. The question just occurred to me as we were floating."

"Let's." And with that, Soraya began swimming toward shore, swimming in strong, graceful strokes through clear tropical water, something she would never experience again, ever.

Colfax tried to catch up to her, but he fell behind. When he reached the beach, she was drying off with a towel, and he was breathing heavily. *She is extraordinary*, he thought. *I do not know what it is about her that . . . inspires me so.*

13
Code Indigo

Soraya and Colfax found Thurman and Ekaterina under a thatched hālau, sitting at a plastic folding table, going over a spreadsheet on a digital page.

Soraya put her palms on the table and said, "Thurman, Kat, Colfax has an idea. We hope it's not too late."

They looked up. "It's never too late until it's too late," Thurman moaned.

A quintessentially Thurmanian quip, Colfax thought.

Soraya asked if they had calculated the savings to the weight budget without Murty and Srinivasa.

"Of course. That made possible an increase in biomass so we could acquire the additional species and their provisions that Colfax requested. And because we've moved the launch to the center of the launch window instead of the end, we have some additional fuel savings. It's always good to have a buffer," he said. "Why? Did you want to squeeze in one more rufous-crested thing-a-ma-bob or long-billed watchamacallit? I'm afraid it *is* too late for that."

"We're not thinking about birds," Soraya said.

"We are concerned about you two," Colfax continued. "You must have considered joining us. With what happened in Iceland and Kenya, with Murty and Srinivasa still in hostile hands, you must know how much danger you will be in after we are gone. Sooner or later, the oligarchs will locate you, wherever you go to seek refuge."

"We're non-repros, Colfax. We're not essential. We are not worth twenty billion Americredits," Thurman said.

"Are you saying that a non-reproductive life is not worth living on Mars?" Colfax replied. "And how long will your money retain its value if the collapse you fear is indeed inevitable? You seem to have become so preoccupied with our future that you have failed to plan for your own."

"We can't simply disappear," Thurman replied. "We have duties."

"You seem to have overlooked a potential danger," Colfax snapped, "something we cannot afford for you to do."

Soraya interjected. "Ekaterina, remember what you said when we were at the rendezvous point in Iceland, about what the oligarchs' henchmen do to get information?"

"Yes."

Soraya leaned down, her knuckles resting on the plastic tabletop, her eyes inches from Ekaterina's. "Were you lying to us?"

"No. Why would I lie? I'm no *izhivaya suka*. I do not lie," Ekaterina replied, standing so quickly as she spoke that her plastic chair tipped behind her.

Soraya straightened and folded her arms. "Then this could be happening to Murty and Srinivasa now. *And it could happen to you. And to Thurman. If you stay behind*."

Thurman spoke. "Yes. It's a risk we have to take."

Colfax erupted, slamming his hand on the plastic tabletop. "Damn it, Thurman! No, it is not. It is categorically *not* a risk you have to take. And if you do not care about protecting yourself, you damn well should care about protecting Ekaterina after all you have accomplished together. But if that is not sufficient, what about us? What if they tortured you and got vital information from you? What if they put you under duress to help them construct a new LVRV, and what if at the next launch window they sent thirty assassins up to kill us all and make room for a desperate oligarch's cronies? They would do it. They would do anything. They would do it in a Tokyo minute. I know you have the perspicacity to ascertain that my concerns are both salient and irrefutable."

Colfax watched Thurman's eyes dart to Ekaterina's and then to Soraya's, just as they had done that day at the rendezvous point.

"Perhaps we should have considered this," Thurman said, his tone still a growl. "But such a decision is too grave to make at the last minute. Ekaterina and I will go into hiding, as planned. We can go even darker, as they say. We have the means."

"Not here," Colfax said. "As of tomorrow, Gilligan's Island will be known. Satellite trackers will expose you. You will not be safe anywhere. The world has grown small. And who knows what they have already learned from the two crew they have already taken?"

Soraya again leaned over the table, this time, her face inches away from Thurman's, still seated. "*What is possible is possible*," she said firmly, almost angrily. "I have heard you say this many times. You shouldn't dismiss a possibility that could be for the good of the mission. And that could save Ekaterina's life, not to mention your own."

Thurman frowned and turned to Kat. "Your thoughts?" he asked through clenched teeth.

Ekaterina walked across the hālau and looked out over the ocean. "I am a fighter, Thurman. I do not run away. I fight until I win or die. I cannot run away. But . . ."

Thurman stood and walked over to her. He moved close behind her as she continued. "But perhaps this isn't running. Perhaps this is choosing a different fight. Instead of fighting against killers and plunderers here, instead of fighting against selfish idiots, cultic zealots, and heartless thugs here, we need to fight *for* something, *there* . . . with good people at our side, people we trust, people we . . . love."

For the first time, Colfax saw some physical sign of the affectionate dimension of their relationship. He noticed how Thurman's hand tenderly touched Ekaterina's shoulder. He noticed how she leaned back, ever so slightly, into his touch. He noticed how she turned and her eyes rose to his face. He noticed Thurman touch her hair, and he heard a tenderness in Kat's tone as she said, "Thurman Howard Thurman, we are partners in this. There is nothing more for us here. Soraya is right. It is better for the mission to go, and better for us too. *Resheno*."

They embraced. Soraya and Colfax stepped away to give them some privacy. The old couple whispered to each other for several minutes, and then Colfax and Soraya saw them walking briskly toward a small office in a nearby trailer, the one with a satellite dish beside it. They followed to see how they could help.

Colfax was still damp from swimming as he entered the trailer, its antique air conditioner making more noise than warranted by its meager success in cooling the air. Still, he felt a shiver.

Ekaterina was making a call, not through her bracelet, but through a laptop that was almost as old as the air conditioner.

"Silva. No, everything is according to plan. I am sorry to wake you. I was wondering about Murty and . . . OK. At least it's not bad news. Yes. All is clear for launch. Yes, but there is one change. Yes, significant. Thurman and I are initiating Code Indigo. Yes, full auto-destruct. Yes, for all of Category A. Exactly. Keep B and C systems intact and running under their usual aliases. Yes. I want everything on Category A to disappear as soon as you can make it so. Yes. The only backups will be on Mars and on the LVRV. They're safer there in every way. So, yes, everything, as we've discussed in the Code Indigo protocol. This is clear? That's all you need to know.

"Us? Exactly according to Code Indigo. Except with one adaptation. We will be joining the crew of the last voyage." She listened for a moment before continuing.

"Yes. Absolutely. One more thing. I would like you to distribute all Macopro crypto-currency resources to all Category A staff in equal portions as a severance bonus. This will be untraceable and will help them until they find new work. I know, but they deserve this. Be sure Srinivasa and Murty are included, for their families' benefit even if . . . and continue to . . . yes, of course you will. Yes. Just make it disappear from our corporate account and appear in equal portions in their personal alias accounts. Clear? No, no. You know we prepared for this, Silva. Please. Please. Other arrangements. I want you to repeat back to me what I am asking you to do. Yes. Yes. Yes. Yourself included. This is a big responsibility for you. Are you sure . . . Everything else we need will be handled through other means, just as we have arranged. That is all. You will do this? Thank you. Yes, of course. You are most welcome. No, no, please don't cry, Silva. It is all for the best. All shall be well, one way or another. And you will continue to lead the Category B and C staff under their legal entities until you hear from one of us, or a person who authenticates in our stead. Clear? Goodbye, Silva. Code Indigo. Thank you. For everything. And enjoy . . . your new home. And name. Kiss your little girl for me. I hope she won't hate us for where you will be raising her."

Kat seemed disoriented for a long moment after she ended the call.

"Well. It is done," she said at last. "We will disappear from Earth to join you on the final voyage. A rumor will be disseminated that we have been killed and our enemies will rejoice. As part of Code Indigo, Silva will disseminate the news that Macopro will cease operations because Mars Base has failed and its founders are dead. All our senior staff will relocate and be given new identities. They will all believe, except for Silva, that we are—"

Thurman interrupted, "As soon as we take off, Soraya, you will be in charge. You are our captain. We will be part of your crew. Our old lives as rogue oligarchs will be over forever. Thanks be to God for that."

Thurman looked at Ekaterina and took a deep breath.

For a brief instant, Colfax thought his old friend looked ten years younger. His face, his skin, even his wrinkles, seemed changed; there was a steady radiance about him. "Everything essential for the voyage has been triple-triple checked. Everything for Earth is in Silva's capable hands. We can easily make the final arrangements for the two of us later tonight, and we can augment needed provisions from the surplus on the space station. We'll just have to program in the robotic transfer. I will have the staff here re-install Murty and Srinivasa's seats and cocoons that they had removed. Silva is already taking care of everything else remotely. Kat, our lives just became simpler. Let's take the rest of the day off. It is Christmas Eve. It is our last day on Earth. Let's go swimming, one last time."

Ekaterina looked like she was going to argue, then shook her head, smiled, and said in Ukrainian-tinged English, "We are going to a red desert planet. Why not swim while we can, one last time, in the emerald-blue Pacific?"

"One last time," Soraya repeated, as they left the trailer. Then she turned to Colfax. "It sounds like our help isn't needed. I want to take a shower one last time on Earth. Who knows when I'll feel really clean again?"

They walked back toward the main building together, both a little surprised – happily so – that the crew would now be ten again, not eight.

Soraya turned to walk to her room and Colfax watched her, the subtle sway of her hips, her wet hair on her bare shoulders. He stood alone in the common area of the main building.

What do I want to do one last time? he wondered. Suddenly, unexpectedly, the old black hole opened up underneath his feet, that aching void of loneliness.

He felt there was only one thing he must do one last time: *check his message feed*.

He didn't give himself time to consider why he wanted to do this, or whether it was a good idea; he simply ran back to the trailer and found that Ekaterina had left the 2030s-era antique laptop powered on and logged into the satellite connection. He navigated around a few dead ends and made his way to his message feed. One last time.

His inbox had 1,257 messages. He scanned from the top. From his editor. From his financial advisor. From Ann's sister. He skipped them.

There it was. A message from Hailey. And another, and another. Maybe a dozen. He selected them, started at the bottom, and read up.

He began to narrate to himself the story of what he was reading.

Otto left again, but not before throwing Hailey against a table and breaking a rib. That cretinous bastard.

She needs me. She is sorry.

She was a fool to trust him, to choose an unstable man who betrayed her repeatedly instead of a stable one who was only good to her. She was never as happy as when we were together.

Where am I? Why is there no answer to her messages?

She apologizes for hurting me. She feels like an addict who relapsed. Yes, she has a broken rib from Otto's act of violence, but what she did to me was worse. She broke my heart, and she is sorry.

She pleads for forgiveness.

She tells me she wants me to be the father to her boys. They saw Otto beat her. They need a better man in their lives. I should be that man.

She asks if there is someone else. Is that the reason I have not responded? Or perhaps I cannot ever forgive her. She does not blame me. She dares to hope I will call today.

She apologizes for not trusting me. She fears she has made things worse by her previous message.

She is worried I have done myself harm.

She is sorry for thinking that.

She is afraid. Why the uncharacteristic silence?

Her older son is angry at her for "driving Dad away, and Colfax too." She needs my advice.

She is sorry that she is so needy.

She misses me, even my "smarty-pants vocabulary."

Her most recent message, sent this morning, is short, agonizing: "Why won't you answer me?"

"I cannot do this," Colfax said out loud. "I must not abandon her like this."

And there it was. The one last thing Colfax wanted to do: to be with Hailey, on Earth, for the rest of his life, whatever that would mean.

A one-way voyage to Mars is no place for an aging poltroon like me, he thought. *With Thurman and Ekaterina on the crew, I am no longer needed. Eve will be fine, and she will understand.*

He began sweating, breathing heavily, his pulse reverberating in his chest. *Let Thurman go, and Ekaterina. I shall stay here. With Hailey by my side, I shall struggle to survive against Earth's coming chaos. That is a noble enough challenge without launching myself through the vacuous expanse in a metal tube.*

He opened a message and typed Hailey's address. Then, out of the corner of his eye, Colfax noticed a refrigerator across the room, and next to it sat a cabinet that might contain something he might need to bolster his resolve.

Part II

The First Trimester

14
Boundary Condition

It was about 22:00 on Christmas Eve. Eve was still awake, putting finishing touches on the departure ritual Soraya had asked her to design. There was knock on the door, gentle but firm. "Eve, I need your help." It was Soraya's voice.

Eve was in the oversized T-shirt she wore for sleeping. She thought of grabbing a pair of pants, but Soraya added, "It's urgent."

When Eve opened the door, Soraya said, "It's your dad."

"He's not . . ."

"I'm afraid so."

Colfax had got drunk occasionally when Eve was a child, but his drinking intensified when she reached adolescence. He cycled from binge to shame to pleas for forgiveness to promises of improvement, followed by forced and excessive cheerfulness, short-term sobriety, followed by the inevitable relapse into the next binge. By the fourth or fifth cycle, Eve's mother was ready to leave, but she endured with the help of a support group. Eve also sought support and therapy when she was in college and graduate school, and she kept her distance from Colfax as much as possible during those years.

Her dad always enjoyed the art of insult. Sober Colfax used arcane words as his weapons, taking double pleasure in humiliating his victim by using words the victim didn't understand.

Drunk Colfax was less articulate but even more vicious. Eve still winced when she recalled some of his drunken tirades when she was in graduate school.

He became sober for a few years when he was offered his dream job at the EPA, but during and since her mother's illness,

Eve knew that he drank on occasion, and then, always to excess. Even so, her relationship with her dad had warmed since her mother's diagnosis. Watching Ann's decline softened Colfax and made him a better man, Eve felt, tapping into a reservoir of compassion and tenderness that she never knew he had.

Eve assumed Thurman and his team had checked out Colfax's history with alcohol. It was hard to imagine they would have missed both his drinking problem and her fertility problem. So, she didn't obsess about the possibility of relapse, although it did cross her mind a few times. But the look on Soraya's face just outside her doorway – embarrassed and pained – reminded her of the look on her mother's face years before, and instantly she felt overcome by the sick, stale smell of bad memories and feelings of shame.

Eve jogged barefoot after Soraya in the moonlight from the main building past the office trailer and then to the hālau where Colfax was lying on his side, flecks of vomit stuck in his goatee and a pool of it spread on the wood floor in front of him. There was an empty bottle of white wine on the floor nearby and a nearly empty bottle of vodka still cradled in his hand. He was crying in long, pitiful groans. His glasses were nowhere to be seen.

From past experience, Eve knew Colfax could be mad drunk or sad drunk. When mad drunk, he would be blunt, crude, and merciless. When sad drunk, he would wallow in self-pity that went beyond pathetic to paranoid to just plain silly. To see someone so brilliant reduced to either the mad or the sad state was deeply disorienting, not to mention, for a daughter, embarrassing.

"Colfax, I've brought Eve here. I'm going to let the two of you talk for a while," Soraya said, and then gently withdrew to the porch of the office trailer nearby.

Eve sat down cross-legged in front of her father and tried to prepare herself to listen without reacting to his well-rehearsed triggers.

"I cannot leave," Colfax sobbed. "I cannot evaporate to Mars. I love Hailey and she needs me. I need simple, undiluted happiness. I have no need for a contrived adventure. I have no need for an ex-extra-extra-terrest . . . challenge. I simply need a humane modicum of happiness. I have too much on Earth to leave behind." He started blubbering like a pouting child. Clearly, he was sad drunk, for the moment at least.

"OK," Eve said, holding out her hands in a calming gesture. "I'll miss you, Dad. But it's your life and your decision, and I support it. You should know that your choice doesn't change mine, as we agreed. I'm still going. This is my path now."

He awkwardly pushed himself up into a cross-legged sitting position, his spine hunched over, his thinning hair disheveled like a madman's. "Please do not go, Eve!" he said, slurring his words, speaking with too much volume and spit, gesticulating erratically. "There will be nothing but trouble for you there on that desolate planet. I know we are clusterfucked here on Earth. But you shall be even more ignominiously fucked on Mars. Wherever we go, we fucking humans bring our fucking human selves along for the fucking ride. The problem is us, the human species, the whole damned fucking species. We did not evolve properly. We got ahead of ourselves. Between us and extinction, the only thing that matters is the happiness of love. Eve, one must find someone to love before the lights go out. That is the only thing needful, for me, for you." Then he leaned forward and cupped his hands around his mouth with an exaggerated whisper: "And besides, if you go, your little secret might come out."

His eyes glared at Eve in a way that scared her for an instant. But then she heard words form in her mind, words she did not want or need to say aloud: *I hate you. I hate you. You bastard, I hate you.*

He was still glaring at her, but all fear was gone within her. She felt nothing . . . except for a faint sense of condescending pity mixed with a stronger sense of disgust. *I know he thinks he's uniquely brilliant*, she thought. *But I'm every bit as brilliant. The only difference is that I have no need to perform my brilliance constantly.*

She was uncomfortable with this retreat into moral superiority, and the second she acknowledged it, the truth spoke itself within her: *My problem isn't showing off. My problem is needing to save everyone and everything. That's why I wanted him to come on the last voyage. I wanted to save him. But some things are so fucked up they can never be un-fucked. When will I realize that?*

Colfax lowered his eyes and found his vodka bottle. He sucked it for its one last swig, hoping for more than the bottle contained. Then he tried to throw the bottle away, but both his aim and strength were impaired, and the bottle spun and slid into Eve's knee. That's when she noticed that his glasses were beside his right leg and would be crushed if he leaned right. She crawled closer, careful to avoid the pool of vomit, retrieved them, handed them to him, and he clumsily put them on with two hands.

Then she saw him switch from sad to mad drunk in a second, mad with a dose of grandiosity and pomposity mixed in. "Therein lies your problem, Eve." He almost spat her name. "You have never been in love. You are not capable of understanding because you have never known love as I have. Yes, you were engaged to that bastard *Colin*. But what was he? A selfish cretin and he dropped you like a . . . piece of spoiled meat. That was not love because he was incapable of anything so elevated. So now, you are alone in this world, and being alone is the most pitiable thing that can befall anyone. No wonder you want to piss your lonely life away on a lonely planet. Not I. I have too much self-respect for such a destiny. I have love! Someone *loves me! Me!*" He was bellowing at full voice now, thumping his chest, a hollow patriarch, a pitiful King Lear.

Eve knew it was fruitless to try to reason with him in this condition, so she didn't argue or react, as much as she wanted to.

She asked him a few questions and listened to his rambling answers. When he said something about Hailey, she stood up, alarmed. If Colfax tried to reach Hailey with unencrypted communication, whoever was out to stop Macopro could know about their whereabouts – right now.

"Dad, did you speak with Hailey, or did you just b-mail her?" Eve asked, her voice suddenly stern.

"She b-mailed me and I attempted to call," he said, morosely. "But the wretched server here allows no outgoing calls. This is a damned prison, with Ekaterina as our dominatrix warden and Thurman as her hunched-over weakling assistant. So yes, I successfully b-mailed Hailey that I was away and could not call. And I told her I loved her with all my heart. And . . ." He flipped to sad drunk and started crying again – for a moment.

"Dad, did you reveal anything to Hailey about where you are or what you're doing?"

His head snapped up and his eyes, red and glassy in the faint light, again glared. That last draw on his bottle was kicking in and his capacity for speech began to falter: "Do you think me some sort of ignorot . . . idnoram . . . igniotic . . . fool? I signed those stupid papers for Thurman, that you burned in the fire. I would never violate that agreement. I have interg . . . integrity. You do not trust me. You never did. You think of me as a famned didiotic stool. You neither respect me nor dever nid. If you desprected me, you dever would have joined that cr-crazy cult. That broke my heart, you know. And if you had not got so religious, you would have found love. There is nothing less attractive in a woman than religion, and it is even worse in a man."

Eve so wanted to remind him that Ann was a dedicated Lutheran when he met her, and that being drunk was even less sexy than being religious. She restrained herself. Colfax hung his head again. Now that he was cycling so rapidly between mad and sad, she suspected he might simply fall asleep.

Eve mostly believed him about not revealing anything to Hailey. And she hoped she wasn't a fool for doing so.

He gradually slumped to his right, his head touched the floor, and he started to snore. For several minutes she stared at him feeling first pity, then disgust, then nothing. She took a step toward him and looked down upon his puke-stained face.

"You were wrong about me never being in love," she whispered, knowing he couldn't hear. "You never asked me about other relationships after Colin. I certainly never offered such personal information to a selfish asshole who wouldn't hesitate to use it against me later."

But he was right about the cult, she thought. Eve had joined a group with cultic tendencies back when she was in college. Since her parents raised her with no religion at all, she was curious when a good-looking fellow invited her to Campus Christian Fellowship during the first week of freshman year. She was immediately drawn in by warm and friendly people who weren't getting drunk and high all the time and who weren't having casual sex with as many people as possible. That was refreshing to Eve.

By midterms, she became a convert, a true born-again believer, and Colfax had reason to be worried, especially when she came home between semesters and told him he was going to experience "eternal conscious torment" in hell because he hadn't "accepted Jesus as his personal Lord and Savior."

I sounded like a little religious robot, repeating the phrases I had absorbed as a member of CCF, she mused as she watched him snore. She remembered his tirades about her "bullshit dogma." They hurt enough when he was drunk, but even worse when he was sober.

Eve remembered joining her parents on a skiing vacation over winter break. Colfax drank vodka, they got into an argument, and he called her *credulous, ductile, docious, a willing cog in a crypto-fascist cult machine, sycophantic, solipsistic, sententious* and *tendentious* . . . words which hurt all the more when she later looked up what each one meant.

Eve stood over him, staring down at his rounded body on the floor of the hālau. It was clear he wasn't going to wake up anytime soon. Soraya had called Thurman and Ekaterina, and the three of them walked toward the hālau gingerly. Eve met them halfway and shared some background with them, trying to be discreet but accurate.

"I imagine this disqualifies him from the voyage," she said. "But I want you to know that I'm still in. No matter what."

Then, without expecting to, Eve started to tear up. "I have to admit something to you, Thurman: unconsciously, I didn't want to leave Dad behind because . . . because I was worried that without me around . . . this would happen; he would slip back into his . . . old self-destructive ways. It was a lousy reason to bring someone along. I'm sorry. Ever the caretaker."

Thurman came and put his arm around Eve. "Look, Eve, I knew your father when he was an arrogant, out-of-control, self-important frat boy in college. I saw him sink pretty deep into some self-destructive behaviors back then, and then I watched him pull himself together and become a great leader, a great man. So, I'm not going to count him out yet. Besides, what he feared for Kat and me would be an equally great danger for him if he stays on Earth. Let's clean him up, get him to bed, and see how he is after a couple hours of sleep. The truth is, we are lacking good options. Bringing him is a problem, but leaving him behind at this point is a risk too."

Ekaterina could see that something was bothering Eve. "What is wrong, dear?"

"I hope you understand, but I would very much *not* like to have to talk with him about this in the morning. I'm his daughter, and I need to stop being his caretaker. Certainly not in this situation. It's a boundary condition I have to set."

"You are wise in this, dear," Kat said. "My father had a similar disease. Thurman and I are your father's peers. We will talk with him. We will handle this."

Soraya spoke up. "Actually, I'm the captain. I should be the one to talk with him, professionally speaking. I will wake him at two and we will have a decision by our gathering time at three." She paused. "The only problem with this plan is that if he decides not to come, you will have no real opportunity to say goodbye."

Eve didn't hesitate with her reply. "That's OK. Dad's not one for goodbyes anyway." And with that, Thurman and Kat shook Colfax to semi-awareness, helped him to his feet, and took him to his room as Eve went to her room. "I hope he can shower himself," Eve whispered, and then corrected herself. "It's not my problem."

She reviewed the departure ritual she had created, practiced what she would say, and went to bed around midnight. *Strange*, she thought as she turned out the light. *I really have no feelings about whether he comes or not. It's out of my hands, and I'm OK with that.*

By the time her bracelet woke her at 2:30, she had re-erected a familiar emotional wall between her and her father. His drinking had ruined too many important days of her life in the past. She was determined not to let him ruin this day, either by his presence or by his absence.

She didn't see him when she began leading the ritual, and she felt no emotion when she concluded that he would be staying on Earth: no emotion except a shiver of relief.

15
Transfer of Trust

The crescent moon had just risen when the crew gathered at 03:10, dressed in clean and pressed navy-blue jumpsuits, their helmets under their arms. The breeze was moist and mild, the temperature about twenty-five. They could hear the gentle sounds of pre-dawn: palm fronds rustling in the humid warmth, waves lapping on the beach not far away, a bold gecko squeaking from a nearby bush, the crackling of a fire Eve had arranged to be lit in the center of a circle of logs and limestone rocks.

Eve welcomed everyone and explained that their ancestors from all their cultural traditions had created rituals of passage to mark important life transitions for tens of thousands of years. "I hope this simple ritual of gratitude and transfer of trust will be meaningful for all of us," she said. "I've drawn from a wide variety of cultural traditions to design it, at Soraya's request."

Then she led them in facing into the four directions of the compass. In each direction, she led in a prayer or read a reflective meditation from a different spiritual tradition. Then they formed a circle, facing inward, and Eve invited them to gaze by firelight into the faces of their fellow crew members. "We're leaving a culture that set us in competition with one another," she said, "or left us all worrying primarily about ourselves. But going forward, we can no longer see ourselves as competitive or independent. We must be interdependent. The common good is our starting point. We matter to each other. We belong to each other. In these moments, I invite us to open our hearts to one another and to give our hearts to one another."

She paused and let this silence continue for several minutes. She knew it already, but could see that her father was not in the circle. She was relieved, and sad, but mostly relieved.

Next, she invited them to look past their companions across the circle, to look out at the world bathed in moonlight and starlight, and to offer thanks to Earth's rich web of life of which they had been part their whole lives. One by one, nearly everyone spoke. The reverence was palpable:

"Thank you, oceans," Soraya began.

"Thank you, wind," Ekaterina continued, followed by several others: "Thank you, soil . . . Thank you, rain and snow . . . Thank you, evolution . . . Thank you, trees and ferns and prairie grasses."

When Ikemba added, with equal reverence, "Thank you, burritos. Thank you, basil pizza. Thank you, Nigerian rum," everyone laughed and clapped.

When the laughter died down, Eve asked her colleagues to close their eyes and silently offer, in whatever words felt right to them, thanks to the ultimate source of all they had received on Earth, whoever or whatever they might understand that source to be.

Then she had them turn their circle outward, and she asked her colleagues to speak aloud, one at a time – whoever was willing, a hope or prayer or intention for the Earth and all their brothers and sisters, human and nonhuman, whom they were about to leave behind.

Refa spoke first: "That humans will be good, and the Earth will be well. And that Dr. Murty and Dr. Srinivasa will be found and set free." One by one the others followed.

For the final element of the ritual, Eve asked everyone to lie on their backs facing upward, with their feet toward the fire. She walked around the circle, inviting them to feel their weight on the Earth, to acknowledge the pull the Earth had upon them all; to feel gratitude for all it had given them, and to hold grief for all the harm human beings had done to it. She reminded them that every cell in their bodies was borrowed from the Earth so they were really a living expression of the Earth itself, energized by the sun. "We are Earth children, each one of us," she said.

Then she reminded them that Earth's gravity was all they had ever known, and so its pull upon them was real and undeniable. She asked them to simply feel the gravitational pull of the Earth, to hold that feeling of belonging for seven full minutes in silence, returning gently to it each time their thoughts took them elsewhere. She gently struck a singing bowl to begin this time of silence.

Then she joined her colleagues on the ground. The grass was moist, and for a few moments, all she could think about was what a terrible idea this was, that everyone would be damp and uncomfortable, and that Soraya would regret trusting her. But then she took her own advice and returned to the feeling of the Earth's gravity, and the accompanying realization that for all her life, she had been held by the Earth. After a few minutes, she felt, to her surprise, that she was falling into something like a visionary state.

Her imagination raced from one scene to another – that first home she remembered in New Jersey, her second-grade classroom, the salt-water aquarium at the doctor's office, playing Frisbee with her little terrier Jack, swinging at the park with the rusty gate. Each thing – the carpet in the New Jersey home, the polished floor of her classroom, the crystal-clear water of the aquarium, Jack's warm wet nose, the rhythmic squeak of the swing – each thing seemed unspeakably precious in its physicality. The scenes and sensations flashed and blurred from one to another so quickly that, for a second, she felt they fused entirely into one timeless single experience that caused her to gasp. At that instant, the timer on her bracelet clicked in her implant. She stood, wishing she had allowed ten minutes instead of seven. She sounded the singing bowl and began walking slowly around the circle again.

She then invited her colleagues to feel the upward pull of the sky – the invitation into immensity and infinity, to exploration and adventure. She reminded them that the unknown weight and pull of what beckoned beyond the Earth was far greater than the familiar weight that held them on Earth. She suggested they transfer their trust from the Earth to the sun, because although they had drawn the molecules in their bodies from the Earth, they had derived virtually all of their life's energy from the sun.

"Even on Mars," she said, "we will be drawing our life from the same sun, and its energy will be with us on Mars. Let's hold that realization: that at the end of our long journey, the same sun will provide us with all the energy we need to survive and to thrive." Once again she asked them, when their thoughts wandered, to gently return to a feeling of dependence on the ultimate source of energy, sustenance, life, and love – not just the sun, but the mysterious source and center from which all the suns in all the galaxies were derived. She told them that after several minutes, one by one, Soraya would touch them on the shoulder, inviting that person to rise in silence and enter the Ark. This time, she ran her wooden mallet around the rim of the singing bowl with increasing firmness. She sustained the sound at its peak volume for several seconds and then let it slowly fade. Then Eve joined her companions, lying on the Earth, awaiting her turn to be summoned to the Ark.

She was unprepared for what happened almost immediately. Some began to sniffle, then cry, Dei-Lin and Soraya especially. After a few minutes, others began to smile, even laugh – including Ikemba and Eve herself. She felt an unexpected and joyful exhilaration so powerful and huge that she felt her heart might burst. *We're doing this*, she thought. *We're actually doing it!*

Then, for a few minutes a deep silence fell on them all.

One by one, Eve would hear the sound of someone rising, then the scuffle of feet moving to the aircraft and the Ark. When Soraya came and touched her left shoulder, Eve rose and saw the ground crew from Gilligan's Island standing silently in a line that led to the ladder by the plane's left wing. They greeted each crew member with silent smiles and wet eyes, the men of the ground crew shaking each crew member's hand, the women smiling and embracing them, some of the older women kissing them on each cheek and then pulling them in close so their foreheads touched. "Sa-bo, sa-bo," they whispered tenderly. Last in the line were the pilot and co-pilot of the Airbus, an older Korean man and a younger Korean woman who saluted them with a sincere dignity.

It was dark, still three hours before sunrise. The sliver of a silver moon gave little light from its location in the eastern sky. Eve stood to the side, her hair blowing across her face like blonde smoke. For some reason, she wanted to be the last to board the Ark. She didn't know whether to laugh or cry as she stood there, feeling too much for words. Soraya and Dei-Lin were the last two to climb a wooden step ladder into the vessel.

A wooden step ladder? Really? She looked up and saw Dei-Lin climbing from the ladder onto the huge wing of the Airbus, and then scrambling on her hands and knees across the wing toward a rope ladder that hung down from the Ark's entry door.

Eve put her foot on the first rung of the ladder and began hoisting herself up.

On the second step, the tears came. Joy, yes. Fear, a little. But both were tinged with a sadness she had known since she was a girl, a sadness only her father could inspire. *Let it go*, she told herself on the third step. *Leave it all behind*, she whispered on the fourth. She knew, of course, that would be easier said than done.

When she reached the wing, she stayed on her knees as Dei-Lin had done and crawled alongside the bulging fuselage of the huge aircraft. She came to the rope ladder just as Dei-Lin disappeared from it into the Ark. Dei-Lin's head appeared through the hatch. "If we can survive this part without breaking our necks, getting to Mars should be a breeze," she said flatly. "Can you believe it?"

Eve pulled herself up the rope ladder and Dei-Lin offered her a hand. "Just a minute," Eve said. She turned and looked once more out over the Pacific, the waves glowing faintly in the angled moonlight. *Goodbye*, she thought. And then came words so simple, innocent, and tender that she might burst: *I love you. I'll miss you. Thank you, dear Mother. Thank you.* She knew her thanks were directed at everything and everyone she was leaving behind.

She clasped Dei-Lin's extended forearm and entered. Once inside, she saw two rows of seats, three seats in the front row and four in the second. The first seat on the first row was vacant, and there she tethered in. Her fellow crew members, including Soraya and Dei-Lin, were abuzz with duties, but her duties, for now, were completed. She felt a wave of exhaustion fall over her like a heavy blanket, emotional exhaustion from the exchange with her father in the hālau several hours earlier, and a kind of spiritual exhaustion as well, from the intense responsibility of leading the ritual. She closed her eyes and felt herself letting go, letting go, letting go.

It may have been ten minutes later, maybe twenty. Eve gently awakened. She felt that a sense of relief and acceptance had spread through her body. She opened her eyes and looked around the Main Cabin. To her right, Nikau and Refa had tethered in. Toward the front of the Ark, she could see through the open hatch into the Bridge.

The Bridge was like the cockpit of an airplane but wider, with a seat for the pilot in the center, a seat for the co-pilot to the left, and a seat for the captain to the right. Mounted on the hatch itself, there was an additional jump-seat that could be folded down for use when needed. The pilot and co-pilot seats were surrounded by control panels full of control sticks, buttons, screens, dials, toggles, faders, meters, keypads, and other devices she wouldn't know what to call. These control panels covered the front, sides, and ceiling of the Bridge – anywhere Ikemba and

Dei-Lin could reach while tethered into their seats. The front viewport, what would have been the windshield of a car, was about one meter high and three meters wide, but Eve could only see about half of it through the open doorway in the wall that divided the Bridge from the Main Cabin.

Eve looked up. Above her arched the rounded inner hull of the Main Cabin. Beneath the flat deck under her feet were storage compartments in which their seats would be stored between launch and landing. That storage area, empty now, would also be loaded with a lot of other gear and supplies they would soon retrieve from the supply station in orbit. A metal railing divided the seating deck from the open cylindrical space that made up the rest of the Main Cabin. Unable to turn around, she imagined the closed oval hatch eight or nine meters directly behind her. It led to Decks 2, 3, and 4. She was fascinated, having only ever seen the Ark's interior in hologram form back in Iceland.

Eve waited. Soraya, Ikemba, and Dei-Lin were still busy on the Bridge with last-minute duties. Her colleagues were chatting quietly, beside her and behind her, but Eve sat in silence. Soraya came and kneeled beside Eve. She looked in Eve's eyes and said, "That ritual was perfect, Eve. None of us will ever forget those sacred moments. You are the right person for this job. I give thanks to Allah, the merciful and compassionate, that you are with us. Never forget this: we need you. We need what you bring us. You belong on this crew and you belong on Mars."

Eve smiled, blinked and swallowed hard, feeling too emotional to respond other than with a nod. Soraya tested Eve's tethers, then touched the back of her hand to Eve's cheek. Oddly, Soraya's gesture reminded Eve of her mother straightening her clothing before sending her out the door to go to school.

Soraya then joined Ikemba and Dei-Lin on the Bridge and pulled the hatch shut behind her.

Now, tethered in, Eve realized that communications were coming in through her implant. She heard Ikemba's voice, then

Dei-Lin's, then the voices of the Airbus pilot and co-pilot. She started to feel anxious. Her disquiet was not primarily claustrophobia relating to her surroundings, nor fear about the vast distance to Mars, nor concern about the impending stress of takeoff, all of which she felt to some degree, but rather, it was a rising sense of terror about still being on Earth in the presence of human beings who would kill this crew if they could.

Her thoughts raced back to what happened in Kenya and Iceland. She imagined how some oligarch's terrorist team might somehow attack before they could take off from Gilligan's Island, using information from their two kidnapped colleagues. A bomber recruited from among the kitchen staff, lured by the promise of a million Americredits or rubles? A weaponized drone launched from an unseen boat just offshore? A computer virus encrypted in the vessel's code by a hacker? Eve found herself clenching her jaw, squeezing the armrest of her chair, even tensing her toes in her boots.

Then, suddenly, an explosion did occur, but it was one of laughter, not bombs. Ikemba addressed the crew through their implants, perfectly parodying the typical spiel that flight attendants used to give back when commercial air travel was more common. Ikemba began with a hilarious set of instructions about seat belts, rest rooms, and carry-on luggage, leading to this dramatic conclusion: "Ladies and gentlemen, do not raise your tray tables to their upright and locked position, because you have NO TRAY TABLES! There will be NO SERVICE, NO SNACKS, NO DRINKS. And please notice that there are NO EMERGENCY EXITS! Did you hear me? NONE! Once we take off, you are STUCK! If there is an emergency, you'd better hope I know what I'm doing, because YOUR lives are in MY hands until we arrive on Mars!" Then he let out his loudest mad scientist crossed with evil dictator laugh, which got even Kat chuckling.

Ikemba then spoke in a perfectly calm voice: "Thank you for flying Macopro. Enjoy your flight! Before we take off, Dei-Lin and Gabriela have some of the latest space news. Gabriela and Dei-Lin, I'll hand over to you."

Gabriela began. "Well, my friends, the news from Mars is very bad. Mars is so very, very sad."

Dei-Lin asked, "Why is Mars so sad, Gabriela?"

"You want to know why? OK, Dei-Lin, I'll tell you. He and Saturn have been in this long-term, long-distance relationship. Mars is very romantic, you know. When they started dating, Mars would send cakes, donuts, croissants, and other spacetries. When he proposed to Saturn, he gave her some beautiful engagement rings. But then just last night, they broke up, and now Mars is broken-hearted. Do you want to know why Saturn dumped him, Dei-Lin?"

"Why did she dump him, Gabriela?"

"Saturn said she only wanted a plutonic relationship. Can you imagine that?"

Instead of laughing as she usually did, Gabriela remained silent while her companions groaned. "Do you want to know what's even worse?"

The whole crew joined Dei-Lin and asked in unison, "What's even worse, Gabriela?"

"Saturn won't return the rings he gave her." More groans followed, but Gabriela's tone remained deadpan. "Mars got so angry he turned red and asked Saturn why she didn't love him the way he loves her. You know what she said?" Dei-Lin and the crew responded in unison, and Gabriela replied, "Saturn kept saying, 'I just need some space. I just need some space.'" More groans, but still no laughter from Gabriela, who added, "The only planet sadder today than Mars is, of course, Uranus. Do you know why Uranus is so sad, Dei-Lin?" Everyone joined Dei-Lin on cue, and Gabriela replied, "Well, if I were named Uranus, I'd be sad too, wouldn't you? But Uranus is so sad because the Sun just announced that the solar system is changing Uranus's name, and Uranus likes the new name even less. Do you know what the new name is, Dei-Lin?"

This time, before anyone could say anything, Dei-Lin delivered the punch line, and she delivered it perfectly, as a question: "Urectum?"

And at that, groans and laughter filled Eve's implant.

This joyful, raucous liturgy of distraction perfectly quelled Eve's anxiety, and no thought of terrorists or oligarchs returned throughout the rest of the launch.

Another five minutes of waiting passed, and then takeoff began. Eve felt the slow bumpy acceleration on the asphalt, the momentary fear that they would run out of runway before lifting off, then the long, steady, gentle ascent. Nobody spoke. The old A380 roared through the atmosphere for about forty minutes, and then came the moment when the spacecraft separated from the aircraft – seven distinct bangs in rapid succession, like machine-gunfire.

Immediately Eve felt the first rush of weightlessness – for her, the feeling that a bubble was rising from her gut through her throat to her neck and then spreading across her brain, like riding a roller-coaster over the crest, but the expected post-crest fall never came. She counted the gentle glide, nine seconds, giving the aircraft time to descend and veer away before rocket ignition.

Suddenly the Ark's engine roared and Eve felt the chest-crushing pressure of extreme acceleration. Just as she felt she couldn't take any more, the intensity of the acceleration doubled, and then doubled again. Eve felt her eyeballs pushing back into her eye sockets so intensely she feared that they might burst. She found it impossible to inhale, then sensed that she was about to pass out, and then she passed out momentarily, only to awaken into the slow release of blissful zero G, bliss that was quickly followed by the soapy feeling in her mouth that precedes throwing up.

Because of their hasty departure from Iceland, the majority of the crew never reached their fourteenth "treatment" in the

Gauntlet, so their bodies had not formed the neural pathways necessary to protect them from launch nausea. To minimize sickness, they had eaten little during their last day on Earth, and Gabriela had dispensed powerful anti-nausea injections just before the departure ritual. (She had a relevant joke for each person as she gave them their shots. For Eve: What do you get when you cross a tortoise and an injection? A slow poke.) The injections worked, but barely.

16
A Place as Beautiful as This

Because Ikemba was the only member of the crew who had experienced space flight before, when they achieved Earth orbit, he came to the Main Cabin and helped them put into practice what they had learned in recent days and weeks in theory . . . first, moving around the Ark in zero G, and later, more delicate things, like eating, drinking, and using a zero G toilet. They had seen training videos about these activities, but being there was . . . different. It felt to Eve a bit like arriving at a new college campus and being given an orientation by an upperclassman, except that the campus was at the bottom of the ocean and they were expected to breathe underwater. It was not just a new place, but a totally new kind of place.

Once everyone got reasonably comfortable moving around, Soraya brought out a small cloth bag and opened it. She pulled out a pair of glasses, or goggles, or something in between. "These are AR glasses. The letters stand for augmented reality. They will be essential for your daily life on the Ark," she said. "Those of you who normally wear glasses will find that they correct your vision, so your existing glasses will no longer be necessary. They will be linked with your bracelet and ear implant, and they are integrated with the Ark's quantum computing systems. We'll show you how to use their various functions in the coming days. You will find them quite amazing. They will become your microscope, your telescope, your digital page, your reading device, your personal theater, and more. We are giving them to you today because they also will serve as your still and video camera. Anything you want to record, you can easily do so, with both audio and video." She then turned to Dei-Lin, who was the resident AR glasses expert.

Dei-Lin distributed a pair of glasses to each of the crew. "These *args* will be really helpful for daily life on the Ark," she said. They joked about the style and the name, but soon they were thoroughly intrigued as Dei-Lin guided them in arg use. Their first opportunity to use them would come in a matter of minutes, after they docked with Macopro's unmanned orbital supply station.

Although only two LVRVs were launched every twenty-six months or so, Macopro launched both manned and unmanned supply rockets much more frequently. These cargo ferries carried water, equipment, supplies, fuel, and thorium-salt mini-reactors to the station, from which they could be loaded onto the next LVRV. This allowed each LVRV to launch with minimum payload when escaping Earth's gravity, the most fuel-intensive part of the voyage.

Docking went smoothly. The station's robots transported voyage-essential cargo and fuel cells into the storage bay below Deck 4 without incident. As the cargo was being loaded, a huge container of ice that had been stored at the station was melted and pumped into a thick jacket just beneath the LVRV's outer skin. This jacket of water would serve the needs of the crew, the plants, and the animals, but it also served another essential purpose: it helped shield the crew from solar radiation and galactic rays, which would constitute one of the greatest dangers of their interplanetary journey. Most of the water would be discharged into space before landing on Mars to lighten the ship during descent.

Once the voyage-essential cargo was loaded and the cargo bay was re-pressurized, the cargo had to be stowed. That was the crew's job, and it gave them their first opportunity to use the args. When they approached a cargo container, an inventory code on the container signaled on their args, and in the upper right corner of their field of view, a list of the container's contents appeared. Below it, a 3-D floor plan of the Ark appeared, highlighting the location in which each item was to be stowed.

If their earlier orientation to zero-G life felt like a campus orientation, they now felt like they were moving their gear into their dorms. The hatch into the cargo bay was narrow, so crew members had to propel themselves into the hold individually, choose a container, and gently push or pull it through the hatch. Then it would take anywhere from twenty to forty minutes to stow each item from the container in its proper place, guided by their args. The empty container, made of a canvas-like cloth, could then be folded and stowed for use on Mars.

They quickly discovered that moving things in zero G was trickier than they expected. Ikemba tried to coach them. "Yes, you can lift an eight-hundred-kilogram thorium-salt mini-reactor as if it were a suitcase, but . . . the question is, once you lift it, can you stop it before it hits the wall and blows us all to pieces?" he said. He was exaggerating, but he made his point. As they stored their gear, there were a few tense moments, but Eve was pleasantly surprised by the amount of laughter they shared.

In other portions of the arg field of view, additional information was constantly appearing. Dei-Lin told the crew that, eventually, all of this information would make sense, and that within a few days or weeks, the args would feel like a natural extension of their bodies and minds.

They had two more Earth orbits to complete before shifting into the Hohmann Trajectory Orbit that would take them in a long, gentle arc to Mars. They took turns at the windows. The port window was turned toward Earth and the starboard looked out into space. Eve was eager for some time at the port window to get a view of Earth that she had never seen before and would never see again.

When her turn came, she was glad to be joined by Nikau and Refa, members of what they were calling, somewhat uncreatively, Team Culture. They invited Ekaterina to join them. Kat was a tough woman, and she knew more about space flight than the other three. But she didn't have the "benefit" of even one session in the Gauntlet. She looked like she was very drunk or very sick or very angry, or all three at once.

The four of them gathered at the window just as the islands of Indonesia were coming into view below them. Tender green patches of forested mountains, marked with jagged brown scars, would become momentarily visible in gaps that opened in the white blanket of clouds. Then the clouds would return until they would get a brief glimpse of the magic blue of the Indian Ocean. They immediately experimented with their args to take videos and photos. The telephoto power of the args was almost beyond belief.

The clouds fell behind them and Australia stretched to the south. In the distance they saw the narrow tip of green along the southwest coast, the thin verdant strip along the north coast, and the vast expanse of reddish gray in between. As usual, much of Australia was on fire, and the lines of smoke were easily visible. Even though she had seen thousands of pictures taken from space, looking down on her home planet with her own eyes filled Eve with a sense of awe and aching tenderness. Sharing the experience with two young artists and a wise older woman made it feel even more poignant.

Soon Papua New Guinea stretched beneath them, its forested mountain spine fading to lighter green near the coastline, streaked with spiderlike scars of brown with smoke rising from the edges. A shallow sea glowed like an iridescent emerald between the mountainous island and Australia.

"How can we leave a place as beautiful as this?" Refa asked, clearly not expecting an answer. "After everything we've done to her, she is still . . ."

"How could we damage and destroy something as wonderful and precious as this?" Nikau replied. After a few minutes of shared silence, Nikau added, "Look, is that the northern tip of the Aotearoa, my ancestral home? I never got to visit it. And I never will. I never will."

Refa put her hand on Nikau's shoulder, which Eve noticed because Refa hadn't before this point impressed her as a particularly warm or empathetic person.

Soon they were over the vast expanse of the Pacific. No one spoke, and no one could look away. Their launch site in Kiribati was too tiny to pick out from space, but when they used their args to magnify and seamlessly integrate what they saw with computer-generated images, they could discern the runway, the main building, the office trailer, the hālau, the beaches, everything.

After a long stretch of magnificent blue ocean dotted with white clouds, they could see Mexico, and north of it, where California should be, they saw the blue-gray smudge of fire smog. "Still burning," Eve said. "It's hard to believe after all these years there's anything left to burn."

Directly beneath them, they saw the narrow strip of land that joined North and South America.

"I visited Central America. I was right there," Refa said, a wistful tone to her voice. "Just six or seven months ago, with the New York Youth Orchestra. Mexico City, Guatemala City, Managua, San Jose, and Panama City. I can make them out now. I never could have guessed I'd be seeing them from this vantage point. We played Dvořák and Copeland, my favorite Western composers." She hummed a few familiar bars from the Second Movement of Dvořák's *New World Symphony*, as the Central Range with its four great volcanoes passed below them. As she hummed, Eve noticed that in her args' lower left field of view, the name of the symphony became visible. Eve mentioned this to Refa, and Refa called Dei-Lin to come over. Dei-Lin showed Refa how to focus her eyes on an item in the screen and blink to select it. Then she showed her how to activate a share function, and soon the four circled around the window were listening to a symphonic rendition as the soundtrack to their aerial tour of Earth.

By then they were over the Caribbean. Eve could only imagine what Refa and Nikau saw through their artists' eyes as they looked down on Cuba, Haiti, and the Dominican Republic.

"I'll never see such blues again," Refa whispered. "We don't even have words for such colors, not in Arabic, not in English. At least I get to see them once. I hope I can remember this scene when I'm living in a rust-red world. No image on a screen can capture this. I feel like I just fell in love. With everything. Everywhere."

"Perhaps, having seen it with our eyes, we will see images on screens differently in the future," Ekaterina said, her voice uncharacteristically gentle. "We can only hope."

"I hope you're right, Kat," Refa replied. She reached over and hugged this woman, who was the age of a grandmother; again, a surprisingly tender move for a teenager who made such a fierce first impression. "But even without any vids, I don't think I'll ever forget what I see, what I feel right now."

A few more moments passed in silence.

"You guys, I feel . . . I don't know what I feel," Nikau said. "I mean, I am an emotional person, but this feels . . . almost scary. Like, what we see is so beautiful, but I feel so sad. It's . . ."

Refa spoke. "It's not just you, Nikau. I feel the same thing. It feels . . . kind of like a funeral. A beautiful funeral."

"I think this is what they mean by the overview effect," Eve said. "Many astronauts have experienced it, when they see the Earth from above. There was a famous actor who played an astronaut back in the twentieth century, William Shatner. When he was ninety, he got to travel into space for real, and I remember reading his description of the experience."

"What did he say?" Nikau asked, their eyes still gazing through the window.

"He felt the contrast between space . . . the lightless, cold, lifeless expanse of space . . . and the vibrant colors of the Earth.

And it made him feel an intense love for the Earth and, at the same time, profound sadness about how little we humans appreciate her," Eve said.

"I'm not ninety," Kat said, "but I feel like I've never really understood the Earth until now, now as I'm saying goodbye to her forever. *Bozhe miy.*"

It was soon time to surrender the port window to their colleagues, and not long after that, it was time to tether into their seats for leaving Earth orbit, and acceleration. Rather than a single short and intense acceleration to cruising velocity, the crew would experience a carefully timed sequence of rocket firings over about an hour.

This firing of the rockets was less dramatic than the firings during launch. Even so, after two or three bursts, Eve felt dizzy and disoriented. She lost the sense that they were moving forward; instead she felt that they were sliding from side to side or tumbling end over end. She told herself that this feeling was a consequence of her inner ears and brain, not of reality, but the feeling was still unpleasant. Later, she noticed that her hands ached from clutching the armrest so hard for so long.

The bursts kept continuing, every few minutes, so just as she began to feel more normal, the vertigo returned.

Ekaterina and Thurman had exchanged seats with Refa and Nikau, so now they sat to her right. After twenty minutes or so of acceleration, Eve looked over at the older woman, wondering how she was faring. Kat's eyes were open and unblinking; she appeared to be staring at the ceiling through her arg.

"Are you OK?" Eve asked.

"I am listening to Dvořák again," Kat replied, "and looking down on the South Pacific using the arg video function. It is helping me survive the damned nausea. You'll notice I have a bag in my hand, just in case."

Eve lifted her head to see Thurman to Kat's right, his eyes closed, absolutely motionless.

"Thurman, how about you?" Eve asked.

"Did you know," he answered, speaking very slowly in his raspy bass voice, "that to escape Earth's gravity, we traveled at over eight kilometers per second? That is 28,800 kilometers per hour. Over the last twenty minutes, we have more than doubled that speed. So, for an older gentleman traveling that fast, I would have to say I'm doing pretty damned well."

Eve noticed him smiling ever so slightly, his eyes still closed, and she knew he was OK.

"What music does for me, numbers do for him," Kat said, without emotion.

After another hour or so, Dei-Lin and Soraya unstrapped from their seats on the Bridge and floated back to face the rest of the crew in the cabin. "Congratulations," Soraya said, "we are in our beautiful, curved trajectory to rendezvous with Mars in two hundred and seventy days. Unless there's a problem, we won't need to fire the rockets again for about two hundred and fifty days, when we will begin gradually slowing down so that we can be gently captured by the gravity of Mars. Congratulations. We're on our way!"

As the crew's applause subsided, Dei-Lin said, "The LVRV has one more trick up its sleeve. I'm sending a live camera feed to your args. Ikemba is about to deploy the solar array." Eve and her colleagues saw a view from a camera mounted just above the Bridge, looking back over the dorsal ridge that ran the length of the vessel, with the Ark's vertical stabilizer perfectly bisecting the Earth behind them. Just as they began oohing and aahing over the view, a slit appeared along the center of the ridge and four racks of solar panels gracefully unfurled. They stretched to their full length and adjusted to face the sun behind them.

"We're a dragonfly," Eve said out loud, her eyes brimming, "a solar-powered dragonfly."

A few seconds later, Ikemba came through the hatch. "I've done my job, everyone, at least, the first part of it. Now it's time for you to do yours."

They unstrapped themselves and stowed their seats in a long-term location, guided by their args. As they did so, Soraya spoke into their implants: "We are syncing our clocks with the Valles Marineris settlement. By the Mars Base clock, it is now 21:30. We will have our first meeting at 07:00. You have done well, my friends. We are underway. I've asked Ikemba and Gabriela to review sleeping arrangements, so let's assemble down in Deck 2."

Ikemba led the way and showed everyone where their hammocks, called cocoons, were stowed. He explained how to rig them and strap themselves into them, and how to use their sleep helmets to shut out light and sound. He explained that the cocoons and sleep helmets were woven with dense, thick filaments of a special shielding material. This thick fabric would provide extra protection from radiation while they slept. "That's a big deal," he explained. "Radiation levels out here range from one hundred and fifty to a thousand times higher than back on Earth, depending on the form of radiation." Ikemba then nodded to Gabriela.

"Each night," Gabriela explained, "you will take a radio-protective medication designed to enhance rapid tissue repair while you sleep. That's why we want you inside your cocoon for at least eight hours every night. Your body needs that time of rest in a space of maximum protection so that it can repair itself from the radiation damage that comes along with space travel."

As Gabriela distributed the medication, Ikemba continued, "Think of it like this. Our first line of radiation defense is the LVRV itself. The Ark's skin and structure include shielding materials made from boron nitride nanotubes. They absorb and disperse cosmic and solar radiation. Then, as a second line of defense, the Ark contains a protective water jacket. Water, it turns out, is an excellent radiation barrier. Third, your underwear, jumpsuits, and knit space caps are made from radio-protective fabrics. Fourth, your cocoons and helmets provide additional shielding at night. Then, the nightly radio-protective meds boost our own bodies' ability to repair damage while we sleep. Put that all together, and we reduce our chances of long-term radiation damage. But these protections only work if we use them consistently and strictly according to protocols."

Eve recalled learning about radiation damage from a training vid, but after Ikemba's instructions, she was eager to pull herself into her cocoon. She wasn't especially tired, but she was eager for some privacy to process the last twenty-four hours, especially the ugly scene created by her drunk father in the hālau before launch. Soon, though, all unpleasant thoughts of that incident were gone, and she fell deep into a series of dreams, swimming in emerald seas and soaring over folded green mountains, with Dvořák as her unfailingly elegant soundtrack.

17
Song of the Redwing

When Eve felt someone touching her shoulder through the cocoon, she didn't awaken all at once. From dreams of swimming and flying, she suddenly found herself riding a bicycle down a steep hill, skiing in the Rockies, and rolling down a hill as a child. Then, the pleasant dreams became nightmarish and she felt herself falling, falling, falling. Suddenly she was awake, shuddering, replaying the ugly scene with her father in the hālau.

She pulled off her helmet, opened her cocoon, and saw Nikau smiling, their faces just inches away from each other. "Rise and shine, Eve," Nikau said. "It's time for day two in space. *Wā parakuihi*. Breakfast time! Refa and I ate already. Umm . . . You-know-who is down there in the galley. You can't avoid him forever."

Eve got dressed, activated her arg, and managed to brush her teeth without emitting too much spittle into the air of Deck 2. When she pushed down to the little galley area near the bottom of the deck, there he was, tethered to the wall, arranging squeeze tubes of food and a pouch of coffee in the air in front of him.

Her father hadn't been present for the ritual. Eve was grateful for that. He must have entered the LVRV at the last minute, in those few moments when she'd dozed off. He had then tethered in directly behind her and never said a word, nor did anyone say anything to him.

She'd passed him once during their first day in space, near the cargo bay hatch when they were stowing gear. Neither spoke nor acknowledged one another. *It's funny*, Eve thought as she prepared to encounter him, *that on a small vessel with ten people aboard, two people can successfully avoid each other so well.*

"Good morning," he said quietly as she pulled herself along the handholds on the wall, down toward the galley. "Nice glasses."

"Everybody's wearing them these days," she replied.

"Eve, I am truly sorry. No doubt my despicable performance in the hālau brought back a plethora of unsavory memories. Mercifully, I cannot remember everything I said, but what I do remember was inexcusable. I feel ashamed. Thankfully, Soraya has assured me there is no vodka on board."

Eve nodded, then asked, "What about Hailey? I thought . . ."

"Soraya helped me with that as well. She painted a vivid picture of what it would be like to be a torture victim in the hands of an oligarch seeking information on Macopro. That description and some black coffee were sufficient to sober me up quite efficaciously. Under her direction, I wrote a message to Hailey with a delayed send. Hailey should have it by now."

"What did you say?"

"I told the simple truth: I am away on a project. It is a highly classified mission funded by an oligarch, related to my environmental work, and I will be gone for more than two years, having signed agreements that forbid me from going into details. I told Hailey that she will need to move on in her life without me, just as I must do the same. And I said that I am not as good a man as she thought. I was vague, to be sure, but I spoke truthfully. Especially the 'not as good a man' part."

"Hmmm." The less said, Eve felt, the better. "Headache?"

"Affirmative. About what one would expect after combining a hangover with this launch. Worse than the headache, though, I am worried about how I have hurt and embarrassed you, not to mention Thurman, Ekaterina, Soraya. At least the injection Gabriela administered before launch successfully pre-empted the worst of what might have occurred in terms of, shall we say, gastrointestinal upset. How did you fare in that regard?"

"About as you'd expect," Eve said, and then made eye contact with Colfax for the first time since the hālau event. "Let's leave it on Earth. We've got nine months and millions of kilometers to put between us and the past. But don't you ever . . . Ever."

She didn't finish her sentence. She didn't need to.

For the next few minutes, they sucked their tubes and pouches of breakfast together without speaking, letting physical proximity and the ritual of eating gently restore some sense of normalcy, if not warmth, between them. It was a familiar ceremony, albeit with unfamiliar food, that somehow reduced the gap . . . reduced it, but didn't bridge it.

At 06:55, Soraya reminded the crew through their implants that their first morning briefing was about to begin. Eve pushed up past her father toward the Main Cabin. Just as she grabbed a handhold, Colfax grabbed her left foot. She bent over to face him, surprised and a little annoyed to be stopped.

"Eve," he said, "I was too ashamed to participate in the ritual before launch. And too hungover. But Soraya told me what it entailed, and I would like to tell you what I would have said."

"OK," Eve replied, a little coolly. "OK."

"When you asked everyone about our intention for the Earth, I would have said that I hope . . ." He looked down awkwardly, then continued, "I hope the wood thrush will survive. And the European redwing. So many species have been lost, but those two . . . they will always be special to me," he said. "Whatever happens to humans, the birds have been nothing but spectacular, and they deserve to survive."

"You always called those two your 'spark birds,' the birds that sparked your love for ornithology. So, I understand," Eve said. She paused, searched her memory, and managed to whistle the descending tones of the redwing's call, first five, then six, then seven notes.

"That is the song," Colfax said. "I'm pleased you remember."

"I could never imitate the wood thrush call. Too complex and otherworldly. Time for our meeting," Eve said. Her father let go of her foot, and Eve launched herself from the handhold toward the Main Cabin as if flying were her normal mode of travel.

When Eve and Colfax passed through the hatch, Soraya was chatting informally with Refa and Nikau. She explained that decades ago, when planning for Mars voyages, scientists discussed putting the crew into artificial hibernation. Their assumption was that a voyage of between two hundred and three hundred days would be insufferably boring. When actual voyages began, though, crews discovered that there weren't enough hours in a day to accomplish all they needed to accomplish between launch and landing.

"That's especially the case for this crew," Soraya said. "Because our mission is about more than engineering for physical survival. Our mission is to help Mars Base go beyond survival to flourishing, and not just human flourishing, but the development of whole flourishing webs of life. We know the two are inextricable, and in fact, are not two things at all, but one. Today, our launch is behind us and the work of the last voyage begins."

The first crew meeting on the Ark had an awkward start. The ten travelers tried to figure out how to float in a way that made sense, but soon they were all drifting in odd directions. After some laughter and ineffective attempts to reorganize, they finally arranged themselves in two circles, each with five people, one slightly above, one slightly below. They used Velcro tethers on their jumpsuits to attach themselves from each hip to anchor strips on the cabin wall. From that day forward, they called this arrangement "meeting formation," and without being asked, they proved themselves creatures of habit by always choosing the same location in the formation. In "meeting formation", they could see the faces of all their colleagues.

Soraya's first order of business was to tell the crew the new date and time.

"If you look at your bracelets, you'll see that we've synced the Ark with Mars time at Mars Base in Valle Marineris. So, it's no longer December twenty-sixth, 2056," she said. "The date is 06.22.11, and the time is 07:07. From this moment forward, we're orienting ourselves to the Martian day, which is slightly longer than an Earth day. From now on, midnight occurs a fraction of a second after 24:39:35."

She nodded to Ikemba, who continued. "We're maintaining the idea of weeks, which will be as arbitrary on Mars as they were on Earth. On Earth, months are based loosely on the twenty-eight-day cycle of the Moon. In fact, the English word *month* is derived from the word *moon*. As you know, Mars has two moons, Phobos and Deimos, and they're of no use in establishing a Martian month because one circles Mars every seven hours and the other every thirty hours. By the way, they're much smaller and nearer to the surface of Mars than Earth's moon is to Earth, and neither is round. Inhabitants describe the larger and nearer moon, Phobos, as a shiny potato. It appears to the human eye about a third the size of Earth's moon. The smaller and more distant moon—"

Soraya interrupted, "Thanks, Ikemba. I think you have a future as a teacher, when your work as pilot is through."

"I never thought of that. I think I would like it . . . being a teacher," he said. "I'm planning to retire from my current career as a pilot right after we land, you know."

With a small smile, Soraya continued. "As Ikemba said, we're keeping the Earth month, but standardizing it at thirty days. Since the Martian year is 687 days long, we're working with twenty-three months, with the final month being shortened by three days. Perhaps someday we'll create names for the months, but for now we'll just use numbers."

Ikemba interjected again. "On Mars Base, they set year one as the year of our first landing. So, Earth date June second, 2044 became 01.01.01 on Mars. Since then, 1.9 Earth years have passed for every year on Mars."

Once they had calendars and clocks more or less sorted, Soraya explained that she had studied the previous voyages and what could be learned from them. "Think of this voyage as space school," she said, "and the time will pass remarkably quickly. We all have a lot to learn and a lot to prepare for.

"Physically," she said, "we have to master the daily rigors of zero-G life, with new ways of exercising, sleeping, eating, bathing, and attending to other bodily needs. Socially," she continued, "we have to learn to adjust to life together in this very confined space, including addressing and resolving frustrations and conflicts. This will serve us well on Mars, since accommodations there will also be tight."

She took a moment to glance around at her colleagues. "Intellectually, we need to learn all we can about Mars itself, including the planet's geography and geology, the history of the colony's first years, and basic information about our two hundred or so soon-to-be neighbors and colleagues."

Ikemba once again jumped in. "We'll also need to use time in our voyage to study our vid bank," he said.

Then Soraya deftly redirected: "Thanks, Ikemba. You're exactly right. Gabriela, will you take a few minutes to explain the vid bank?"

Gabriela leaned over from the top row so she could make eye contact with those in the circle slightly below her. "Each of us has been assigned specific skills to study. For example, our clothes won't last forever, so some of us will use the vid bank to study sheep shearing, yarn-making, knitting and weaving. Others of us will learn to turn flax, bamboo, and cotton into thread and fabric. Others of us will study pottery, forging metal, agriculture, aquaculture, and all kinds of electronics. We also need to study the more technical skills, from regolith engineering to atmospheric mining to metallurgy to solar panel construction to computer programming and circuit design. So, when we arrive, we'll enter into apprenticeships with colleagues on the base who are practicing these skills. And . . ." Gabriela flashed her most innocent smile, "if you would like to become my apprentice in being an entertainer and chief morale officer, just ask me."

"I'm sure you'll have at least nine applicants from the Ark, Gabriela. But seriously, as Gabriela said, there are no stores where we're going," Soraya told them. "Everything we need, we must make. Broadening our skill set will be essential."

Gabriela continued, "As many of us as possible will need to know as much as possible about as many skills as possible. Knowledge that would be dispersed among tens of thousands of people on Earth will need to be shared among about two hundred of us. So . . . we all must be students, and we'll all need to join Ikemba in thinking of ourselves as teachers as well."

At that moment, Eve saw in a deeper way why combating suicide was so important. Each resident who died took with them essential knowledge that may not have been duplicated in another resident's understanding. That realization went through her like a shiver.

"More immediately," Gabriela said, "we'll each have daily housekeeping duties on the Ark, which will mean learning how to operate waste dehydrators, food rehydrators, clothes washers, air scrubbers, battery rechargers, the bio-composter, and the like. There's no reason to be bored on this voyage."

Ikemba added, "The solar array that we deployed yesterday will need minor adjustment every few days, too. I'll oversee that, assisted by Dei-Lin."

Soraya said, "Yes. Each of us will have additional daily responsibilities. For several of us, that will mean tending the animals and plants on the ship and preparing them for Mars. We're something of a traveling zoo, aquarium, and greenhouse, with precious living cargo. Others of us will have other primary duties. Eve, would you tell everyone about your team?"

"My team will be developing a plan for a vibrant and sustainable Martian culture," Eve began, "while seeking to understand the causes of the suicide epidemic and looking for ways to preempt future suicidal ideations. Easy to say, but if I think about it too much, I feel absurdly unqualified for such a task. I console myself that anyone who felt qualified would be . . . unqualified, on the basis of arrogance."

Soraya then began bringing the meeting to a close. "We're going to have to make time for rest and fun, individually and together, on this tiny Ark. Video games, chess, party games, vids, art, whatever it takes to make sure that we relax and enjoy ourselves for a few hours each day. And, Gabriela, we will be depending on you in your unofficial capacity as chief morale officer."

Colfax raised his hand and asked about golf, and Soraya told him there were unlimited opportunities just outside the cargo bay.

"OK, I shall take a pass on that for now," he said. "I have heard about those micro meteors and how they can speed through a human skull before the victim even knows what hit him, or her."

Eve spoke next. "We have two of Earth's best young musicians with us, and although some of their larger instruments are disassembled for transport, they each have a few smaller instruments readily available. So, we can expect some live music for our night life."

Nikau beamed and displayed a thumbs-up, while Refa nodded once, her smile barely discernible.

Nikau then asked about checking on news from Earth. Soraya began, "I'm sorry, Nikau. That won't . . ."

"But we were told . . ." Nikau began.

Soraya looked at Thurman. He nodded. "Thurman has some . . . some news that we didn't feel it appropriate to tell you yesterday," Soraya said.

Eve felt herself tense.

18
Eye Roll

Thurman looked down at his hands as he spoke, his voice even deeper and his pace of speech even slower than usual. "Since we survived the abduction attempt on December second in Iceland, our colleagues have experienced a series of synchronized cyberattacks at our offices in Copenhagen, Seattle, and Vilnius. There was another car bombing and abduction attempt at our Kenyan launch site just a few days ago. So, whoever has been after us already knows too much about us. We have no reason to believe that our launch yesterday was detected, but we have every reason to believe Macopro remains the object of someone's very keen interest. So, just before launch, we made a grave decision. We initiated Code Indigo, which involves the complete termination and erasure of Macopro as an ongoing entity. The last thing we want to discover is that two years from now, a shipload of armed troops is en route to take over Mars Base on behalf of a desperate oligarch who has captured Macopro's assets and knowledge base. In short, there is no Macopro left. It is gone."

Eve felt a chill spread among the crew as the words "complete termination and erasure of Macopro," were spoken, and then Nikau groaned, "Oh, God, no."

Thurman continued. "Kat and I realized, thanks to input from Soraya and Colfax, that it was simply too dangerous for us to remain on Earth because of the information that could be extracted from us through torture, drugs, or both, which explains our last-minute decision to join you on this voyage. Code Indigo resulted in a complete scrubbing of our computer systems, dispersal of our staff under assumed identities, dispersal of our assets, and dismantling of our corporate offices. That is why I say, as of launch time yesterday, Macopro no longer exists, which means there is no communication center to relay messages to or from Earth. We are on our own. All our eggs are in a very small and fragile basket on Mars."

Dei-Lin leaned in and asked, "Why didn't you tell us all this sooner?"

"It was a judgment call we had to make," Thurman said. "I know you are very sensitive to secrecy, Dei-Lin, and I apologize. I am telling you now."

The hum of the Ark filled the cabin. The crew remained motionless in their meeting formation, no one speaking a word, each deep in their own thoughts.

Gabriela broke the silence. "Let us hope and pray that the loved ones we left behind on Earth will remain safe and well." Eve noticed that Gabriela's normally bright eyes were now glistening. In zero gravity, her tears couldn't fall; they could only pool in her eyes.

Nikau asked, "Without support from Macopro on Earth, are we, like, in trouble?"

Thurman replied, "Our missions have always been self-contained, and after undocking from our supply satellite, every voyage depends more on Mars Base than on any of our resources or personnel on Earth. Of course, we had various scenarios planned for emergencies – Code Yellow, Green, Blue, Indigo, Violet, and so on. It's part of our method to plan for any possibility. But you should know . . ." Thurman cleared his throat before he could continue to speak, "You should know that this is the most difficult decision I have made in my entire career. And I have made plenty of tough ones."

"If Code Indigo meant the dissolution of Macopro, I would hate to imagine what Code Violet might have been," Colfax added, implying a question.

"It involved all the provisions of Code Indigo, plus a pink cyanide tablet that all Macopro senior staff carried on their persons at all times," Thurman replied, flatly.

Eve looked around the circle. Nikau looked distraught. Even Dei-Lin and Ikemba seemed shaken. Eve searched for the word to describe what she sensed they were all feeling, knowing that they had broken off all possibility of communication with Earth. "Bereft" was the first word that came to mind.

Soraya caught Eve's eye. Without words, Eve knew that Soraya wanted her to offer something – consolation, guidance, something. Eve had no idea what to say, but she opened her mouth anyway, hoping something would come.

"Friends, I think we should take a break for a few minutes and allow each of us to process this news. If you need to be alone, I recommend you go to Deck 2, 3, or 4, and let's maintain those spaces as quiet for the next few minutes. If you need to talk to someone, then stay here and speak among yourselves. I will stay here to process this with anyone who needs to talk. Soraya, would that be OK? Could we reconvene in thirty minutes?"

"A good plan, Eve, but let's make it forty-five minutes."

Eve untethered and went to hug Nikau, then Ekaterina, then Thurman, and finally, Gabriela. Others joined her. The only people who left the Main Cabin immediately were Ikemba and Colfax. The other eight stayed to comfort one another and to attempt to process the news Thurman had just shared.

Soraya floated up to Eve and whispered a request. Eve nodded.

They returned to meeting formation at the appointed time, and Soraya looked at Eve.

Eve spoke. "Soraya asked if I would find some part of one of our Earth traditions to bring us together as we reconvene after hearing this disturbing news. I thought of a Buddhist meditation that I learned, oddly enough, from an Irish Catholic nun who was working in a Greek hospital in a displaced persons camp full of mostly Muslim refugees from Kurdistan. It goes like this:

May you be filled with lovingkindness.
May you be well.
May you be peaceful and at ease.
May you be happy."

Then Eve invited her colleagues to repeat those words after her, speaking words of blessing and healing to one another. After they recited the blessing three times, Eve explained that the original Buddhist blessing used the word "I" instead of "you." So next, she invited them to close their eyes, place their hands on their hearts, and speak the blessing to themselves three times.

May I be filled with lovingkindness.
May I be well.
May I be peaceful and at ease.
May I be happy.

Finally, she invited them to think of those they had left behind on Earth and to repeat the blessing three times more, but this time, with the word "they."

May they be filled with lovingkindness.
May they be well
May they be peaceful and at ease.
May they be happy.

After a few minutes of silence, Eve said, "I know it won't be easy, but I think we're ready to continue our work."

Soraya thanked Eve and then made eye contact with each crew member as she spoke, her voice strong and her tone commanding: "Much of our daily work will happen in our subteams. Eve leads Team Culture, which includes Refa and Nikau. Gabriela leads Team Biome, consisting of Dei-Lin and Colfax. Kat and Thurman, I'd like you to join in with that team too, as Team

Biome will have a lot of lives in their hands. My Lead Team includes Gabriela, my first mate; Ikemba, our pilot, and Eve. Just so you know, Ikemba will be spending every free moment doing landing simulations, and whenever Biome Team can spare her, Dei-Lin will join him in practicing the landing process."

Soraya continued, "Our night will last from 22:00 to 06:00, and we will dim lights and observe silence on all decks. The galley is always open, so you can serve yourself when you're hungry. We will eat our dinner meal together at 18:00, and in general, we'll reserve after-dinner hours for recreation, exercise, leisure, and reflection. Several of us are keeping journals of our voyage, and others may decide to use their args to create video logs. After-dinner hours are a good time for that."

Soraya then typed on the digital page that she wore on her left thigh, and assignments for the day appeared on the arg of each crew member.

Eve's morning was set aside for a meeting with Team Culture. Then she was scheduled to spend the afternoon with Ikemba, who would teach her to use the exercise equipment that would be so important for maintaining health in zero G. Then there was a list of vid tutorials she was supposed to watch before dinner. She had been chosen to specialize in sanitation on Mars. Not her first choice, but it was important, she knew, so she anticipated becoming an expert in composting toilets, waste-water purification, material recycling, and so on. *Shitty work is holy work, too*, she whispered to herself.

"At some point during the day," Soraya said, "Gabriela will call you to Deck 4 for a medical exam. You'll have an exam every twenty-one days so we can monitor how you're doing in zero G."

"That's right," Gabriela said. "Twelve times during the voyage I will be taking numerous body measurements. That is because I cannot check your weight. You all weigh nothing now! Congratulations . . . it's called the Deep Space Diet. In other good news, you'll all be getting taller in zero G. Without gravity pulling you down, your spine will lengthen. So, enjoy the growth spurt! Think of this as your second adolescence. But with more mature behavior, I hope. Colfax, I'm looking at you."

A few people chuckled, and she added, "I will also be checking your blood pressure, strength, reflexes, and mental acuity. I'm not a physician, but I've been trained as a medic, and you can come to me with any medical issues. I will pretend I know what I'm doing, and then I will consult the database to find out what I should do to help you. Of course, for help of a more personal nature, Eve is the person you should see. I will specialize in biological health. She'll take care of more spiritual needs. And she actually knows what she's doing."

Soraya picked up from Gabriela. "Eve, there has never been anyone with your capacities on a previous voyage. Gabriela is right; you are a natural person for us to come to with more personal matters. But no less important, I know that we all were deeply moved by what you have done for us, before departure and again this morning. I would like to ask you to develop a simple morning ritual for these daily briefings, and perhaps we will see the value in a monthly or weekly ritual as well. We will each have a daily regimen for physical exercise; I think we should experiment with appropriate group exercises for our internal well-being and collective morale. Would it be possible to begin experimenting as soon as tomorrow's briefing?"

Before Eve could answer, she noticed a slight eye roll from Colfax across the cabin. Any ritual sounded too much like religion to him, she supposed. He quickly recovered his composure and turned his frustration into humor: "But please, Eve, refrain from the offering plates!" He didn't get the same response to his attempt at humor as Gabriela did. Then he pushed it farther: "It is never right to charge victims for their torture."

Dei-Lin ended the uncomfortable silence. "With all due respect, Colfax, I want to say that I was probably the most skeptical person of all when I heard we would be having a *ritual* before launch. I am definitely not a religious person, and definitely not a spiritual person either. But those few minutes were very meaningful for me. I feel the same about the . . . words, whatever you call them . . . that Eve just shared. I mean, my God, in light of what's been happening on Mars, I am happy to be a guinea pig for Eve's work. Maybe volunteer is a better word than guinea pig . . . and it's certainly a better word than victim."

Eve replied before her father could argue. "Thanks, Dei-Lin, I'm honored to work on this, and glad that these experiences have been helpful. I will depend on everyone's feedback, positive or negative, as I experiment. In fact, negative feedback will be as helpful to me as positive, as long as it's expressed constructively," she said, careful not to look toward Colfax. "I will do my best to make sure it is nothing like torture, and if it is, I'm sure I'll hear about it." This time she pointed at her dad and gave her most exaggerated eye roll.

Everyone, even Colfax, laughed once more, and with that, Soraya sent the crew off to their duties.

It's going to be a long nine months, Eve thought.

19
Talking Whale

Eve needed to decide where her small team could meet. The plants and animals needed to be set up for the long voyage on Decks 3 and 4, so Team Biome was at work there.

Soraya and Ikemba were already conferring on the Bridge. They needed to schedule the five emergency drills that the crew had to practice and perfect until they could complete their tasks in a specified time: a radiation drill for solar flares, a depressurization drill for micro-meteor impact or hull failure, a system-fail drill for computer malfunctions, a crewmember-down drill in case of sudden illness or injury, and a life-support drill for some failure in life-support systems. So far, every previous voyage had faced at least one radiation emergency, and each of the other emergencies had occurred at least once to at least one crew. So, the drills were important, and they would begin soon.

Ikemba also needed to configure the computers on the Bridge for landing simulations that he and Dei-Lin would practice endlessly in the coming months.

That left Deck 2 open for Eve's team to use. It seemed like a lot of space for just the three of them.

Once their cocoons were stowed, the cylindrical space of Deck 2 was wide open except for the back-to-back toilet and bathing compartments near the top of the deck, and the galley benches on the opposite side near the bottom. Refa, Nikau, and Eve moved down to the galley benches and tethered themselves in, as if sharing a meal. That felt to Eve like an appropriate setting for their team of three.

Eve pulled her digital page from its holder on her left thigh and flattened it to its full size. A table was unnecessary since it floated in front of her. First on her agenda, she introduced a check-in.

"Refa, Nikau," she said, "I am honored to be your team leader. I take this responsibility very seriously and I will do my best to bring all of myself to our work. I am depending on both of you to do the same. To begin each meeting, I want to ask you to share how you are, how you feel, what you're bringing to our work for the day. Your honest self-reporting will help us be supportive of one another. To give you an idea of what I mean, I'll set an example by going first. I didn't prepare anything for this, because part of the idea of a check-in is to be spontaneous and honest."

Eve took a breath and looked at her teammates. "The first thing I need to say is that I'm still feeling a little off-balance from my dad's comments a few minutes ago. You can imagine what it's like having your father . . . well, I'll speak with him about that later in private. Right now, I want to put that whole situation aside so I can concentrate on our work together. With that out of the way, I am . . . about to explode with excitement. I look at each of you and I feel like the luckiest person on Earth – I guess I should say *in the solar system* – to be working with you on such a meaningful project."

She took another deep breath. "I'm only ten years or so older than you, Refa. But I must say that I feel a bit old at the moment too, not in a superior way, but in a way that I think I should explain. Nikau, I think you'll understand, because I think you were about twelve when I was born.

"When I was growing up in the 30s, that was still the era of public schools, the unmonitored internet, free education, and free speech. It was before the mega-pandemics of the 40s. It was during the Cold Civil War, before the various factions in the United States began to routinely defy the federal government. It was before the *politicult*, when the global oligarchs were pulling strings but not fully controlling their puppets in government, religion, the newsfeeds, and the military around the world. I know how all that changed around the time you were born, Refa, so I understand that your baseline of reality is so different. I guess the reason I want to say that is to make clear that your different perspective as our youngest crew member is important to me.

"And that applies all the more because I was born with white skin and all the complexities that go along with that. I hope that both of you will feel that I lead with respect for you as my equals, and I hope we can model the kind of mutuality that we know the world – I guess I should say humanity – needs, wherever it is, on Earth, on Mars, or in between. If you ever feel that my whiteness is blinding me, please tell me and I promise to listen. I promise."

Nikau leaned in. "Eve, your skin is so pale that your whiteness is blinding *me*!" They pretended to shield their eyes, and Eve laughed. Refa smiled but didn't laugh.

Eve didn't want to lose her train of thought, so she turned serious again. "I don't have to tell you how important our work will be, and how difficult. We will make mistakes. But even when we aren't making mistakes, we will be misunderstood, and there will be plenty of criticism. Some people, when they're afraid or under stress, find the only way they can validate themselves is by tearing down someone else.

"Because of the suicides, we will be entering a very tense situation, so we have to expect antagonism. When we arrive, we will need to expand Team Culture from the three of us to, I hope, at least seven or, ideally, ten, drawn from the whole Mars Base community. But for now, Team Culture is the three of us, plus whoever else on the Ark would like to join us from time to time. This is our mission, to begin to develop a vision and plan for a joyful, just, peaceful, and ecological culture on Mars, and to use only joyful, just, peaceful, and regenerative means in doing so.

Your gifts in music and art will be central to those regenerative means. With that goal in mind, I'm ready to get to work."

She looked to Nikau to her right, and Nikau began with a suggestion. "In Māori culture, and it's similar in many Indigenous cultures, we have something called a *tokotoko*, which is like a talking stick. It authorizes a person to speak in a gathering. It was a big deal in my grandmother's generation when women took the tokotoko and had equal authority as men after all the years of colonization and male domination. Anyway, Eve, it might be a nice thing to use something like a tokotoko in our check-in each day. I know we don't have any sticks on board," they said, unzipping the top few inches of their dark blue jumpsuit. "But this," they said as they removed a necklace with a carving of a whale as its pendant, "could work. One of my cousins carved it from whalebone. It reminds me to speak true and be true to who I am in my bones." They cradled the "talking whale" in their hands throughout the rest of their check-in.

Nikau took a deep breath and began: "Oh, God, you have no idea how much I need to tell somebody this. I've been homesick since departure, like a little kid away at summer camp for the first time. In my cocoon last night, I had to hold a towel over my face so you all wouldn't hear a grown adult crying." As Nikau said the word *crying*, tears began to form and their brown eyes brimmed.

"It hit me last night that I will never speak to my friends again, or my family. In our culture, family togetherness is life. My grandmother always used to say, '*Ehara taku toa i te toa takitahi, engari kē he toa takitini*,' which means basically that nobody succeeds alone: we only succeed together as a family. And my grandfather used to say, '*Waiho i te toipoto, kaua i te toiroa*,' which means, 'Let's always stick together and never drift apart.' They're both dead now, but in Māori culture, they're still with me, and when I speak their words, their wisdom lives on in my life, in my being, in my bones.

"Back in Alaska, it almost killed me to say goodbye to my parents, my aunties and uncles, and all my cousins. They were so proud of me because of my musical career. And they were grateful because I was able to give them a lot of money from those days. They were proud of me for my music therapy work too, but it hardly paid me enough to live on, so I couldn't share with them. Anyway, they threw this big going-away party for me when I left for Iceland. Of course, because of the Macopro NDA, I couldn't tell them where I was going or that I'd never be back. I just told them I was going on a special project with my new job and I would be gone for a while. They all were kind of happy I'd gotten a 'real' job that wasn't in music or psychology, and of course I told them it was with one of the respectable mega-corps, since I couldn't tell the whole truth. My cousin Gideon said he thought I must be working for an oligarch because I was being so secret, and I only laughed and said, 'If I was, I couldn't tell you.'

"Anyway, I felt so dishonest, and I couldn't let them know how sad I felt about leaving them. I had to pretend to be so happy when they were all making jokes about me finally being a star again and raking in the big Americredits, and all that. I felt especially bad to be deceiving them because a lot of my relatives are Pentecostal, and they were, like, praying for me and speaking in tongues and prophesying that I would prosper and that sort of thing. That was powerful for me because a lot of Pentecostals reject family members who come out as nonbinary. But in this case, I guess being Māori – and being family – trumped being Pentecostal. Anyway, I wish I could at least tell them the truth so they could be proud of me for being the first Māori in space and on Mars, if we get there. That would mean a lot to them because our people have always been explorers, you know?"

Neither Refa nor Eve spoke because Nikau held the carved whale, but both knew Nikau could feel their empathy for Nikau's situation. Nikau dried their eyes on their jumpsuit sleeve in the most innocent way and continued.

"When we were looking through the window at Earth yesterday, when you all were talking about how beautiful it was, I was working really hard to keep it together, because I suddenly felt that for the rest of their lives, my friends and especially my family will be missing me and wondering whatever happened to me. They will never think of looking up . . . that I might be up here in space. If I could have turned around and gone home at that moment, maybe I would have. But I'm glad I couldn't. I'm glad I'm here. I'm handling it. I'll get through it. I guess you're my friends now, and my family. You're all I've got. I'm glad to get that off my chest, and now I'm ready to get to work."

When Nikau passed the whale to Refa, she stared at it for a few seconds, then looked up at her colleagues. "First, I need to say that both my parents were fighters for peace, and they both died by violence. Then my brother was killed by a cop in New York, and most of my cousins are in jail or in a refugee camp somewhere if they aren't in their graves already. It's been that way for my people for over a hundred Earth years. Nikau, if your people were explorers, mine were survivors who held on against all odds, even when we were squeezed to the very edge of existence. So, it's a little hard for me to relate to your discomfort about your dad being here, Eve, or your homesickness for those you've left behind, Nikau. I wish I had family to put up with, or to miss, or to miss me. On the positive side, I guess I'm used to being on my own.

"I grew up in a land they call the holy land, but I call it the unholy land because of its injustice. I think I could easily have become a terrorist if just a few parts of the equation were different. I had so much fire, so much . . . fury. If you don't know what rage and resentment feel like burning in your bones . . . you should know there have been times in my life when I could have blown up the whole world, just to stop the injustice that I didn't start but had to live with every day, every second. At least I found a place to channel my fire . . . in music, in art, in creativity. And in activism too. My mother took me on my first protest march when I was still in her arms. Feeling empowered to make change and use my voice has been part of me since then.

"I've always been an outsider, on the edge, observing but not really belonging, you know? I mean, what am I? Am I Palestinian like my dad or Israeli like my mom? A Christian, a Muslim, or a Jew . . . or an agnostic-leaning secular atheist? Am I a folk musician or a classical musician, a singer or an oud player, a musician or a painter, an artist or an activist? Am I allowed to be all the above? I sometimes wish I could belong one hundred percent in just one slot and be just one thing. At least I have one place where I feel like I don't stick out, like I'm not a misfit: playing in a band or an orchestra. When I'm making music, I always *feel* and *know* that I am one small but important part of a larger creative process that requires other voices and gifts. It's what your grandmother's proverb said, Nikau. So, holding this carving, remembering the majestic creature it comes from, knowing that something big and powerful validates my voice in this circle as an equal . . . this means something to me. I will not take it for granted. I know the brutal ugliness we're leaving behind us. I know the healing power of music and art. I know the freedom and burden that comes from being who you are, even if it feels like you're in a seething, chaotic storm or a raging fire. So, with that, OK. I'm ready to get to work. Wow. I surprised myself there. Quite a speech, right? This whalebone must be magic, because I don't think I have ever before been that *fasih* . . . that eloquent."

She handed the carving back to Eve. Eve reached out to give Refa a hug, but both realized they couldn't because they were tethered to their benches. The awkward sight of two people leaning toward each other, but just out of reach, made all three burst into laughter.

Eve looked down at the notes on her digital page as Nikau put the whale necklace back on, tucked it in their jumpsuit, and zipped up the neck.

"I want to set the stage for our work by reviewing some basic background on Macopro. Before launch, we were all supposed to watch some training vids on the history of Macopro and Mars Base. But our prep time was cut short, so I want to be sure all three of us are working from the same assumptions."

Eve explained that Macopro's early work was, as anyone would expect, focused almost purely on the technical challenges of building a sustainable colony. NASA, ESA, SpaceX, Mars One, and others had been working on these challenges and learning from one another's setbacks long before Macopro secretly entered the field in the 2030s.

"Macopro quickly gained a reputation for being unscrupulous in borrowing and stealing anything they could from anyone they considered a superior competitor," Eve continued. "Because they imitated, they showed little creativity. Then came the death of the company's founders, which brought Kat to the helm, and then she recruited Thurman to join her. Then the *Excelsius* disaster came not long after that. That's when Macopro went dark and basically started over again. They stopped copying and brought together some of the world's best design engineers, and they came up with three strategic innovations that were central to the Macopro Method."

Nikau spoke up. "I remember all this from the training vids. They were the first to develop a multi-launch strategy, which meant they would launch two Mars-bound vessels during each eight-week launch window every twenty-six months. Everyone else planned to launch one vessel and wait for it to return before launching the next. The multi-launch strategy was a bigger risk for Macopro, but it meant faster rewards."

Refa interrupted. "Is this where the Robot Fleet fits in? I've heard of it, but I don't know the details of why it was such a big deal."

Nikau answered, "Are you kidding? I've always been obsessed with the Robot Fleet. It was the late 30s . . ."

"I was born in 2038," Refa interrupted, "so to me that's ancient history."

"OK, *tamaiti nohinohi*. So, here's the ancient history. Four years before the first manned voyage, not counting the *Excelsius* disaster, Macopro built a supply station in Earth orbit. The whole thing was built and run by robots. It was like a giant weightless warehouse out beyond the Moon's orbit, a little beyond the Webb space telescope. They did this while the satellite wars were still going on, when some countries and oligarchs were shooting down each other's communication and surveillance satellites, so it was all done in secrecy. Then, two years before the first voyage, they sent six unmanned vessels to Mars and established a beachhead of supplies, equipment, fuel, and structures on Mars. It was really amazing. Robots did all the work and had everything waiting for the first two ships of colonists to arrive. It all became public right after the first landing was announced. It was the pinnacle of techno-optimism, the sense that robots plus artificial intelligence would solve all our problems. It was almost a religion for a while in the 40s, you know? Like, *if we do this, we can do anything*."

Eve got the conversation back on track. "Those robots led right into the second innovation. Macopro called it the 5:1 Strategy. Before every manned launch, as Nikau explained, they would send at least five reusable rockets to the unmanned Macopro supply station with food, water, fuel, equipment, and other supplies. That way, the LVRV could escape Earth's gravity carrying nothing but crew, plus other biotic cargo, and the fuel necessary to achieve Earth orbit. Then, robots at the space station would load supplies into the LVRV cargo bays and install fuel cells in the LVRV rockets, just like they did for us yesterday after lunch."

"But it was the third innovation that turned Macopro from global hero to global pariah: the One-Way Strategy. All the other programs planned a voyage and return, but Macopro never planned to do so. To put it bluntly, they only recruited people – like us – who agreed to die on Mars."

Nikau interrupted. "When people first heard about that, Macopro's reputation went down the toilet. People said it was a death cult."

Refa said, "It reminds me of Cortés burning his ships when he got to Mexico. Macopro was doing the same thing, asking people for absolute commitment with no Plan B in sight. I guess that's part of why they've been so successful. So far at least."

Nikau spoke. "Eve, I just noticed that when we refer to Macopro, we say *they*. I never really noticed that before. I wonder why we don't say *we*. After all, we're part of it now, I guess. Maybe we should start saying *we*."

Eve replied, "Actually, Nikau, that's exactly the kind of question we need to consider. We're the last voyage. Now that we've launched and Code Indigo has been implemented, Macopro is finished, and Mars Base is on its own."

Refa added, "So really, from this point on, we're not Macopro anymore. We're . . . I don't know what we are, or who we are. Are we earthlings? Martians? Both? Neither? Who do we want to be and how do we want to define ourselves?"

Nikau nodded. "Being both and neither . . . I guess that's my specialty. And that's the part Macopro never really addressed until Kat and Thurman decided to recruit people like us for this final voyage."

"Yes," Eve said. "Before things started to deteriorate on Mars, I think Macopro assumed that recruits came with a full identity battery that would power them psychologically and socially until they died. They didn't realize that if we human beings don't recharge, our internal psycho-social batteries drain and go dead. On Earth, we could more easily take that recharging for granted because we had the accumulated charge of religion and culture from the past. Plus, we had constant inputs of meaning and identity from the culture – and nature – that surrounded us. But that has been running down even on Earth as we've all seen, even in our lifetimes. Whatever works to help Mars Base could help Earth someday, when Earth is ready, if . . ."

Eve felt she was making a mistake to refer back to Earth. That was no longer their responsibility. So, she shifted focus to where they were going, not to what they had left behind: "I hope you feel how remarkable our opportunity is. All space projects have been sponsored either by a government or by a corporation owned by oligarchs. We're the first one to . . . to have a life of our own, with all that entails. Nobody owns us, not a corporation, not a nation-state. We have nobody to report to, nobody to ask for help from, and nobody to blame, but ourselves. We are free, responsible to one another for our common well-being."

Nikau leaned forward, hands on knees: "And that's a hell of a lot of responsibility. Wow. I guess you're saying that Mars Base is a massive but fragile engineering experiment that needs to become a human community."

Refa added, "And civilization on Earth is a massive but fragile economic experiment that needs the same thing."

Eve nodded. "That's why I wanted to review this history. We need to understand that so far, almost one hundred percent of the creative energy on Mars Base has been focused on the engineering and survival challenges. Even the response to the suicides was handled like an engineering problem: simply send in an expert psychologist to fix it. As Nikau said, it will be our job to try to help this corporation of scientists and engineers focused on survival start acting like a human community focused on belonging and meaning, too. We will employ the arts, philosophy, spirituality, and any other creative means at our disposal. But we have to remember that we're not simply trying to build a replica of what's clearly not working on Earth. We need to become a new kind of human community."

"How about a new kind of multi-species community," Refa proposed.

"How about a *sustainable* multi-species community," Nikau added.

"How about a *generative* multi-species community," Eve said. "Because we have to do more than sustain. We have to generate."

Nikau untethered and floated over to Eve so that Nikau's face was less than a foot from Eve's. Nikau grabbed Eve's shoulders and drew even closer, so she could feel Nikau's warm breath: "Do you realize how cool it is that your parents named you Eve? Do you realize how freaking amazing this is? My Pentecostal relatives would say this was, like, predestined. We're like . . . a second Genesis. Hey, maybe that should be our new name instead of Macopro – Second Genesis? Or maybe Genesis 2.0?" Nikau pushed off Eve's shoulders, floated back to their seat, tethered down, turned to Refa, and opened their hands as if they were about to take a bow. "What do you think, Refa? Second Genesis has a nice ring, doesn't it?"

"Sorry, Nikau. That's a no-go for me," Refa said. "To use a religious term like Genesis puts us back in the old colonial stories that we need to leave behind on Earth. Those stories have already caused way too much harm. We're already drawing from the Noah's Ark myth. I think we've reached our lifetime monotheistic myth limit. Nice try, though, Nikau. We just need some fresh language that isn't so infused with old supremacist ghosts. I never even liked the name Macopro, because the words *colonization* and *colony* are super toxic to colonized people like us, and super limiting, too. To me, they say that what we build on Mars will simply be a colonial outpost of what was already built on Earth. Don't you think we should aim higher than that?"

Nikau looked pensive. "Yeah, it would have been good if Macopro had figured all this out earlier. They might have done a lot of things differently."

"I guess they did the best they could. Now it's up to us," Refa replied. "We're all Eves. We're all Adams. I'm sure our new Eden will have its dangerous snakes and tempting trees, just like the old mythical one did."

"*Ehara taku toa, he takitahi, he toa takitini*," Nikau replied. "My *kuia* – my grandma – sure knew what she was talking about."

20
Progress Report

It was 07.02.19.23:30, fifty days into the voyage.

"If you push too hard with this superstitious Bronze Age alchemy, the backlash will give you whiplash," Colfax whispered, almost spitting. "You know I am far from an aficionado of your shamanistic dissimulation. But neither will I take any satisfaction watching you and your micro-team of pseudo-mystics go up in mega-flames. The ritual hocus-pocus is execrable enough now among people to whom you are known. Think of when we get to Mars. You will have almost two hundred people who will see you as a snake-oil charlatan if you remain heedless of my remonstrance and counsel. They will distrust you from the start and soon resent you if you make even one false step. You only have one chance . . ."

"To make a first impression," Eve finished his line with a touch of mockery in her voice. Funny that such a brilliant man so careful of his vocabulary would repeat such a tired twentieth-century cliché.

Eve was tethered to her father's left at the galley bench. Her food tubes, bags, and pouches were floating in front of her in a neat row, undisturbed by Colfax's vitriol. She was trying to remain patient, but finally she exploded.

"I guess it's hard for you," she said, whisper-shouting and measuring her words carefully, "to watch your daughter succeed. It's hard for the great Dr. Colfax Innis to share the spotlight with his little girl, or to acknowledge his little girl has grown up to be his adult peer, and on this voyage, at least, to have more prominence than he does. It's hard for you to acknowledge that I know things, I see things, important things, that you are blind as a boulder to. You know who you remind me of?"

Colfax took a sip of recycled water from his pouch and said nothing, his pursed lips and forced calm neither inviting nor declining Eve's offer.

She kept her voice low, calm, and strong: "You remind me of your father. You have become him. He did his best to impose his beliefs on you. He couldn't accept you as different. He had to berate you and pressure you into conforming to his beliefs. That's you, now. And you've become me too, that late-adolescent me who came home from college to try to impose my new-found faith on you. You're right, Dad: I was wrong to do that. I was naive and arrogant and cultish and insulting, and I've apologized repeatedly. And I've also grown and changed. But here you are – sixty-four now? – and you are acting a lot like I did at my worst, and like your father did. I remember how sincere I felt when I told you that you were going to hell. In my mind, I was just showing concern for your eternal soul. I had no idea what you had gone through, what you were as a complex adult, what you knew and saw that I didn't. I had no idea how ridiculous, how predictable, how utterly pathetic I sounded to you. Because I was still practically a kid, and you were an adult."

Eve turned her whole body toward him and lowered her voice fully to a whisper for emphasis: "You think I'm still an adolescent, but you're acting like an arrogant, crotchety, bigoted old man – like your old man. You have no more idea of who I am than your father had of who you were. You are absolutely oblivious to what's going on with me – in here." She pointed to her chest. "And in here." She pointed to her head.

Colfax reached out and took a bag of nutrition bars that floated in front of him. He unsnapped it, slowly extracted a bar, then re-snapped the bag so no crumbs would escape. He lifted the brown bar to his mouth and took a bite. Over the hum of the Ark, Eve could hear every chew, chomp, and swallow. The sound of his jaws, teeth, and throat made him seem so . . . animal, physical, mechanical. Her reaction was visceral.

He is just an aging bag of protoplasm, a set of deteriorating biological systems, she thought as she watched him. *He needs to ingest matter to keep his systems from collapsing. His teeth need to grind the matter up so that his stomach juices can reduce it to slurry so his intestines can extract enough sugars, fats, and proteins to keep the fragile system functioning. And it will all end up as shit in the end, food for worms. Sure, he has an amazing brain, but even that isn't what it once was. I'm tired of being intimidated by him. He's just a man. A fragile, aging shit-factory . . . who is also a noisy eater.*

When the bar was gone, Colfax touched his fingers to his lips to capture any remaining crumbs, which added to Eve's disgust. She knew that behind his falsely calm exterior he was preparing a verbal counterpunch. That's what he always did.

So, she punched again first. "When I look at you, you know what I see? I see a bitter old patriarch who has lost control of his little kingdom and desperately wants to get it back. It's tragic, on a Shakespearean level."

Colfax froze. His jaw clenched. Eve braced herself for the counterpunch.

But it never came.

Her father seemed to contract, to withdraw. "Strong words," he replied, then paused. "There may be a grain of truth in them, in spite of their ingratitude and vitriol. I need time to . . . cogitate." Then he gathered his bags and pouches, unbelted from the bench, stowed his supplies in his locker, and pushed off toward the lower hatch. Just before he passed through to Deck 3, he turned back toward Eve. "I need to tell you one thing," he said.

Eve nodded. *Here it comes*, she thought.

"When I was your age, I knew I had a drinking problem," Colfax began, "along with a problem with consternation – in fact, one could call it a mean streak. I worked assiduously to control them both, and I would do so for weeks, sometimes months at a time. And then I would binge with vodka or with viciousness, or both, because as you know, they went together. I hated myself for this weakness all through my thirties. I kept my head down and did my work, knowing I had this dark secret, feeling like an abject failure, which fueled my work as compensation. I desperately hoped that someday I could overcome my shame so I could . . . fulfill my potential."

Eve nodded, although she had no idea where this was going.

Colfax continued, "When I hit forty, I reached the sober conclusion that I would never achieve lasting sobriety and I would never tame my mean streak. So, I decided that I would have to succeed in my work in spite of them. And I think I did pretty well, considering."

Colfax read the confusion on Eve's face and responded. "You wonder where all this blather is going. Well, here is my point: in ten years, maybe twenty, you might come to realize that everyone has some shame that they carry, some failure, some unfixable weakness, including you. They don't succeed in their work because they have conquered that weakness, but because they have learned to live with it, to work on in spite of it. Their personal failure is the caliginous twin . . . the Jungian shadow if you will . . . of their public success."

Eve was about to say, "I still don't understand," but Colfax said her words for her.

"You do not understand this yet. You still think that people can be perfect, or nearly so. If they're not perfect, it is the result of a lack of effort – or prayer or ritual or therapy perhaps. That naivety is a byproduct of your religious zeal, no doubt. As a result, people will always disappoint you, beginning with your father. Someday I hope you will see the necessity of imperfection, its unspeakable pulchritude, the courage it requires, even . . . the humility. I hope you see this for the sake of others, and for your own sake." His tone was neither accusatory nor defensive. It was reflective, even wistful, Eve thought.

Then Colfax disappeared awkwardly through the hatch to the lower decks, presumably to commune with his birds.

Before she could process her father's parting words, Eve's arg clicked with a message from Soraya. "I need you on the Bridge."

She pushed up from Deck 2 through the Main Cabin to the Bridge and pulled the hatch shut. Soraya was alone, strapped in the captain's chair. She wasn't looking out into space. She was looking down at her hands. She swiveled her chair as Eve positioned herself in the jump seat on the back of the hatch.

"I just received a transmission from Mars Base," Soraya said. "They held their elections back in Month Four, and three people, Chase Granby, a psychiatrist, Naomi Watseka, a soil scientist, and Sisavanh Cherubandith, a medical doctor, were elected to the Triad. I will be in contact with them every few days, either with text or vid transmissions. They have a lot on their plates right now, but they're very mindful of our arrival in Month Fifteen, and they seem especially interested in Team Culture's work."

"It's encouraging to hear that. My dad seems to think that there will be some hostility or at least resistance to our role when we arrive," Eve replied.

"Colfax may just be projecting that across the kilometers," Soraya said, sounding slightly annoyed. "Anyway, the Triad asked me two questions about you. They wanted to know if you are authorized to preside over weddings."

"Well, I suppose I'm a natural candidate to do so," Eve replied. "I've never officiated a wedding but I've been to plenty, and I'm happy to learn. What else?"

"They asked for a progress report on Team Culture's work."

"What's the lag time in communication now?" Eve asked.

"It's still about twenty-eight minutes, fourteen minutes each way, so we're a long way from chatting. Everything will be monologue via text or vid until we're close enough to begin deceleration. By then, the delay will be around twenty seconds – ten seconds each way, and real conversations will be choppy but possible for about half of each day, when Mars Base is facing us. For now, I'd like to record an interview with you through my arg and send the vid file so the Triad can see you and hear your own voice. I'll try to ask the questions I think they need answers to at this point."

"OK. That makes me a little nervous, but I can see why it would be a good thing. When would we do this?" Eve asked.

"I was thinking now," Soraya replied, unblinking.

"Yikes. Just let me take off this cap and do something with my hair. First impressions, you know," Eve said.

Soraya smiled, and Eve shot back to her locker on Deck 2. The crew normally wore knit caps during their waking hours, in part because the Ark was heated to only eighteen degrees, but more importantly because the caps contained a silver-polyethylene mesh liner that reduced cosmic radiation from reaching their brains. But what was good for the brain was not so good for the hairstyle.

Of course, without the cap, zero G meant her hair would puff out like a peacock's tailfeathers.

Eve used the mirror on her locker door to quickly brush her hair and then pulled it back with a silver clasp her mother had given her on her sixteenth birthday, perhaps the most precious single item in her small allotment of personal objects. *Funny*, Eve thought. *I never noticed that. The dragonfly on the silver clasp looks a lot like the Macopro logo*. Then she flew – literally – back to the Bridge where Soraya was making notes on her digital page.

Soraya started the recording and introduced Eve to the team.

"Chase, Naomi, and Sisavanh, it really is a pleasure to speak with you," Eve said. "I must admit I feel a bit awkward addressing you by your first names, but since Macopro policy eliminated special military, political, or academic titles, I'll . . . proceed. As a summary statement to get us started, I'll begin by saying that

Team Culture has identified our key objectives and we're making progress on them."

Soraya asked, "Could you summarize those objectives?"

"In our first phase," Eve began, "we're trying to identify the most beneficial psychological and sociological elements in Earth religions and ethical traditions, so we can emphasize those highly beneficial elements in human culture on Mars."

Soraya interrupted. "Some people, maybe even most people in the Mars Base community, will question whether religion has any beneficial elements at this point in our evolution. What would you say to them?"

"It depends on what you mean by religion," Eve said. "If you mean dogma and temples, conformity police and political manipulation, it would be hard to disagree. That kind of religion has proven itself a failure, both in what it has done and in what it has left undone."

She realized that the Triad probably had no idea of her reference to the Book of Common Prayer. She felt it best to stop there.

"So, you define religion differently," Soraya said, implying her question.

"As you can imagine, this is my whole life's work, my whole field of study, so I struggle to define religion in one sentence, but here's a start: I would say religion is an essential evolutionary survival strategy by which we seek meaning, belonging, and purpose to sustain and enhance both our individual and social lives, and usually this coherence is conveyed through a cosmic story."

Soraya nodded slightly, encouraging Eve to continue.

"As science continually expands and enriches our understanding of the universe around us, we face a continuing challenge to understand the universe inside us as individuals and the social universes we create and inhabit . . . as families, as communities, even as a species. The academic disciplines and practical traditions of religion help us to reflect on what it means for us, individually and as communities, to be conscious and responsible agents in society and in the cosmos at large. We haven't come close to outgrowing our need for religious reflection, and I doubt we ever will. What we have outgrown is the need for religions that answer questions nobody is asking and that fail to address the challenges we actually face. One of the most urgent challenges we face is the articulation of a new story, a cosmic story that creates a matrix of meaning, belonging, and purpose to help us survive and thrive, whether we are on Earth, on Mars, or . . . in between."

"Perhaps . . ." Soraya said pensively, "perhaps the problem is the word *religion*?"

"No doubt, religion is a problematic word. In a positive sense, religion is about restoring our interconnections . . . within ourselves, to one another, to the environment, and to the source or the whole, what some people call God and other people name in other ways. I have to acknowledge that, to most people, religion means a bunch of anally retentive people with no sense of proportion who strain out dust particles and swallow boulders. That's the reason our team isn't called Team Religion, but Team Culture. Surviving has been a herculean task on Mars so far, but without a dynamic culture that promotes human thriving, then I fear that merely surviving will prove . . . insufficient. That's why we're seeking to derive resources from Earth religions that can help the Mars Base community develop a thriving culture. Those resources won't be our ceiling, but they can provide us with a floor upon which to keep building."

Soraya asked, "Are you trying to create a synthesis of all Earth's religions? Maybe drawing out their common elements?"

Eve paused, nodding slightly, blinking as she searched for a way to answer concisely. "I often hear people say that all religions are the same, and there's some truth in that. They have common elements, for sure. But as someone who has studied all the Earth's major religions in some depth, I can tell you that saying all religions are the same is a lot like saying all forms of government are the same, or all fields of science are the same."

Soraya smiled, as if to say, "Go on."

"They have their commonalities. But the truth is, different religions are engaged in different research projects, to put it in scientific terms. They're trying to solve different problems, problems unique to their contexts. And they're bringing unique resources to bear, based on their unique histories and geographies. So rather than throwing all of Earth's religions in a blender and creating a kind of religious soup, I think it's better to say that we're looking for unique resources from each religion to address our common human problems in our current situation."

"I wonder how you work that out as a member of a religion yourself," Soraya said. "How would Team Culture deal with, say, my Muslim background, or Sisavanh's Buddhist background, or Naomi's background, which I believe is Crow – or Apsáalooke?"

Eve smiled. "Every religion has its own unique treasures to offer, and perhaps it has corresponding shadows or weaknesses or even flaws. As a Christian, I want to understand my faith's deepest treasures so I can appreciate them myself and make them available to others, and I also want to own its flaws and shadows so I will always remain humble and avoid inflicting them on others. I want to always remain curious so I can receive the unique insights and strengths that people from other traditions offer me. In that way, my Christian identity is enhanced by insights and resources from others, just as I hope they are enriched by the insights and resources that I bring. To me, this is an expression of being good neighbors to one another. We don't suppress or deny our differences, we aren't divided by our differences, and we don't try to eliminate our differences by imposing one way of seeing on everyone. Instead, we are mutually enriched by our differences. What we hold in common is our common desire for the common good. And, I think, a sense of humility, a sense that we don't know it all, that we are imperfect and have something to learn because . . . because we all have a shadow side that is hard to acknowledge."

"What about people – the majority of us, I imagine – who may have some distant religious heritage, but don't practice any religion?" Soraya asked.

"I don't really divide the world into religious people and non-religious people," Eve said. "To me, everyone is concerned about meaning, belonging, and purpose, so that makes everyone religious, whether or not they adhere to any specific hierarchy or doctrinal system. What I said about different religious traditions applies equally to people who might call themselves secular or atheistic or agnostic. I'm deeply interested in the unique gifts that they bring to the table. They have good reasons for not affiliating with a religious tradition, and they see things that people inside religious traditions might miss. And I would assume the opposite would likewise be true."

"Two final questions for now, Eve," Soraya said. "Can you tell us a bit more about your team, and their religious backgrounds, and yours too?"

"I'd be glad to. I should say up front that I'm the only member of my team with formal training in religion, including the psychology and sociology of religion, philosophy, and related subjects. The truth is, people like me are a kind of endangered species these days. Demand for our expertise is pretty low, at least outside of very rigid in-groups. And finding someone with my background who would be willing to . . . to go on a voyage like this . . . according to Thurman, it wasn't very easy.

"My two colleagues are artists. They're musicians, primarily. One also has training in visual arts, and both write poetry, and they love literature and film. What they bring to the team is not so much religious knowledge or even formal religious experience but artistic vision, plus open-mindedness, plus a deep sensitivity to the beauty and wonder of the universe and the glory and squalor of the human condition. Thurman and his team, as you know, do – or I guess I should say *did* their homework in recruiting. Nikau Ruka is a nonbinary musician and artist and comes from a Māori culture. Nikau's parents were Pentecostal, and Nikau self-describes as spiritually open but not specifically religious. Some of you may have heard of Nikau's band, which was popular some years ago . . . It was called The Beast in the Jungle, which was an allusion to a short novel by Henry James.

"Refa Barghouthi is Palestinian. Her mother was a secular Jew from Jerusalem and her father was a non-practicing Christian from Ramallah. They met as peace activists, and in one of the tragic ironies that are too common in the Middle East, her Palestinian father was killed by a bomb planted by a fellow Palestinian, and years later her Jewish mother was shot by the Israel Defense Force during a peaceful protest. After the loss of her parents, Refa lived in New York with an uncle. After all she's been through – and I haven't told you the worst parts, it's no wonder Refa describes herself as an 'agnostic-leaning atheist.' I've also heard her say that peace and art are her religion. For both Nikau and Refa, traditional religion seems like a relic from the ancient past. Yet they are passionately committed to exploring the meaning, belonging, and purpose I spoke of earlier, and art is their vehicle or path.

"As for me, I do identify as a Christian. I'm devoted to Jesus and his moral and spiritual vision. I see each religion as a language, and although I've tried to become multi-lingual, the Christian tradition, especially the Christian contemplative tradition, became my spiritual mother tongue. Nikau and Refa find that explanation somewhat odd, but interesting. My mother was a quiet Lutheran and my dad, as you will soon discover in person, is a vocally anti-religious ex-Methodist, so I guess you could say their perspectives are part of me as well."

Soraya leaned back for her final question: "Can you share with us some of your preliminary findings?"

"Three key words keep coming up for us again and again in our conversations. First, *story*. We realize that, historically, Earth religions at their best told framing stories that helped people make sense of the past, find meaning in the present, and build a bank of virtue and wisdom for a better future. Unfortunately, over the last several hundred years, the stories told by our religions have largely remained frozen in time and aren't helping us as we need them to. We all know about the demagogues in recent decades who have found religion to be the secret to activating authoritarian personalities and mobilizing them for violence. That's why so many of us have such deep and legitimate suspicion of religion. But our need for life-shaping stories remains. Refa once said that she feels like a trapeze artist who let go of the old stories but is still flying through the air with no new story to grab onto. Sometimes she's not sure if she's flying or falling. In fact, I've wondered—"

"That's a powerful image," Soraya interrupted, gently nudging Eve along. "So, story, and . . ."

"The second word is *desire*. We humans are creatures of desire, and at their best, Earth religions celebrated and nurtured some desires and challenged or redirected others. We feel that Mars culture will need to engage in deep conversations about the most essential desires that we want to encourage, and the most problematic ones that we want to challenge, channel, or redirect. And then, of course, we'll have to deal with the *how* question – how do we strengthen desirable desires."

"Story, desire, and . . .?" Soraya asked.

"The third word may surprise people, because it's an archaic word: *ritual*. We feel that we need to create rituals that help us bond to our shared stories and strengthen our desirable desires. In fact, we've been experimenting with some rituals on our voyage, and the results have been positive and instructive."

"Speaking of rituals, Eve," Soraya said, "the Triad asked if you have experience of performing weddings. They have been discussing how soon the community can begin forming family units and adding new members to the community through birth, since this is the last voyage."

"No specific experience with weddings . . . yet. But I'll be glad to begin preparing now," Eve replied.

Soraya took off her arg and pointed it at herself. It reminded Eve of the era of "selfies" that her parents laughed about from their youth. "Colleagues, if I could add a personal note. I come from a long line of secular Muslims. I have never practiced any religion, although I have read a little of the Sufi tradition of Islam. I must say that the rituals Eve and her team have constructed have proven deeply meaningful for everyone on our team, almost, and I look forward to further conversation with you on these matters over the remaining two hundred and twenty days of our voyage, and then after our arrival. Please send me any additional questions, and we will reply promptly. Soraya Rasul, ending transmission."

Soraya replaced her arg and Eve could see Soraya's eye movements ending the recording and transmitting it to Mars.

"Was that OK?" Eve asked.

"Perfect," Soraya replied. "Look, Eve, we both know that suicides are at the top of everyone's minds there. They'll be able to take those three words – story, desire, and ritual – and see how they relate to their situation."

"I hope so," Eve said, sounding uncertain. "I was interested in the question about marriage rituals. It seems like a strange time to bring new life into the community, when there is so much death. But then again . . . it's nice to have people see rituals as a good thing."

"I do think even your father will come around, eventually," Soraya said.

Eve stowed the jump seat, opened the hatch, and grabbed the door frame to propel herself back down through the Main Cabin to Deck 2.

"Eve."

She stopped herself and looked back. "Yes?"

"There's something else I need to tell you." Soraya looked . . . afraid. "But it needs to stay between us."

"OK." Eve turned back toward her captain and clicked the hatch shut.

"It's not good," Soraya said.

Eve moved closer, floating between the captain's and the pilot's chairs. "Has there been another suicide?"

"Well." Soraya's jaw clenched and her gaze locked with Eve's. "The Lead Triad thinks at least one of the apparent suicides may have been . . . a murder. A murder, that is, staged as a suicide."

21
Fighting on Both Sides

There was a lot to hate about being trapped on a tiny vessel with nine other people, Eve thought on the ninety-first morning of the voyage. After anyone deposited solid waste in the toilet, opened the SDH (technically, sludge dehydrator, but the crew used a different s-word), or put dehydrated sludge in the worm composter, within a few minutes the aroma was detectable from the Bridge to Deck 3.

Deck 4, of course, had its own set of smells. Because of the exercise equipment, it often held a faint bouquet of locker room with a sachet of damp socks. But those scents were often overwhelmed by the smell of the animals housed there. The design team in Iceland added a special air-filtration system for Deck 4, along with a rubber diaphragm to cover the hatch opening. (The crew called it the doggy door.) It was supposed to contain odors when the hatch door was open, but their designs were . . . insufficient, especially because of the two puppies aboard. Although they were small, furry, incredibly cute, and clad in doggy diapers, in zero G their urine occasionally eluded their diapers and the odor of ammonia became . . . insidious. That had earned them the names Pooper and Peony.

If Pooper and Peony on Deck 4 weren't bad enough, Deck 2 had its own funk each morning when the crew emerged from their cocoons, unleashing a pungent mixture of stale farts, bad breath, and sweat. It was unpleasant enough with ten of them. Eve wondered how earlier voyages had smelled with more than twice that many aboard.

As annoying and even disgusting as these features of Ark life were, the worst thing by far, the single thing Eve hated the most, was this: *there was nowhere to go to have a fight.*

Since privacy was nonexistent, the crew tended to avoid the arguments that really needed to occur. If there were a Geiger counter for passive-aggressiveness, Eve thought the Ark would be in the red zone.

Everyone knew that Colfax and Eve's names would be at the top of the list of radioactive relationships. They periodically had a restrained public spat, but they couldn't find the privacy to process what they so obviously needed to process in depth and at length – and at full volume.

Late one night at the end of the first trimester of their journey, Soraya approached Eve. "We all love you and your dad," she said, "but the tension between you two is becoming embarrassing and draining to us all. I'm happy to try to serve as mediator."

"Thank you," Eve replied. "I may need you to mediate later, but first I think I need to try one more time."

There was a "message all" function on their args that they hardly ever used since they were within earshot of one another one hundred percent of the time. But at about 21:00 that night, Eve used that function to send out this message:

> I would like to reserve Deck 4 starting at 21:30 to have a private meeting with my dad. I will be closing the hatch, with Soraya's permission, for at least an hour, because I expect it to be loud and ugly. I'm sorry for the inconvenience, and please wish us well. (Dad, please join me on Deck 4 at 21:30.)

Eve felt driven to this rather extreme step by something that had happened earlier that day at morning briefing.

For a while after launch, at Soraya's request, Eve and her team led a morning ritual at each daily briefing. But after some weeks, they backed it off to every second or third day, largely due to complaints from Colfax and Ikemba, who felt that the rituals were "serial overkill," to use Colfax's term. Eve was pretty sure Ikemba wouldn't have complained if her dad hadn't pressured him to do so, but she was fine with the decision. It meant less work and responsibility for her, and it was better than the alternative the crew discussed, which was to divide the crew by having some come early for the ritual and others not.

That morning, she had prepared something new by combining a well-known prayer from St. Patrick in the Christian tradition with some moves from Tai Chi and Qigong. After the ritual, Dei-Lin expressed thanks and asked Eve to explain the origin of the prayer and the moves.

Most of the crew always seemed to enjoy both the rituals and the explanations Eve offered, so Eve took a few minutes to explain. She was enthusiastic because St. Patrick was one of her favorite characters in the Christian tradition and she also loved Tai Chi and Qigong from ancient Daoism and Confucianism. Eve recalled a scholarly article on the resonance between the Daoist idea of *chi* and the idea of the Holy Spirit in Christian thought. On top of that, the moves were extraordinarily enjoyable to execute and beautiful to watch in zero G.

Eve knew she was walking a fine line. The rituals she designed had meaning in and of themselves, without needing explanations about their origins in Earth's religious history. Eve understood that some crew members had less curiosity about the historical background of the rituals and would rather just experience the physical movement without explanations. But when Dei-Lin and others asked questions, Eve felt she owed them what she knew. This was, after all, her life's work. On top of that, now that they were a third of the way into an extremely long voyage, it wasn't like they didn't have a minute to spare.

Eve had been talking for maybe five or six minutes when Colfax raised his hand, and without waiting for Eve to recognize him, began with, "Eve, dear . . ."

It would be hard for some people to understand how offensive that word "dear" felt to Eve. She remembered how her father used to say, "Ann, dear," whenever he was about to patronize her and pull implicit patriarchy on her. To Eve, the word dripped with ironic contempt, and she instantly felt ablaze with rage.

"Eve, dear, we are willing to eat our sausage," Colfax said. "But I, for one, do not need to know how it was made."

Eve wanted to offer some advice as to where Colfax could shove his clichéd sausage but instead said . . . nothing. Rather, she spoke through closed teeth: "Soraya, I'm done for today."

Dei-Lin had seen this pattern one too many times, and she was sick of it. She was tethered directly above Colfax, and she quickly untethered from the wall just enough to bend over to see him eye to eye, upside-down, of course. "Excuse me, Colfax, but she was answering a question *I* asked. If you have a quarrel, it should be with me . . ." – she paused for a half-second and added, "motherfucker."

"No offense intended," Colfax said, with a smile Eve could only describe as obsequious, a description she knew he would contest.

"You two have enough crap between you that it would clog the SDH," Dei-Lin said. "You need to dry this shit out. We're all getting damn-straight sick of it."

Soraya then intervened with one word. "Agreed." Then she added, "We'll trust you two to take Dei-Lin's eloquent advice, for your benefit and ours, as soon as possible. Let's move on . . ."

So, when Eve's "message all" came through, she knew that everyone except Colfax was silently applauding and thinking, "Finally!"

At 21:30, Eve pushed down to the hatch of Deck 4, pulled open the slit in the doggy door, and quickly looked in. The lights were off and Colfax wasn't there, so she decided to linger among the plants on Deck 3. They were thriving, thanks in large part to Dei-Lin's green thumbs (the crew joked that both of hers were green) . . . not to mention the excellent fertilizer co-created by the crew, the animals, and the worm and isopod colonies Gabriela tirelessly cared for. In spite of the smell that wafted up from

Deck 4, Deck 3 had a kind of magical feel because an array of lights was positioned in the center of the space facing outward, equidistant from the cylindrical walls, with plants growing out from the walls toward the central lights. The walls themselves were lined with tubes of plastic, each with different strains of algae, a few red, some brown, and many shades of green. Dei-Lin loved to point out the bubbles of oxygen that accumulated in the tubes, indicators of what the algae would someday do on Mars.

In the center of the space, inside the array of outward-facing lights, there was an open tunnel where Eve loved to sit and meditate. She felt surrounded by green, bathed in gentle light, and soothed by vibrant vitality from all directions. That ambience seemed like a good place to compose and center herself while waiting for her father.

But he didn't come. *He'll probably come fashionably late on purpose, just to act like he doesn't really care and put me off balance*, she thought. Finally, at 21:35 she decided to move down to the bottom of Deck 4. *At least one of us will model maturity and punctuality.*

As Eve pushed through the diaphragm, she was enveloped in animal warmth, humidity, and odor. She went to the control panel, adjusted the lights to a moderate level, and raised the air-filtration setting. The doves started their gentle cooing and the parrots made clicking sounds with their beaks. One that Gabriela had named Messi started saying, "¿Qué pasa, Messi? ¿Qué pasa, Messi? ¡Hasta mañana!" A few crickets chirped uncertainly. The puppies roused themselves from sleep and whimpered, so Eve opened their pen and scratched their ears as they floated among their doggy toys. "You flying puppies are growing fast, but you're going to be really confused when you have to learn to walk again in gravity!" she said, giving each of them a treat to keep them quiet. Then she shut their pen and moved slowly around the walls, peering through clear glass at fish and through mesh at birds, prairie dogs, and lizards, all appearing strangely akimbo because they had no gravity to orient them toward an up or a down. Below these cages, behind closed doors, hibernating and brumating animals slept in refrigerated containers.

At the far end of the cylinder, there was an insulated hatch to the cargo bay that always stayed closed because the bay wasn't heated. Exercise equipment was bolted to the bottom of Deck 4, around the closed hatch.

Eve tethered herself to the seat of an exercise bike, directly across from a bench used for resistance strength training. (Traditional weights were worthless in zero G.) That place had become a popular seating arrangement for one-on-one conversations. Eve looked in the lower left corner of her arg: 21:38. *Way beyond fashionably late*, she thought. *It's not like he's stuck in traffic*. Just then, her father's head popped through the doggy door.

Eve had assumed Colfax would float down and tether himself on the bench across from her. He didn't. Instead, he pushed himself through the slit in the doggy door and hovered just inside the hatch, his arms folded.

"I learned a long time ago," he said, with a steely voice, "not to let a colleague delineate both the time and place of an inquest *and* the seating arrangement too. I would rather *not* begin a meeting that I am being publicly shamed into attending with you trying to quite literally put me in my place. I am no dullard."

Eve didn't want to create new damage to their already damaged relationship with ill-chosen words. But even she had her limits. She exploded.

"You miserable, arrogant, manipulative piece of patronizing . . .!" She left off the final word, untethering herself so she didn't have to crane back her neck to see him. "I'm sick of your power games. I'm sick of your insults. I'm sick of you second-guessing and criticizing everything I *do*."

Eve surprised herself with her ability to scream.

Colfax was already interrupting her, which was a bad sign. Equally bad – the angrier he became, the more pretentious his diction became. Since he'd already dropped a "dullard" and an "inquest," Eve knew his verbal heavy artillery were sure to be unleashed soon.

"Patronizing? Power games?" he shouted. "*You* are the churlish, jejune autocrat who incessantly flogs *me* with your regressive, obscurantist ideology!" His arms were not folded anymore. He started pointing at Eve and himself with exaggerated motions. "Can *you* imagine how hard it is for *me* to endure *your* touchy-feely woo-woo voodoo each morning? *I* signed up for a mission to Mars, not an implacable cult leader's indoctrination camp! Your perpetual disapprobation renders me bilious."

Eve was already shouting back: "Look! If you have a better place for us to conduct this so-called inquest, please, be my guest. If you don't want to sit here, choose someplace else!" With that, she lifted herself from the seat of the bike. "At least I took the initiative to set this up. *I* for one don't *enjoy* passive-aggressive behavior . . ."

Eve intended to push herself off the bike so Colfax could choose where they would sit, but her launch from the seat had not been as gentle as planned. She found herself moving away from the bike at the bottom of Deck 4 and toward Colfax at the top with considerably more speed than she intended, and to make matters worse, she had no way of stopping herself. Halfway through her tirade, she realized she was going to slam right into him. By the time she said "passive-aggressive behavior," Colfax had to reach out and grab her by the wrists to stop her in mid-air.

". . . as much as *you* do!" Eve finished her sentence, her face a few inches from her father's.

So here we are, Eve thought, breathing heavily, *both mad as hornets, close enough to bite each other's noses*. Her father looked enraged: his jaw clenched so hard his goatee trembled. They stared at each other for two full seconds.

Eve thought that they might laugh, that they might both see the absurdity and childishness of their attitudes.

But they didn't.

"OK, then. *You* take the bench and *I* shall take the bike," Colfax said.

Colfax then flew directly to the bike, also pushing off with a little more force than intended. He hit the bike with a jolt and scrambled to tether himself in place, trying, and failing, to save some modicum of dignity.

Eve pushed her body halfway through the diaphragm, pulled the metal hatch closed, then pushed down to the bench and tethered in.

Now, they were both in a sitting position, eye to eye, a comfortable distance apart, trying to overcome a really difficult start to a really difficult conversation. Eve struggled to calm her breathing and keep her hands from shaking with rage. "Well?" she asked, opening her arms awkwardly. "Maybe you'd like to begin?"

The doves, parrots, crickets, and puppies, she noticed, were dead silent.

That's when she heard it, faint at first, but unmistakable. Coming in her implant. Music. First horns in long, slow, subdued tones. Then a crescendo followed by a roll on the tympani, then sweet, sweet strings. Colfax got a strange look on his face. He obviously heard it too. He gave one of his famous eye rolls.

"Where is *that* coming from?" Colfax said. "I never heard music in here before."

"It's in your implant . . ." Eve thought, *stupid*, but didn't say it. "Refa. It's from Refa. Dvořák's *New World Symphony*, Second Movement. She loves Dvořák. So does Ekaterina. So do I."

"Trying to soothe the savage beasts? A little trite?"

"It's not for *us*. I mean, it's not for *us* to listen to. Look in your arg: it says *audio all*. She's trying to give the rest of the crew something else to listen to, other than hearing our yelling echo through this whole LVRV, which, as I'm sure you, the great scientist, already realize, transmits sound waves quite well. She's giving us a gift of privacy. We can simply mute our implants." Eve touched her wrist just as the tender English horn solo began and Colfax did the same.

Now Eve was the one with folded arms. Colfax's hands were on his knees. The ever-present hum of the Ark seemed to grow louder as the seconds passed.

"Well, we are not off to the best start, are we," Colfax said, trying to modulate his voice in volume, but keeping the edge on its tone. It was obvious he had prepared his speech. "I shall speak my piece. I have done my best to be pliant and to follow your leadership with alacrity and ebullience. Normally I am neither irascible, cantankerous, nor bellicose. But I have surpassed the limit of my quiescence; I resent being repeatedly subjected to your vapid mixture of flatland psychology and sanctimonious religion."

Eve couldn't contain herself: "That is so unfair. That is so . . . *insulting*! Are you intentionally trying to humiliate me?"

Colfax matched her rage and intensified it: "Do you want to know what humiliation looks like? It looks like a globally respected scholar who was briefly a White House cabinet-level official having to sit like a ductile schoolboy at the feet of a child whose diapers he once changed and whose tuitions he paid through his own hard labors. And do you want to know what humiliation looks like? It looks like me having to feign interest and agreement with your daily moralizing when *I know your secret*, the deception upon which your very presence here depends."

Eve felt a rush of adrenaline. She restrained an impulse to slap her father, something she had never even thought of doing before, even in his worst drunken tirades. Through clenched teeth and with a lowered voice, she snarled, "You fucking hypocrite. That is a low blow, to bring up my fertility at a time like this. I seem to recall you saying something about Thurman's lack of diligence not obligating me to become loquacious. Remember that? If I have anything to be ashamed of, it was accepting moral guidance from you in that very situation. So, what are you saying: you're going to blackmail me? I stop fulfilling my responsibilities or you'll go tattle on me to your pals Thurman and Soraya? Is that what this is about? What do you want them to do, stop the rocket and make me walk home to Earth?"

Colfax squinted and decided to pivot. He returned to the little speech he had obviously scripted and rehearsed: "Repeatedly, I have gently endeavored to assist you in steering away from this sententious folly, but you remain stubbornly obdurate. Your ritualistic shamanism reeks with manipulation and . . . falls beneath the dignity of a scientific mission. And beneath my personal dignity as well. Although I *am* your senior, I am willing to be treated as your equal, but I will neither be deprived of free choice nor reduced to the supine position of one of your groveling thralls." He was jabbing his index finger an inch from Eve's chin.

Eve tried not to, but the urge was too strong: she started to laugh.

"What? Are you mocking me, you disrespectful . . .?" Colfax yelled. "You make my point by your mockery."

Eve bit her lip. "Dad, you said 'stubbornly obdurate.' That's a redundancy. Come on, Dad, you're better than that. That kind of *repetitive redundancy* is beneath the dignity of a great mind like yours."

Colfax glared at Eve, unblinking, as if he were a steel statue. Eve had gotten a word in edgewise and so had broken his flow. She rested a beat, gained her composure, and cued her response.

"Look," she said, "you seem to forget that we have a captain on this vessel, even if we don't use the word much." Her volume began to crescendo and the tempo of her words accelerated. "And *Captain* Soraya Rasul sets the agenda. You're right. In some ultimate sense, you *have* no free choice. If you don't like that . . . well, it's too late to turn back. You're stuck with my so-called vapidity as long as *Captain* Soraya Rasul empowers me to lead. And not just for six more months. You may be stuck with it for the rest of your life, because the Triad on Mars supports my presence on this voyage! *They do!*"

The word "do" echoed for a second like a note in a sounding bowl. Eve hoped the rest of the crew still had Dvořák up to full volume.

Colfax regrouped fast and came back at full force: "See? You are gleeful to pull rank and force me to do things that I find . . . intellectually reprehensible and desultory. That is the epitome of autocratic and quasi-dictatorial leadership. I know: you will reply that the rest of the crew finds your cute little cultic acts to be *meaningful*" – he mocked the word as he said it – "but I find them to be *fatuous*. They grate on my intelligence like steel on steel. I refuse to capitulate to a regime under which I have no choice and no say—"

"Just a minute," Eve interrupted and immediately realized she shouldn't have. She tried to recover, modulating her voice. "May I?" He nodded once, but barely. "I notice that you said – for the second time – you have no choice and no say. You *are* given a say. You have the same right as anyone to express yourself. But being given a say isn't the same thing as being given the power to veto what everyone else, including our captain, wants!"

"For all your talk of empathy, young lady . . ."

"Young lady? Don't you *dare*!" Eve shouted that last word. "I am a thirty-one-year-old full-grown woman and it's time you started treating me like an adult, you patronizing little—" Eve was glad, in retrospect, that Colfax didn't let her finish, because the body part she was about to name would have gone too far.

"For all your talk of empathy, *Eve*, you show precious *little* for my situation." His eyes didn't move as he spoke.

Eve paused. Something inside told her to shut up and listen. Her heart was throbbing like a pipe drum in one of Dei-Lin's playlists, but she felt herself regaining control. "You are right. I have no empathy for your situation. I feel so hurt, so insulted, so wounded by your behavior that I have only been thinking of myself." She took a long breath. There was no way she could compete with his pompous vocabulary, so she consciously tried to change key and speak simply: "And that's not fair to you or right of me."

They both turned their eyes to a point beneath one another's feet, resting for a few beats, making room for one or the other of them to improvise at this impasse.

"I'm listening. I want you to tell me how you're feeling," Eve said, hoping a breakthrough was imminent.

"*Feeling*? See? You are still framing this fracas in your touchy-feely woo-woo parameters. Another prime example of you trying to remake me in your divine image! I am not a *feeling* guy, Eve, if that remains unclear after all these years. I am a conceptual guy, a thinking person. And I am weary of you making me feel inferior simply for being who and what I am. I am an intellectual. I am rational. Without apology!"

"I get that. Point taken," Eve said, nodding, her eyes finding his for the first time in a while. "I want you to tell me what you're *thinking*."

"Thank you. Here is the essence of what I think, which I have tried to explain on numerous occasions, and to which, so far, you remain utterly insensible. Perhaps this time you will let my meaning gatecrash through all your damnable moralistic and self-interested filters." He took a long breath and lowered his voice. "Eve, people cannot sustain the kind of intimacy you keep trying to create. People need space – trapped as we are in these tubular confines. This need for space matters even more for intellectually focused people like me. The need will be equally intense on Mars. Look, I am a research scientist and policy analyst, which means I ask questions and look for satisfactory rational and objective answers. Even in my ornithological work, I counted specimens and assessed population strength and designed species survival plans. My colleagues and I did not sit around and talk about how we felt about birds. Our motivating emotional experiences were manifest not by verbalizations but by our active embodiment."

"But, Dad, you and I both know you love birds," Eve replied. "You have deep feelings for them."

"Of course, but that is not the point. Most of the residents on Mars are engineers, and they resemble me more than you. When they see a problem, they do not want to explore their feelings about it, nor do they want to probe their deeper meaning." He put finger quotes around *explore*, *feelings*, and *meaning*. "They want to solve it. Black and white. Problem, solution. That is how they – or most of them, anyway, will be. You think I have been hard on you. Perhaps I have. Perhaps I have done so intentionally to prepare you for what you shall surely face, because believe me, on Mars, you will be crucified."

That was a strong word, and they both knew it. They were still mad as hell at each other, but Eve could feel that they were finally connecting, at least a little. They were moving from adversaries to allies. They were both on the same side, with Colfax trying to be understood and Eve wanting him to succeed. Eve didn't want to break that fragile alliance.

"So, if I understand you . . ." She was trying to soft-pedal her anger, rendering her voice as controlled and unemotional as she could, trying to find some note of resonance with his inner state. "If I understand you, you're saying that you're not trying to attack me, or disrespect me, or undermine me. You're trying to protect me. Because you love me. And you're afraid that I will fail."

He took off his arg and ran his left index finger below each eye, from the inside corner to the outside. He looked for a second like a fragile boy. "Well, fear has nothing to do with it. But, well, yes. Perhaps it does. And love, as you say. Of course. Why else would I act as I have? Have I not tried to tell you this a million times?" His internal exaggeration editor must have corrected him: "Or at least seven or eight times. Or at least once." He put back on his arg, and managed a faint smile – mostly sincere, and partly sad. "There. Now I have said it again."

Eve had the urge to untether and hug him. But they still had too much unfinished business for that. She decided to ask a question, but she needed to ease into it: "I believe you. Now I need to ask you something. Because you love me, and you know I am a feeling person, can you imagine how it has felt for me to have you constantly sniping at me and complaining, even undermining me in front of other people? Can you imagine how disempowering it is for me, a woman in her thirties, to have her father vacillate between the roles of patronizing patriarch, personal antagonist, and classroom troublemaker?"

Eve didn't mean to appear emotional, but when she said "antagonist," her voice cracked, and it sounded like she was about to cry. Now Colfax started to untether, probably, she thought, to hug her, but she held up her hand. "It's OK. We need to talk this through. Rationally."

"Eve, I regret that. I have no desire to be your antagonist, or any sort of obstreperous troublemaker. I can be a petulant ignoramus sometimes, as your mother well knew. But I trust you will believe me: I do not want you to fail. I want . . ." He didn't finish the sentence. Eve thought she knew why.

It seemed like they had come to the end of a movement, but the symphony wasn't over yet. They needed to rest for a moment, to sit with some silence until they were ready to move forward.

"Dad, do you even understand what I've been asked to do?"

"Of course. You have been asked to service the emotional needs . . . if you want to call them the spiritual needs, I can live with that . . . of the Martian colony, of which we will soon be part."

Anger flared up in Eve. She wanted to scream at him: "You imbecile! You blunt-edged dimwit! You cretin!" They were words she had heard him use since before she knew what they meant. She restrained herself. Not knowing what to say, biting her lip to keep from crying, Eve looked down and watched her right thumb dig into her left palm.

"You are unsatisfied with that answer," Colfax said. "You would describe your role on this mission in another way."

She nodded and waited to see if he really wanted to understand.

"OK. I am listening. Try to help me see it. I evidently do not."

She composed herself. *God, help me make this clear*, she whispered in her thoughts. This was the window she had been waiting for, the chance to help him see.

There could not have been a worse time for a message icon to flash on their args, a blue pulsating light, followed by a voice in their implants: "Eve and Colfax, we need you in the Main Cabin immediately. This is urgent."

"This is not good," Colfax said.

"No, it's not."

They both untethered and pushed to the top of Deck 4. Eve parted the slit in the doggy door, opened the hatch, and heard yelling. "Wow," she whispered, her heart pounding again. "Fighting on both sides of the hatch."

22
Shouting All at Once

When Colfax and Eve joined the crew in the Main Cabin, Soraya, her head bowed, was listening to Dei-Lin yell at her from the opposite wall. Colfax and Eve held their position at the hatch, not wanting to interrupt.

"You had *no* right to keep a secret like this from us. No *right*! We are not *children* that you have to protect from the *truth*." When she said *children* and *truth*, she shot both index fingers out toward Soraya, as if she were pulling two pistols from their holsters.

Soraya's face looked pained. "Dei-Lin, you may be right. But I had a choice to make, and I did what I thought was right, knowing what I knew then."

Dei-Lin's eyes were locked onto Soraya's. "We deserve better leadership than that," she said. "Maybe you just don't have what it takes."

Thurman spoke up. "Dei-Lin, may I remind you that Soraya is the captain of this vessel, and you are a member of this crew, and . . ."

"With all due respect, Thurman, I have not forgotten that," Dei-Lin said. "I am not forgetful, but I am . . . enraged that our *captain* has withheld information that could result in this crew flying into a death trap. She had no right to keep life-and-death information to herself."

Eve had a hunch about what was going on: news of the murder was out. Her gut told her that Soraya needed her to speak up. "Dei-Lin, she told me," Eve said, quietly but firmly. "I kept the secret too. We both struggled with whether we should tell you all."

Dei-Lin glared down at Eve between her feet. "And to think I used to trust you," she said. Then she turned to Soraya. "Only Eve? You didn't even tell Gabriela, your first mate? How do you feel about that, Gabriela? Or how about Ikemba, your pilot? How do you feel about that, Ikemba? I feel *betrayed* right now, and I imagine you both must feel the same way too, even more so," she added.

Gabriela spoke, not in reply to Dei-Lin, but to Eve: "You had better tether in, because the bad news you already knew just became worse."

Eve caught Soraya's eye, and she nodded. Father and daughter took their usual places in formation.

"What happened?" Colfax asked as soon as he was tethered in.

Soraya looked grave. "A few minutes ago, I received a transmission from Mars Base. There has been another murder."

"*Another?*" Colfax repeated. "I was never informed about the first one." He glanced at Thurman, whose face looked like stone.

"That's what I said," Dei-Lin responded. "I can't believe information like this was withheld from us. And it's not just another murder."

Eve looked at Soraya, confused.

"The video message I received was from Sisavanh Cherubandith," she said. "Chase Granby was murdered, and Sisavanh and Naomi Watseka were wounded; Naomi quite seriously. It looks like an attempted coup."

"What?" Colfax asked. "Why?"

Thurman spoke. "Soraya, perhaps you should play the vid for us. It might help us all to see it . . . in the interest of full transparency."

"I would, except . . ."

"Except what, Soraya?" Dei-Lin challenged. "More secrets you want to keep? It's time to get everything out . . . out in the open."

Soraya was shaken but still in control. "I didn't share news of the first . . . incident with you because I didn't want to burden you with information that we can't do anything about for six more months. In addition, I was told that there was evidence for a murder, but it hadn't been proven yet. I told Eve because . . . because I needed someone to tell. Now, I regret not telling you all, because the burden that we will all share is about to get much greater than any one or two of us can bear alone. I will play the vid for everyone, but perhaps I should let Gabriela see it first, privately, since she is my first mate. It was especially bad judgment to keep this from her."

"It's too late for that," Ikemba said. "Let's see it. Together. Now."

"It's OK," Gabriela said quietly. "It's OK. Go ahead, Soraya. I understand. You needed to tell someone, and Eve was an excellent choice."

"Yes, go ahead, by all means," Kat added. "*Bystro*."

Soraya worked her bracelet, then her arg. Sisavanh Cherubandith appeared on the args of the crew. Most had never seen his face before. His hair was black and thick, pulled back in a ponytail. His skin was brown and the left side of his head was covered in a white bandage, his right eye swollen shut. Soraya pressed another button and the vid began.

"Soraya, it is with great sadness that I send you this message. Our colleague Chase Granby was found dead this morning. It was not a suicide, and he did not die from natural causes. Naomi Watseka was critically injured, apparently while asleep. Her throat was cut."

At this point, Sisavanh held his forefinger and thumb to the bridge of his nose. He breathed deeply, apparently trying not to break down.

"Those who did this intended her death, but they narrowly missed the critical veins and arteries. Still, her blood loss was significant. My colleague, Dr. Fikira Mwangi, quickly identified the members of the crew with compatible blood and transfused her as soon as possible. This saved her life, although we do not know if there will be brain damage from blood loss, or if she will be able to speak normally, as her voice box was compromised."

Again, he paused and breathed deeply. "We have restored order, and we know who the perpetrators are, and we are searching for them now.

"I wish this were the full extent of our bad news," he added. "But it is not."

Soraya touched her bracelet and the vid paused. "Before we proceed, I need to tell you that what you are about to hear is deeply disturbing."

Several nodded as if in confirmation that they were ready, and she unfroze the vid.

Sisavanh continued. "There is no easy way to tell you that we have not been fully honest with you. We have withheld other information."

Dei-Lin muttered, loud enough to be heard, "There's a lot of that going around this solar system these days."

"We reported to you that we had been suffering from a string of suicides. That was the truth, but not the full truth."

Ekaterina gasped. "*Gospodi*," she said in Ukrainian, then translated to English: "Oh, my God."

"We have indeed had suicides. But we have now accumulated evidence that leads us to believe that at as many as four may have been cleverly staged murders. You may ask why we did not inform you fully. I feel great shame in telling you the answer. We feared that if you knew the truth, you would not come."

"Damn right we wouldn't," Ikemba spat.

"Damn right," Dei-Lin echoed.

"They are descending into Calhoun's behavioral sink," Colfax interjected, musing aloud, "or the irrational antagonism syndrome of Biosphere 2."

"The previous Lead Triads made the decision to maintain this deception. When my colleagues and I were elected, we in good conscience could not continue it. We planned to tell you in a matter of weeks, but in light of recent events, I have decided to tell you the full truth now. No one, including Dr. Thurman or Madame Deripaska, knew of this. We on the Lead Triad withheld the truth from you and your crew. We are solely responsible."

Eve looked over toward Thurman; he and Kat were staring into each other's faces, motionless, expressionless.

"I can tell you that I voted for full disclosure immediately after our election, two months ago, but my colleagues said we should wait. As a member of the Triad, I take full responsibility for our decision, and I apologize for the unacceptable situation it puts you in now.

"I need to say, finally, that we are in desperate need of your assistance. We have tried to contain and remedy this situation, but obviously, we do not have the skills or knowledge to do so. Please . . ."

For a moment, Eve thought the vid had frozen, but then realized that Sisavanh himself was frozen, struggling to speak. He gasped, then continued, "In Lao, my first language, I say from my heart: *Phuakhao khoothdnoa*. We are truly sorry. Please forgive us. And please do not give up on us. We need your help. I am Sisavanh Cherubandith, ending transmission."

The room immediately erupted, some people speaking to Soraya, some to the person next to them, some to nobody in particular or everybody in general. Then speaking turned to yelling, and fired by pent-up emotion, people started untethering, which only added to the sense of pandemonium as they drifted at random angles and gesticulated weightlessly.

Only Refa stayed tethered, tapping on her wrist, and then . . . everyone heard it except for Colfax and Eve, because they had muted their implants. The rest grew silent and gradually drifted back into formation and tethered once again. Colfax and Eve realized the others were hearing something the two of them didn't, and they quickly un-muted their implants. Eve recognized the piece, Barber's *Adagio for Strings.*

Before re-tethering, Soraya flew over to Eve. "Can you . . . do something? To help us process this?"

"I'll try," Eve said. "But I'm not sure people will trust me now. Starting with Dei-Lin."

"You can't let one person's doubt outweigh the trust everyone else has for—"

"It's not just Dei-Lin. It's also my dad, and Ikemba . . ."

"But I trust you. And I'm telling you that this is when your most confident leadership is most needed," Soraya said. She touched her lips to Eve's ear and whispered: "I need you to do what only you can do. We all do. Even if your efforts fail, you have to try."

Rather than tether, Eve pushed down to the bottom of the Cabin, near the hatch to Deck 2. She positioned herself so that everyone could look down to see her. Her presence gave them a place to focus. She closed her eyes and remained motionless, listening to the music and inviting them, by example, simply to listen. She let the song play to the end. At first, there was restlessness in the Cabin. By halfway through the song's eight minutes, most had entered into the music's intensity. Ikemba and Dei-Lin fidgeted, exchanging glances, fists clenching and unclenching.

Eve felt paralyzed, terrified, weightless, but in the worst possible way. She had no idea what to do when the song was over. But gradually, an unexpected word came to mind: *curiosity*. And wherever it came from, that word gave her a place to start.

The last chords faded to nothing. She broke the silence, her eyes still closed, her voice shaky in spite of her attempts to sound calm.

"We are here, right now, in this situation. None of us would choose to be in a situation like this. There is trouble behind us and trouble before us. There is even trouble among us in this little cylinder of metal shooting through space. There is no one who can say a magic word to fix this and make it other than it is. Naturally, we are angry. Confused. Of course, afraid. In the presence of anger, confusion, and fear, our brains seek someone to blame. Soraya would be one easy target. I would be another. Sisavanh would be yet another. If you feel you need to blame someone, that is completely understandable.

"But then who will you blame next, when something else goes wrong? And might someone eventually blame you? Blame will take us deeper into division, which will create more anxiety, which will create more blame, and more division, and with it, more danger. That vicious cycle could, very literally, destroy us. And that danger is not on Mars: it is in this vessel, inside us. So, I invite you to turn in another direction . . . toward curiosity, the desire to understand. Curiosity is an alternate response to anger, confusion, and fear, because blame foolishly assumes it knows more than it does. Curiosity acknowledges how little we know."

Eve opened her eyes and gently pushed herself up toward her colleagues tethered in two circles around the walls. She aimed toward Refa on the upper row, who reached out and helped her stabilize. Eve then leveraged herself between Refa and Dei-Lin and faced the group. "Blame expresses itself in accusation. Accusation leads to judgment and condemnation, which often leads to scapegoating and other forms of violence. Curiosity expresses itself in a question. Questions lead to exploration and communication. So, the most important thing we can do at this moment, this moment when we are tempted to turn against one another in blame and condemnation . . . the most important thing we can do right now is to turn toward one another, to ask a question, not an accusatory question, not a gotcha question, but an honest question, a question that leads us into curiosity. Who would like to go first?"

Across the cabin, Nikau unzipped the top of their jumpsuit and pulled out the carved whale. They pulled it over their head and offered it to Eve. She pushed over and took it. "In Team Culture, we use this whalebone carving as a talking stick, or *tokotoko*. It authorizes you to speak from your heart, without interruption until you pass it to someone else. Nobody can speak twice until everyone has had the chance to speak once. Who would like to be first?"

Dei-Lin reached for the whale and her crew mates passed it around to her.

"I want to know who and what will be left when we get there," she said. "The whole situation on Mars Base could easily descend into chaos, and six months is a long time. I feel no need to blame anybody. I'm just practical. I want to know what we're going to be dealing with. If we continue toward Mars, that is."

Thurman raised his hand. Dei-Lin passed the whale to him.

"I want to know who the perpetrators are. I screened every person so carefully and I feel . . . I feel that I've failed. We . . . I . . . took such pride in our Macopro Method, but it now looks like we're being ruled by Murphy's Law." He looked devastated as he held out the whale. Kat, to his left, took it next.

"I want to know how the previous Triads had the disgraceful dishonesty to deceive us. I mean, what possessed them to do such a thing, and for so long? And why did we not see through their deception?" she asked, insistent. "How could we be so naive?"

Eve realized that Thurman and Kat were expressing a question of curiosity, but underneath, they were still thinking in terms of blame. Thurman was blaming himself and Kat was blaming the Triad. But still, the amount of curiosity present restrained the blame.

Ikemba, on the other side of the cabin, raised his hand. Eve pushed over to Kat and then carried the whale over to Ikemba.

"I am *curious* to know . . . how soon we can choose new leadership, turn this vessel around, and head back to Earth?"

Thurman bellowed: "Ikemba, *no*. That is *not* appropriate."

"I am holding the damned whale, and I have the right to speak, so I'll be damned if anyone is going to interrupt me, even if your name is Thurman Fricking Thurman. We all know why they lied to us. Sisavanh said it. They knew we would be fools to come to a base that's in chaos. There are no police, no courts, and once a crew is out of control, anything can happen. On top of that, between the murder and suicides, the population is sinking dangerously close to the minimum viable population level. When that happens, the whole project is doomed. So, my question is absolutely appropriate. It's the only thing I'm curious about and you're damned liars if you don't admit that you're asking the same damned question but are too damned afraid to admit it."

Ikemba held out the whale in his fist and shook it as he continued to speak. "And if you think it's as simple as turning round, think again. The Earth has moved ahead of us in orbit by now, and we can't catch up to it without using a hell of a lot of fuel, maybe more than we have. So, getting back home is going to take some work, some damn good engineering and some damn good piloting, and no amount of rituals and feelings will make a damn bit of difference because everything comes down to math in the end. I'm already thinking about problems and potential solutions, and every second we delay decreases our chances of making it back. *Every fucking second!*" He roared those last three words and the Ark resonated with his fear and fury.

Colfax had been unusually quiet. He was tethered directly below Ikemba and now he signaled to go next. Ikemba threw the whale toward him and he caught it in two hands. He kept his voice controlled and calm: "I want to know how we will make a decision about turning back or going forward," he said, then swallowed hard. "Is this something Soraya decides unilaterally as captain, or something the Lead Team decides together? I want to know if the rest of us will have any say in the decision. But we need to remember there is a distinction between having a say and having veto power. I am also curious about whether we are all committed to following the decision that we make as a group, even if we personally disagree. Let me say it more personally: I am curious about how many of you will join me in committing to follow the decision of our team, even if it goes against our personal preference?"

Eve saw what he was doing, charting a middle course between Ikemba's flirtation with mutiny and unqualified support for Soraya. He was trying to turn this from a battle of wills – a captain versus a mutineer – to a democratic process. His response could have been better, she thought, but it could have been worse too.

Ever so subtly, ever so gently, Colfax made momentary eye contact with Eve before holding the carved whale out to Nikau, who was reaching for it with an open hand.

"Here's what I'm curious about," Nikau said. "Why didn't Macopro leadership anticipate this? Thurman, Ekaterina, believe me, I don't mean that in a way to blame you or anyone else. I mean it to say that some of the assumptions that were made have now been proven faulty, and if crazy-smart people made faulty assumptions, we might still be holding those same assumptions. I hope that question makes sense."

Refa motioned for the whale next. "My question is more . . . I guess you'd say wistful, or philosophical. Why are we humans so incurably violent? And what can we do about it? Suicides are bad enough. But murder, I mean . . . we take our violence with us wherever we go." She shook her head. "Being human is . . . overrated."

Gabriela reached out her hand. "Refa, my question is almost identical to yours." Refa passed the whale to her. "As a biologist, I have a strong sense of why we evolved to be violent. I have a pretty good understanding of the physiology and brain chemistry of fear and its relationship to aggressive responses in the amygdala. I'm familiar with the relevant vagal nerve theories and research. What I don't know is how we can evolve from here, to transcend the violence and fear that seem to be programmed into us so deeply, by both our genes and by our cultural conditioning. Because very literally, violence may have been a survival strategy in the past, and some people on Earth still seem to think it's a viable strategy. But on Mars, with our colony so close to minimum viable population, I don't think there's much difference between murder and suicide. If we kill each other, we kill ourselves. If we kill ourselves, we kill each other."

Only Soraya and Eve had not yet spoken. Eve felt that Soraya should go last, so she floated to Gabriela, took the whale, then floated back to her normal place in the formation. She tethered herself and said, "My question is . . . I'm sorry, I have been so preoccupied leading this time that I need a moment to think, because my question has changed . . . my question is . . . I'm curious about how we can create a transparent process for addressing Colfax's – my dad's – question."

Eve gently pushed the whale across the space to Soraya. The whale seemed to swim through the air in slow motion, its chain undulating like waves in its wake. Soraya cupped her hands to receive it. Before speaking, she looked around the room. Eve noticed in that moment how beautiful Soraya's eyes were, how dark and kind, how deep and mysterious, all at the same time.

"Here's what I'm curious about," Soraya said. "Haven't we already bound ourselves to our colleagues on Mars Base, whether they're in good shape or in a mess? Didn't we already embark, which means our future, for better or worse, is ahead of us, with them? Do we – and they – have the strength to rise above this, to process the pain and shock of this, and move forward together? I believe we do, but I can't be sure until we make it so."

Then Soraya looked at Eve, wondering what was next. Both of them had been so caught up in the experience that they had no idea.

In that split second when Eve was searching for a next step, Ikemba spoke.

"For me, Soraya, you're asking the wrong question. It's not a matter of strength; it's a matter of survival instinct. When you heard that Mars Base was becoming like that island in *Lord of the Flies*, you had a moral responsibility to tell us, so that we could turn back. Did you hear what that bastard Sisavanh said? He said they were going to tell us in a matter of weeks. And don't you all see why they were waiting until then? At that point we pass the halfway point in our journey and it's too late to turn back. Don't you see? We should all be thankful the lid blew off their deception today. Now at least we know what we're dealing with. We had better hope and pray it's not too late to turn back, people, because we want no part of what is going on at Mars Base."

"Ikemba, no!" Kat said.

"Ikemba, stop it, man!" Thurman echoed.

"Every minute that we go farther towards Mars is a moment when we could be heading back toward Earth. I'm sorry. I don't really care about all your processes or questions or curiosity or rituals or touchy-feely woo-woo, as Colfax says. And fuck your fucking whale. I want to chart the shortest trajectory back to Earth, and I won't rest until I hear the rockets fire to put us on that course."

"Ikemba, please!" Thurman shouted. "This is not what we need. You said it yourself – once a crew is out of control, anything can happen."

"You've lost your moral authority, Thurman," Ikemba said, his low volume indicating more disgust than a shout would have. "It's your turn to 'end your life as you know it,' your life of being in charge. This was all fine when it was other people's lives you were risking, and you were in control from a distance. Now you're in the same hot bucket of shit as the rest of us." Ikemba untethered and pushed, not down to Deck 2, but up to the Bridge. He shut the hatch behind him and everyone heard the lock's crisp click.

Eve's heart sank. All the progress she briefly felt they had made was gone. *At least everyone's not shouting all at once as they were a few minutes ago*, she thought. But in a few minutes, they were. And this time, neither Eve nor Dvořák nor Barber could hope to restore calm.

Eventually, everyone separated. Eve retreated to her cocoon, reading something on her digital page, just to distract her from her own racing thoughts. Then she felt her cocoon shake slightly. Someone was outside.

The voice was an inch from Eve's ear. "Could we talk privately? I need . . . some help." It was Dei-Lin.

Eve emerged and they floated down to the bottom of Deck 4 and belted in. "You have my full attention," Eve said.

Dei-Lin looked beneath her, first to the right, then to the left, then straight down again, and then she lifted her face and her eyes met Eve's directly, almost aggressively. "I'm sorry for what I said about not trusting you earlier. Trust is an issue with me. You don't know much about my background. My dad kicked me out when I was fourteen because I found out he was cheating on my mom. My mom let the bastard kick me out because she would rather lose me than lose him. Imagine how that felt. Then I ran with a gang for a couple years and did some things. I joined the Army because I wanted to . . . well, I don't need to go into all that. But I guess I'm about to trust you now, in spite of my major trust issues."

Eve nodded, meeting and holding Dei-Lin's gaze.

Dei-Lin continued. "I'm worried I may be next."

Eve was confused. "Next?"

"You know, the next . . . statistic."

"You're feeling depressed," Eve said.

"Worse than that," Dei-Lin said, looking down again. "I don't feel anything. Except fucking mad. And I'm wondering . . . what the point is. Of this whole thing."

"This voyage," Eve said.

"This voyage, this civilization, this life, and this existence," Dei-Lin said. "We all know what Earth faces. We've seen climate change coming for over a century, and we sped past all the warning signs, and now it's just a matter of how total the anthropogenic extinction event will be. And the politicians sucked up to the oligarchs and let the masses suffer, and now the whole thing is about to blow up. The corruption. The cover-ups. The cowardice. The politicult. The refusal to see things as they really are."

Eve nodded.

Dei-Lin met Eve's gaze again. "So we decide to go to Mars to make a clean start. But look at us, Eve. Look at us just these last few days. We're no better than the goddamned idiots back on Earth. It's not just the big bad *them*. It's us. It's *us*. It's all of us. We bring our unresolved shit with us wherever we go. We're beyond pathetic. We are fucking doomed. We don't even deserve to survive. That's why they're committing suicide on Mars, Eve. They see it. And now I do too. And I can't seem to unsee it. I think I've caught what they've got. Like Refa said: being human is way overrated."

Eve looked into Dei-Lin's eyes. They were bloodshot and shiny, and their midnight irises became two tiny round mirrors reflecting two of Eve's own faces back at her.

"I know what you mean," Eve said. "Once you see it, it can't be unseen."

23
To Reach Ikemba

It took Eve a long time to fall asleep, and a few hours later, it took a long time for the ping in her implant to awaken her. She heard Soraya's voice asking her to come to the Bridge without waking anyone else.

The hatch to the Bridge was partially open. Soraya was in the pilot's seat in the center, not in the captain's seat as usual. When Eve pulled herself through the hatch and clicked it shut behind her, Soraya motioned for her to take the captain's chair. Eve had the feeling that Soraya had been there for a while.

Soraya's cap was in her hand, and her hair, normally in a ponytail, looked like black fire flaming around her tired face. She didn't even try to fake a smile.

Eve had forgotten her arg, but she noticed the clock on the control console: 03:01. For a few minutes, she joined Soraya staring through the viewport into the darkness.

Mars was nowhere to be seen.

Soraya broke the silence, speaking quietly. "It's funny. I didn't realize that it would always be night here, as long as we were facing away from the sun. Just the other day, I was sitting here with Ikemba. He told me that in about a month, Mars would appear on the right side of the viewport, and gradually move toward the center. Everything seemed fine then."

Eve didn't know what to say. She was still shaken from her conversation with Dei-Lin a few hours earlier, not to mention the near mutiny that erupted before that, and the argument with her father. *What was happening on Mars could happen here*, she thought. *We could turn on each other. We could turn on ourselves.*

"What's your assessment?" Soraya asked, turning toward Eve. "Of our current situation?"

Eve looked down. "I wanted to ask you the same question."

Soraya stared without blinking at Eve, waiting for an answer. "I asked first."

Eve spoke just above a whisper. "I think Ikemba is afraid. When we mammals feel scared, our fight, flight, freeze, or fawn reflexes are activated. Ikemba wanted to flee. When you and Thurman blocked his way, he decided to fight."

"Clearly," Soraya replied. "We all know Ikemba. We all love him. More than any other single person on this voyage, we have entrusted our lives to him. We're all surprised to see him behave like this."

"Maybe . . . maybe that's the key. Maybe he feels our trust and doesn't want to bring us into danger," Eve said.

"That's what Gabriela said," Soraya replied. "I spoke with her earlier."

Eve felt relieved that Gabriela had already been consulted. She said, "I think there's another reflex in play. In the presence of fear, herd mammals like us flock. We pull together. And, right now, I think our danger is that some of us will flock around you, and some will flock around Ikemba. My father is one who . . . seems to fawn over him. Or at least pretend to. They seem to have some male coalitionary aggression pact going. Subconsciously, of course."

Soraya said nothing, so Eve continued. "I'm not worried about Refa. She will be with us. And, of course, Thurman and Kat are with us, and of course, Gabriela. But my father and Ikemba seem to feed off each other."

Soraya interrupted. "Where does that leave Nikau and Dei-Lin?"

Eve replied, "I sense Nikau is very close to Ikemba and my dad, but Nikau is also bonded to Refa and me. I think Nikau will be torn if there is a vote. Dei-Lin is . . . confused, and struggling.

I don't think she really wants a mutiny, but she and Ikemba are super close. Winning a vote by six to four isn't very . . ."

Eve trailed off as she noticed Soraya looking down at her hands. "This isn't a simple vote we're talking about. Ikemba has more power as pilot than any other person, probably including me. Imagine if Ikemba refuses to stand down and becomes uncooperative and we have to restrain him – which I can imagine us needing to do. There are protocols for such things. Then Dei-Lin becomes our only hope for landing on Mars."

"She's smart and strong," Eve said, "but I'd hate to have to trust her to land the Ark. Or to stand by if Ikemba is involuntarily restrained."

"That's why we need to talk to your father," Soraya said. "We need Colfax to reach Ikemba."

"Oh, God," Eve replied. "Even I can't reach my father."

"Where did things end in your . . . conversation?" Soraya asked.

"We were right on the verge of getting somewhere, maybe, but . . ." Eve replied. "We didn't get there. I think we'd be better off talking with Ikemba directly."

"You didn't see the look in Ikemba's eyes when he glared at me. We need to talk to your father first," Soraya said. "And I know what you're going to say . . . that I haven't seen how Colfax glares at you. But I have. Often."

Eve felt her face flush. "I can't, Soraya. Maybe you can . . ."

"Do you think he'll refuse to cooperate?" Soraya began.

"I don't know what to think," Eve replied. "He is opaque to me. A black hole."

"He loves you, Eve," Soraya said. "He hurts you because he doesn't know how to help you. Your groundedness exposes him . . . as brilliant, but ungrounded. He reacts because . . . you've outgrown him."

"He sure knows how to reopen old wounds," Eve said. "I feel like I'm a teenager again whenever he—"

"I think he's afraid, afraid of losing you as you outgrow him, so he foolishly keeps trying to reconnect through reasserting dominance," Soraya said.

"How would you know this?" Eve asked, a little taken aback by her insight.

"I had a father too. And a husband, briefly. Both of whom I loved very much. But they were far less brilliant than Colfax and far more arrogant and . . . violent."

"Please, Soraya, please don't ask me to be here if you're going to talk to him. I think you and Gabriela would do better without me."

"I disagree," Soraya said. "You are the best listener on this crew. You taught us about the power of curiosity. If you will simply be here as a curious presence, I think we can get through to him. I know he can be an ass. But I trust the goodness of his heart, just as I trust the goodness of Ikemba's heart, and I actually think your father will want to demonstrate that goodness in your presence."

Eve took a deep breath and then let out a long sigh.

Soraya pressed a few buttons and spoke into her bracelet. "Colfax, I need you to meet me on the Bridge. And do not wake anyone."

Colfax took long enough to make both Eve and Soraya feel uncomfortable. But he entered quietly, pulled the hatch shut behind him, and tethered into the co-pilot's seat.

Soraya turned to him. "Eve and I need your advice, Colfax."

"I do not envy you for the unpropitious situation in which you find yourselves. I do not envy any of us, come to think of it," Colfax said. "As for advice, I am bereft. Excepting this. Perhaps you should approach Ikemba and petition him for help and advice, as you just petitioned me. Request that he run the scenarios. Tell him you need to know for certain if there is indeed a safe way to return to Earth."

"I didn't expect you to say that," Soraya said, looking down. "Wouldn't that make it seem like I was rewarding him for insubordination? It might even make it seem like I am willing to capitulate." She looked directly at Colfax, eye to eye. "You're making me nervous, Colfax. Do *you* think we should turn back?"

"I do not believe we can return, even if we should, or should want to," Colfax replied. "I have been pondering the situation, picturing orbitals in my mind, and doing a bit of research using my arg and the Ark's computer. Ikemba understands the planetary motion system with more precision than I do, but in my understanding, I am concerned about the speed of the Earth, which is 110,000 kilometers per hour. Theoretically, our top cruising speed out here, adding in the boost of a solar gravitation, might be 275,000 kilometers an hour. However, I believe it would take more fuel than we possess to turn us from our current trajectory and then accelerate into another trajectory. To make matters worse, even if we were able to use solar gravity and the slingshot effect to our advantage in some way, even if we could theoretically plot a trajectory to meet the Earth somewhere on the far side of the sun, I suspect the return voyage to Earth would take far longer than reaching Mars."

There was a moment of silence as Eve and Soraya tried to let that reality sink in. Eve spoke first. "I had no interest in returning to Earth, but as soon as you say it is impossible . . . suddenly, I feel . . . terrified."

"We face two terrifying options," Colfax continued, "landing on Mars in a deeply unstable situation, or attempting an emergency return during which our provisions might run out, and long before that, all the animals on board would perish. Meanwhile, we have not addressed the far from minor detail of landing on Earth: how would we reach the Earth's surface if and when we achieved Earth orbit? The heat shielding on this vessel was made for Mars' thin atmosphere, not Earth's far thicker, more incendiary atmosphere."

"Yes," Soraya replied. "And after Code Indigo, there will be no Macopro rescue party waiting to meet us at the supply station and give us a ride back to Kenya or Kiribati or wherever."

Colfax said, “Exactly. And any rival oligarch with orbital capacities whom we might petition for a ride would likely demand the Ark as payment. We know where that might lead. To save ourselves, we would have to put at risk everyone on Mars, and they are in a precarious enough situation as it is. So, we can turn neither to our founders’ organization nor to a supportive nation nor to Kat and Thurman’s rich friends willing to mount such an expensive effort to rescue us from orbit. But here is my main point: the math is complex, and the calculations would occupy Ikemba’s mind for at least a day or two. I would be happy to help him with the calculations, to walk with him through the process, so to speak.”

“You think that by me asking him to do it, he’ll realize himself how futile it is, and then . . . re-affiliate with the rest of us?” Soraya asked. “Voluntarily?”

“Perhaps,” Colfax replied. “I imagine that he would be working on the calculations already. It is, after all, his job. And he takes his position very seriously.”

Eve risked asking a question. “What is your gut” – she was going to say “feeling,” but edited herself: “What is your gut intuition about whether he will stand down?”

“I think that is the wrong question. I think we should avoid forcing him to stand down. His ego is too big for that, and I speak as one who would know about such things. Soraya, there is no better way for you to reassert your command than by commanding him to do what he already desires to do. But there is another dynamic at play. If you ask Ikemba for his assistance, he will see that you share his fear, which may help him trust you again. Fear is the only thing that makes sense to him right now. If he understands that you share his fear, *you* will then make sense to him. And then, perhaps—”

“I *am* afraid,” Soraya cut in. “It’s just that I’m afraid of many scenarios at once, and our pilot is only focused on the single danger of a complete meltdown at Mars Base.”

"Fear is the propellent that ignites us all, really, far more than we like to think," Colfax replied, looking past Soraya to make eye contact with Eve. "So much depends on us at least being aware of its power. None of us are as rational as we wish we were."

Soraya turned and looked through the viewport into space. "Fear not."

"You are quoting the Bible?" Colfax asked. "To *me*?"

"The Quran," she answered. "When I was a little girl in the U.K., before my father bought us citizenship in the U.S., there was an oval plaque on my bedroom wall. It had a verse written in Arabic, Pashto, Dari, and English, that said, 'Fear not, nor be grieved, and receive good news of the garden which you were promised.' When I had a nightmare or was sick or afraid of the dark, my mother would stroke my hair and recite it to me in each language. I would fall asleep imagining a beautiful garden instead of monsters and giant spiders under my bed. I was terrified of spiders back then."

"Odd. I had a similar plaque on my wall as a child, but with a Bible quote," Colfax replied. "I won it in Sunday school for perfect attendance, perfect attendance that was imposed upon me by my tyrannically religious father, of course. 'Fear not, for I am with you,' it said, in that old-fashioned King James 1611 font. It's ironic, but that font always gave me a perturbative feeling. The font itself, contrary to the message, terrified me. They say that *fear not* is the most oft-repeated command in the Bible."

"It's not surprising," Soraya said. "So much of our brains evolved to keep us alert to danger. Danger is real, of course, but fear . . . fear easily becomes our greatest danger."

That was the only time Eve recalled Soraya breaking from her professional distance and hugging a crew member. "Thank you for your wisdom, your support . . . and friendship," Soraya said as she untethered and hugged Colfax. "You have helped me, Colfax Innis. You have helped us all."

*

The next morning, Soraya met with Ikemba and asked him to come up with a plan for returning to Earth.

He withdrew to the Bridge and kept the hatch shut for the rest of the day. He was visited several times by Colfax and Dei-Lin. Late in the afternoon, the three of them sequestered themselves for several hours. The others were tense, too tense to gossip or speculate about what might be happening.

When the seven were eating dinner, Ikemba emerged from the Bridge. Dei-Lin and Colfax followed. Ikemba floated over to where Soraya was seated and whispered in her ear. They whispered back and forth for a few minutes. Then Ikemba addressed everyone.

He looked shaken. Perhaps ashamed, Eve thought. He told everyone that Soraya had asked him to do the calculations about a return to Earth. He thanked Colfax and Dei-Lin for their assistance in running several possible scenarios. "We have concluded," Ikemba said, "that there is no safe plan for return. So, I apologize for my behavior yesterday. I especially apologize to Thurman and Ekaterina, and to Soraya. I will speak with each of you personally to express my regret. I hope you understand that although I admit I was out of line, I was motivated by my responsibility as pilot to keep you all safe. At this point, the safest of all our dangerous options is to continue our mission. I accept this, and I urge all of us to do the same."

That evening, Ikemba made the rounds to speak with each person privately. Eve experienced his apology as stiff but sincere. He reminded her of someone else she knew.

*

About two weeks later, Eve was tethered in the galley, reading something on her digital page. Refa approached her, but Eve didn't look up. Refa hovered for a long time, and finally spoke: "Eve, I need to talk to you. Not about a Team Culture matter, but about . . . something personal."

Eve slipped the digital page into her thigh pocket, made eye contact, and smiled faintly. "Tell me about it, Refa. I'm listening."

Refa tethered into the bench across from her and leaned toward her. "It's Ikemba. I hate him. And I know I shouldn't, but I do, with all my heart," she whispered, "with a perfect and righteous hatred."

"Did he come to you to apologize in person, after the incident? Did you not trust his apology, his change of heart?"

"He tried to apologize. But I wouldn't let him. I said, 'Save your breath. I will never trust you. I am disgusted by you. I despise you. Completely and totally. You are a coward. And an egotistical one at that.' "

"What did he say?" Eve asked, trying to keep her voice steady.

"He said, 'I accept that. I might have reacted the same way, if our roles were reversed.' That only made me hate him more. But my hatred doesn't sit well in my body. I'm finding it difficult to eat. I can't sleep for more than an hour or two without waking up. I woke up in the middle of a nightmare this morning. In the dream, I had killed him. That scared me."

"So, you regret not forgiving him, not accepting his change of heart," Eve said.

"Oh, no. I do not regret that. I will never trust him, or forgive him," Refa said. "As for his heart, the man has a coward's empty heart. I have no trust or respect for cowards."

"But you are unhappy feeling this way," Eve said. "Otherwise, you wouldn't be talking to me."

"Yes. I am unhappy feeling hatred," Refa replied. "I think hatred is wrong. My parents raised me to know that. Hatred is a sin in my mother's Jewish religion, my father's Christian religion, and my homeland's Muslim religion. My mother always said it is like drinking poison in the hope that your enemy will die. But that is how I feel. Full of hate and poison. And empty of happiness. And unable to change. It has been almost two weeks, and I feel like a whole pot full of poison is boiling inside me. I can't get rid of it."

"If you felt both hatred and happiness," Eve said, "then I would be worried. But I think your unhappiness is what will save you from your hatred."

Eve said nothing more. She only stared into Refa's face, and Refa stared back into hers. They did not smile. They simply stared.

Refa thought, *Eve is so pale. She looks so unwell. How can human skin be that white, almost translucent? It looks like a simple touch would cut it. How can a person look so fragile and yet keep going?*

Eventually Refa broke the silence. "So, what should I do?"

"Let's get back to work," Eve said.

"Work?" Refa asked.

"Yes. We have important work to do, however we feel," Eve replied. "Will you get Nikau? It's almost time for check-in."

"But how can I do this work when I feel such burning hatred in my heart?" Refa asked. "I feel my heart should be at a better place to do our work. This is good work that Team Culture is doing, and my heart is not good right now. I should take the day off, maybe help Team Biome with cleaning animal habitats or something. Maybe cleaning external shit will help me deal with my internal shit. I'm smart enough to know this isn't really about him. It's about me."

"Trust me, Refa," Eve said. "And trust your heart. Your heart is so good that it is grieved by the hatred you feel. Your heart will heal as you do this work, and eventually, the hatred will fade away and the goodness will remain, but even stronger. Sometimes you can't get rid of an imperfection; you have to press on in spite of it and outlast it. And while it's there, you can learn from it, as long as you don't let it control you. I feel sure of it."

Refa did not feel sure of it. But she decided to at least hope that Eve might be right. She pushed down to the lower decks and found Nikau on Deck 4. Nikau was surrounded by salt-water bubbles, the almost spherical bags made of thick, soft, clear plastic that housed marine creatures. She counted five bubbles floating around Nikau like liquid planets, each with its own pump to recirculate, filter, and re-oxygenate its water. "When you can get free, Eve would like you to join us on Deck 2," Refa said. "Team Culture calls."

"OK. I told Dei-Lin I would tend to these bubbles for her. Are you OK?" Nikau asked. "You look . . . different. Your voice sounds different."

Refa smiled and shrugged.

Nikau sealed the port of the bubble they were working on and pushed it gently toward Refa. "This one's done. One more to go."

She caught it like a slow-motion beach ball and gazed at the creatures inside . . . clouds of tiny golden shrimp each the size of a grain of rice, circling the interior of the sphere where some sort of algae or seaweed was growing. She still didn't answer Nikau's question.

Early in the voyage, Nikau had been unusually quiet, maybe a little depressed. But since the near-mutiny, Refa noticed Nikau had become much more talkative again. And now Nikau launched into a stream-of-consciousness monologue as they worked on the bubble: "Sometimes I hold these spheres and I think of Earth. I think that no matter how bad things were there, we shouldn't have given up on it. But then again, what power did we have to change anything there? Just a few hundred old rich people running Earth as if it belonged to them. Meanwhile, there were billions of younger people like us. Billions. It was like they held us hostage. Our voices counted for nothing. And sometimes I think of the potential people of the future, trillions of them who could potentially be born, and the oligarchs never gave them a thought. Like, how can a few hundred selfish old oligarchs get away with what they're doing? It's robbery, really, from the young, from all those who will be born, and from those who will never be born because of them. Sometimes I really wonder, Refa, especially when I work with these spheres."

Refa nodded, smiled, and said, “Me too. I wonder too. Lots and lots to wonder about out there. And in here.”

She saw Nikau look at her for a long second, probably wondering what she meant by *in here*. Then Nikau went back to tending the last bubble.

She waited. Then she helped Nikau stow the bubbles behind their netting. Nikau dried their hands on a towel, put the towel in the dehydrator, and said, “Hey, let’s bring Pooper and Peony with us. They need some exercise and attention. And I could use some playful company too.”

They took the two puppies from their enclosure and each put one under an arm, carrying them like squirmy little footballs up through the diaphragm. They floated through the green of Deck 3, then belted in across from Eve on the galley benches in Deck 2. They let the puppies loose and the three crew members tossed them back and forth for a few minutes like live balloons, both pups growling and yipping with delight. After they tired the pups out a bit, Pooper nuzzled under Nikau’s arm and Peony lodged herself between Refa’s crossed ankles.

Eve smiled. “It will be good to have the puppies with us for today’s work. We humans need some best friends about now.”

24
Interrogate Hate

As Eve pulled up some documents on her digital page, Refa wondered why she preferred to read on her page rather than through her arg. Maybe it was because she was a little older and so preferred the older technology.

For a moment, Nikau and Refa sat in silence and watched Eve read. For some reason, Eve's concentration felt fascinating to observe.

She lifted her head and still didn't speak. Nikau, seldom one to let a silence go unfilled these days, filled it. "So, what are you reading? You seem really deep in thought."

"This is our work for today. It's not pleasant. But someone has to read these messages and process them."

"OK," Nikau said. "What messages?"

"I requested them from Sisavanh Cherubandith at Mars Base. They're the suicide notes from all the . . . I don't know the right word . . . victims? Perpetrators? Suicides? It doesn't seem right to define people by their . . ."

"Why? Why would you want to read them?" Nikau said. "That seems like a violation of privacy. And besides, I thought our main concern now wasn't suicide but . . . gosh, I hate to say it: murder."

"We'll have to deal with the murder or murders, too, Nikau," Refa said. "But there have been a lot more suicides than murders, so I guess it makes sense to start there. And maybe they aren't that different in the end. Eve, has anyone read these already . . . or are we the first?"

Eve was staring into space again for a moment, and then she answered Refa: "I don't know. Some of them were sent to individuals, so I suppose those individuals have read them. Some were sent to everyone on Mars Base, so . . . I imagine that Lead Triad read them all, but I'm not certain. We aren't the first ones to see them. But I think we will be the first to . . . study them, try to learn from them."

"How many are there," Refa asked.

"Twenty-three. Most are short. Open your pages and I'll show you the first three," Eve replied.

Nikau and Refa pulled their digital pages from their jumpsuits and positioned them in mid-air in front of them. Eve sent a share command.

I guess we're skipping check-in today and getting right to work, Refa thought, *which is just fine with me*.

"Here's the first one," Eve said. "The very first."

The three read silently.

> To Whom It May Concern
>
> I am of sound mind. I feel great clarity. I do not want to contribute to this project any longer. We committed ecocide on a beautiful, warm, living planet, and now I find myself here on this drab, cold, dead planet. Perhaps this is our cold hell, a fitting punishment for a consumptive species like ours. Perhaps someday we will become less dangerous to ourselves and others, but I do not see a bridge to there from here. If you have any hope for a way forward as part of the solution, please do not follow my example. I leave no possessions of any significance. I leave with no enemies. To my friends, I say goodbye and thank you for all your kindness. You'll find my remains just east of the metallurgy furnace. I apologize to you for the mess and for any inconvenience. Tito.

Eve spoke: "He sent this to everyone through a delayed-send. He was a materials engineer who oversaw the first round of regolith construction."

"How did he . . . do it?" Refa asked. She had picked up Peony and was petting her fur gently. Pooper was still asleep, nestled between Nikau's arm and elbow.

"He walked out into the sand – a dune of fine-grained regolith, and he dug a hole with a mining backhoe. Then he lay down in the hole, unlatched his helmet, and depressurized. It was night, in Martian winter, so the temperature was something like minus seventy degrees Celsius. When they found him, he was frozen solid, and the wind had partially buried him under red sand."

"Is it a painful death?" Refa asked. "Freezing like that?"

Eve replied, "If you depressurize on Mars, the low atmospheric pressure causes your blood to . . . boil. Instantly. It's like opening a can of soda. Without sufficient air pressure, the blood gases fizz. I think you die in a matter of seconds. Maybe even less than a second. So, if it's painful, the pain only lasts until your brain boils. But it's a cold boil. I suppose like a thousand mini-strokes."

Refa swallowed hard. "Not a super-comforting thought."

Nikau said, "I wonder if that first one was the trigger. I wonder if that first public suicide note set off something in people's minds, like copy-cat crimes back on Earth. Like, you plant an idea in people's minds, and they can't help but think about it."

"I hate to think what that means for us, especially now that we're about to read twenty-two more of these. Were the other notes shared publicly too?" Refa asked.

"Some were. Some weren't," Eve replied.

"Could we read one that was shared privately?" Refa asked, not sure why she was making that request.

"The second one was a private message," Eve said, scrolling down her page. "This one isn't written. It's a vid." First, a still appeared: it was young woman with intensely red hair, obviously dyed. Refa wondered for a second how such vibrant hair dye would be manufactured on Mars. Then Refa noticed that the young woman had a striking tattoo of a green grapevine growing up her neck. A cluster of purple grapes hung below each of her ears, like earrings. Her hand was on her neck, as if she were tending the vine.

"It's from a woman named Hannah. She sent it to someone she was close to," Eve said, and then touched "play," and the still came to life:

> Edgar, you and Hercule have been my two loves here, but Hercule is so sensitive and so overly attached to me. You are the only one I will send this video to, which I know will hurt Hercule, but what can I do, so please don't tell him about this.
>
> I am not sad, really. I am just empty. What is this life for? You know that's the question I can't escape, especially here, where the landscape is arid and sparse, with no clutter, no distractions. I think about this question day and night, and the answer slips farther away from me.
>
> You asked me to read *The Dream of a Ridiculous Man* by Dostoevsky. I finished it in one sitting last night. It struck me as so funny that the ridiculous man mentioned being on Mars and then in his dream went on a journey through space. You must have thought the story would give me a reason to keep living, like you have, but it ended up helping me in another way.
>
> It helped me see that just as the protagonist corrupted the people on the planet he visited in his dream, we will corrupt Mars. We are already doing so. I want no part in that, Edgar. The story also gave me such a deep feeling of compassion for the endless suffering of humanity. I cried as I thought of the little girl that the ridiculous man pushed away. I don't know . . . it changed something for me. I realized that if I had a dog I really loved, and I knew he was suffering as I am suffering, I would put him to sleep. I guess I finally feel permission to extend this same mercy to the tender animal that I am.
>
> Please don't let this make you feel guilty or responsible in any way, Edgar, as if you failed me in some way. I am thanking you

from the bottom of my heart, for Dostoevsky, and even more for what you have meant for me and for our time together. Being with you was the best thing about my time on Mars, and you are a beautiful human being. In every way. You should keep living, no matter what. Please do. Please survive another day. And when they allow it, please find someone and have a baby. Your genes should continue.

I have one request. My grandmother taught me a Hebrew prayer. It's called *El Malei Rachamim*. I am not a believer in God, but you once told me that your grandma was Catholic and taught you to pray. Would you pray this prayer for me, Edgar? Even atheists need prayer at the hour of their death. Please pray this for me, whenever you think of me: "Have mercy upon her. Pardon all her transgressions. Shelter her soul in the shadow of Thy wings. Make known to her the path of life." That is my last wish. I never really found the path of life in my life. Perhaps I can find it as I turn sideways into the light and disappear.

Oh, and please take care of my little plants. They never hurt anyone. They deserve to live. My dream for Mars is that it might someday be green, covered in plants, with some animals, and just enough humans to tend them and care for them, and to cherish them as kin.

That is all. Thank you for your time and attention. I apologize to you for the drama and for any inconvenience. Hannah Mizrahi, ending transmission.

Nikau pulled the whalebone necklace over their head with one hand and offered it to Eve, but she didn't take it. "We forgot check-in today. I think we need some sort of ritual, you know? This is . . . this is . . ."

"I think we're all at a loss for words, Nikau," Eve said. "Let's do this: why don't you hold the whale in silence and give us time to feel with you, to empathize with you, as you take in what we just witnessed. Then when you're ready, you can pass it to Refa, and we'll hold her in silence. Then I'll go last. This way, we can be mindful of our own feelings and feel the concern of each other. Agreed?"

Each person held the tokotoko for about a minute. Eve handed it back to Nikau and said, "We needed that. If you're both OK with it, I'd like us to consider at least one more message today. The next message is also a vid. It went to about a dozen people in the Darwin neighborhood, from a hydroponics expert named Lawrence."

> Hi, Darwin folk. It's my turn. I guess I'm lucky number thirteen. Didn't want to be the last one left standing, you know? Look, behind my perpetual smile, I feel like I'm being eaten slowly by an invisible monster. Karma, you know? One bite at a time, you know? Every day there is less of me. My whole life on Earth, since I was like eight years old, was traumatized by knowing we were destroying our planet through our . . . I don't know, stupidity? Then to come here and feel the low-grade trauma of living in such a sterile lifeless place, and to feel a constant sense of doom with the Fermi Paradox and Great Filter hanging over my head . . . I guess I've had enough trauma for one lifetime, you know? I guess it's time to withdraw my consent and my participation in something so . . . tragic.
>
> You all know I grew up in Florida, which was famous for two things back then: its hurricanes and its heavy censorship. When I left Florida to go to university in New York, I knew I had been brainwashed, so I decided to learn about all the history that had been kept from me in the Sunshine State. I remember feeling like I was waking up from a nightmare into a worse nightmare. All of human history looked like one single catastrophe, one long storm surge from one unending hurricane that was piling wreckage upon wreckage. And I realized that the name of the hurricane was Progress.

So, if you walk three klicks due east from the hot salt tower, you'll see a big flat rock on a hill. What's left of me will be on it. Nice view of the Base from there, you know! Hey, seriously, it's been a blast! But all good things must come to an end, so best of luck, my friends! If you can, survive another day, OK? One more thing: I apologize to you for the trouble of dealing with my remains!

Lawrence ended the vid with a big smile and a thumbs-up.

"You would have thought he was going on vacation!" Refa exploded. "That *al'abalah*! How can he be so casual about something so final! How can he make a human life so cheap, even if it is his own? I hate that guy! I hate all three of these people!"

The animation in her voice woke up Peony, who started yipping. What felt like a little alarm bell went off in Refa's head: *First I hate Ikemba, and now Lawrence, Hannah, and Tito*. She looked at Eve. "You don't have to say anything," Refa said. "I heard myself."

"What?" Nikau asked.

"It's personal," Refa replied. "It has to do with something I shared with Eve earlier, in confidence."

Refa handed her little pup to Nikau, so Peony could snuggle with Pooper.

"I'm confused about something," Nikau said, holding the two little dogs in their arms. "As usual I suppose. What did Lawrence mean by the Fermi Paradox and the Great Filter?"

"The Fermi Paradox," Eve replied, "was a question raised by a twentieth-century physicist who wondered why we hadn't been visited by alien life already. He assumed that with all the star systems in the galaxy and all the time since the Big Bang, some species should have evolved on some planet that would have developed space travel and visited us by now. The Great Filter was a possible answer to the paradox. Basically, hypothesis of the Great Filter says that all species that gain enough intelligence for space travel self-destruct before they can get very far."

Nikau shook their head. "Wow. Lawrence was a downer, but Fermi is worse. I need a break. Lawrence talked about trauma, and I feel it. It's like a headache, but not just in my head. I feel it in my whole body."

"I know what you mean," Eve said. "I've read and reread these at least a dozen times, and it doesn't get easier. Let's give ourselves some time to recharge and pick this up tomorrow."

Nikau said, "Before we go, I want to say something to you, Eve. I'm sorry you have had to carry these messages alone. Even though this weight is heavy, I am glad Refa and I can process this with you. You were right. Someone needs to do this, to take these messages seriously. But, Eve, I don't think we should share these with everyone. Remember what I said about copy-cat crimes. Not everybody is ready for this."

Refa reached over and hugged Nikau. "You are so wise."

"Thank you, Nikau. Agreed," Eve said. "This stays between us. I feel like I need some exercise and then a hot shower to release this . . . tension, or grief, or whatever it is. It helps a lot to be able to share this with you two."

"I'll take the pups back," Nikau said.

Refa waited for Nikau to leave. "Eve, before you go, I have one more question, another personal one."

"OK," Eve said. "You have my full attention."

"How do you keep hope? I mean, we human beings are such a cluster. Just think of those messages. And then that whole Great Filter thing. And Hurricane Progress. And then look at me. I have this little hate-gun inside me, and I'm willing to pull the trigger at a moment's notice. I look inside myself, and I feel that I'm . . . incurable. And here I am, chosen by Macopro for Team Culture. What a mistake. I don't see how you keep yourself from becoming completely cynical. Especially with people like me always coming with our problems. But you always seem, I don't know . . . OK."

"I have my days," Eve said. "I'm no different from anyone else."

"Please don't tell me that," Refa said, her voice cracking. "I need you to be different. I was hoping you might be able to tell me something that would . . . I don't know, encourage me a little. Something from your spirituality. Because I'm kind of at a point where I need it. Seriously."

Eve nodded. She untethered from her bench and pushed over to Refa. She anchored herself by locking her knees onto Refa's ankles, and she rested her forearms across Refa's knees. "You know, Refa, there's this statement in the Christian scriptures: 'In the beginning was the Word, and the Word was with God, and the Word was God.' That English term *the Word* comes from the Greek term *logos*, which means the logic or essence or internal pattern of something. Most of the crew are scientists, so they have devoted their lives to studying the patterns of the physical universe, whether it's patterns of matter and energy, or patterns of biochemistry in plants and animals, or whatever. You have this gift for music and art. And so, you know something about the patterns or logic or essence of things, because you see it and play it and feel it in music. That's what I would focus on: there's a logic that runs through music, a set of patterns and relationships. Maybe that's your way to get in touch with the internal logic of the universe. You've got to find the melody, the rhythm, the beauty, the flow. It's too big, too deep and glorious for words, so you need to trust it and follow it, and never let it go, even though you can never grasp it totally or comprehend it fully."

"I wish I had your faith," Refa said. "My parents had it. Both of them. But I feel like it was burned out of me. At too young an age."

"Oh, Refa, I know how you feel. But think of what's happening down on Deck 3 right now. It's the logos of plants to grow toward the light. I trust, on the days when I can, that we'll all, eventually, grow toward the light."

"What about the other days, the days when you can't trust, when you can't find any melody or rhythm or pattern, just noise?" Refa asked.

"On those days, I try not to make any big decisions," Eve replied, with a faint smile and a wink. "And I stay close to people and things I love. And I remember to be grateful for . . ."

Refa nodded twice, but didn't say anything. She just untethered, hugged Eve, and then grabbed an armful of meal packets from a cabinet in the galley.

She pushed up to the Bridge. Ikemba was there, running a landing simulation on his arg.

"Hey," Refa said. "I brought you lunch. Your pick."

Ikemba gave her his big PR smile, like he was about to sell her something. "Wow! You didn't have to go to so much trouble! Especially for someone you detest!"

Refa realized that Ikemba had no idea just how much she detested him. If he did, he wouldn't make a joke about it. *Typical of a macho egotist*, she thought. *The last to know how disgusting they appear to everyone else.*

"I have a theory, Ikemba, that I wanted to run by you," Refa said. "Two theories, actually."

"I love theories, Refa. Especially when that theory is created by the most beautiful woman in the solar system – well, actually, in the whole galaxy," he replied, his smile stretching even bigger.

Refa gave him the look a teacher gives a rowdy student. "Seriously."

"I am serious, Refa," he replied, and gave her a wink.

"*Khalas!*" Refa exclaimed. "*Ant ghabi jiddaan!*"

"That's not nice, Refa," Ikemba replied. "You forgot that I was raised in Nigeria and worked for Macopro in Kenya, so I know some Arabic."

Refa considered leaving, but she decided to try once more. "I have a problem, and I need your help to solve it."

"Gladly," Ikemba said, unlatching his pilot's chair and swiveling it toward her. "I am your fix-it man. Very handy."

"My problem is that I hate you. I've hated you since you . . . insulted Thurman and started a mutiny against Soraya and nearly destroyed our whole mission." With that, she raised her eyebrows and smiled. "That's my problem."

"Oh, is that all," Ikemba replied. "Then we both have a problem, because I hate myself for that too." His smile disappeared. He pulled off his cap, ran his fingers loosely through his curls, gave them a little shake, then put his cap back on. "We have that in common with everyone on board, I imagine. What I did was unforgivable."

Refa wasn't prepared for that admission. She continued. "I have these two theories about why you did what you did, and I need to know if either of them is accurate."

"OK."

"My first theory is that you are a coward. When you thought about landing on Mars with the trouble there, you became a little chicken and you wanted to run home to your mommy, or perhaps to Mother Earth."

He nodded.

"My second theory is that you are not a coward, but that you love human life, and you did not want to see your human life, or our human lives, senselessly threatened by a violent situation on Mars. In my second theory, you were not driven by fear, but by love."

He nodded again.

"Which theory is true? Or was it something else?"

Ikemba pursed his lips. "Well. To test a theory, you need more than opinion. You need evidence. And I can provide you with evidence for both of your theories. For your first theory, I have to be honest: I did feel afraid. I felt a terror like I have never felt before. The thought of landing among a group of people who were losing all sense of order and trust . . . of having no police, no army, no courts . . . that did frighten me. I would be a liar to say otherwise. Only a fool would let himself fall into the hands of angry, out-of-control humans."

He nodded a few times, as if he were agreeing with himself. "And as for your second theory, Refa, I can say truthfully that I have faced death many times without fear, in the West African Wars and in some other dangerous situations I put myself into. So perhaps it was not fear, but love, as you say. But I cannot be sure."

"You're not helping me, Ikemba. I don't want to hate you, but I think to forgive you, I need to understand you, to understand what brought you to the point where you were capable of mutiny. I still don't understand."

"Do you understand why you hate me?"

"I hate cowards, and I've been working with that theory so far."

"Do you understand why . . . *why* you hate cowards?"

"Because . . . I guess I don't understand why. I could pity cowards. I could see cowards as people who need guidance or training or something. But I don't. I have this gut reaction that makes me hate them."

"A wise old man told me something once," Ikemba said. "He told me to interrogate my fear. And I am trying to do that. Maybe you need to interrogate your hate."

Refa looked down. "Maybe." Then she added, "So how's it going? Your interrogation of your fear?"

"It is making me think a lot about my father. He was a bad man, Refa. A violent man. And he made a lot of money through violence. Maybe I fear that violence is profitable, that it works, that it's the only thing that works in the end. And maybe I fear that I could be like my father. And maybe I fear that if I ended up on Mars Base in the midst of a lot of violence, I would . . . you know, fight fire with fire."

Refa smiled a little, to her surprise. "I like the way you say *fiyah*," she said, and tried to imitate his Nigerian accent with her Israeli-Arabic-Bronx accent. "Fight fiyah with fiyah."

"Does what I have told you add evidence to either of your theories?" Ikemba asked.

"It might. I need to think about it some more," Refa replied. "And I need to interrogate my hate some more too."

"Well, if it would ever help you to talk to me about it, you know where to find me," Ikemba said, then added, "Would you like to stay for lunch? We don't have to call it a date, of course, especially because you hate me so much."

So, she stayed for lunch and she hated him a little less.

25
Traveling Light

Gabriela's eyes were closed, her brow furrowed. She was pedaling hard on the exercise bike at the bottom of Deck 4. The bike beeped to say she had finished ten kilometers at high resistance. She was sweating profusely, but still not fully tired. She dried her face with a towel. *Dios mío*, she said to herself. *I hoped some exercise would purge some of this tension from my body.* She decided to do another ten, but first she stripped down to her underwear. She punched the distance and resistance level into the bike's computer, closed her eyes, and slid back into the zone. Soon her cap had worked its way off her head and was floating behind her. The towel was floating beneath the cap and her jumpsuit was floating just behind the towel.

Above her, Gabriela heard Nikau talking to the pups as they settled in their enclosure. Then she heard Eve enter and say something to Nikau about a good meeting. Nikau asked where Refa went, and Eve said something about a meeting with Ikemba. Then they both laughed. Gabriela opened her eyes, a little annoyed.

Eve was pointing at the jumpsuit, towel, and cap floating behind her undressed friend. The air circulation was pushing them slowly behind her. "Looks like a slow-motion accident scene," Eve said.

"Sometimes you have to travel light," Gabriela replied, managing a smile she didn't feel. Then she pressed some buttons on her bracelet to activate her implant, a way to signal that she didn't want to talk.

Eve pushed down next to Gabriela and did resistance exercises silently as Gabriela pedaled. At about eight kilometers, Gabriela felt that Eve was watching her. She peeked through barely open eyelids and found she was right.

Gabriela slowed to a stop and touched her bracelet to turn off what she was listening to . . . a recitation of poetry by the great Spanish poet Antonio Machado. She pushed *reset* on the bike to end her session. She made eye contact with Eve. Eve tried to smile.

"Soraya is tired," Gabriela said. "I'm worried about her."

"Aren't we all," Eve replied. "Tired, I mean. And worried. About everything. Every single thing."

"She needs us," Gabriela said. "More than before even."

"We all need each other. But I'm not sure what I have left to give," Eve replied. "I feel . . ."

Gabriela paused for a moment, looking to Eve like a tiger ready to pounce. And pounce she did. She leaped off the bike and grabbed Eve's face. Her two thumbs dug into Eve's cheeks and her fingers held Eve's head just behind her ears. Eve was startled, but she didn't sense anger in Gabriela: just intensity.

"*Escúchame, hermana!*" Gabriela whisper-shouted. "There is no road for us. We are walking beyond all roads. Don't you see that? We cannot stop walking. The only road is behind us, where we have already been, and where we can never return."

Eve had never seen Gabriela like this. She felt terribly afraid, even more so as Gabriela continued: "Eve, I know your secret. I know about your infertility. And I know it is solvable. You cannot give up. Yes, you can give up hope. Yes, you can give up knowing what to say or do. Yes, you can feel whatever you feel, terrified, depressed, despairing, empty, exhausted, whatever, I don't care. But you cannot give up, my sister. Because life is not about you or me or how we feel. Soraya needs you, and I need you, and we all need you . . . and all those eggs in your ovaries, they need you to survive, and so do thousands and thousands of their future descendants. And it's not only humans. Just above us, we have animals and plants and genetic material that could well be the only future for hundreds of thousands of species. If we give up, we are selling out their future. Do you understand me?" Gabriela grimaced, and her clenched eyes squeezed out tears, tears that floated like tiny jewels, tiny, perfect, spherical, liquid satellites suspended around her face, each one glittering.

Eve nodded her head. "But . . ."

"No!" Gabriela shouted. "No buts, *querida*."

For a moment, they stared into each other's eyes, noses almost touching, breathing heavily. Then Gabriela pulled Eve's face into her sweaty chest. She held her as if Eve were her own little girl.

Eve began to cry. At first, her crying was silent. But then there were sobs and then long moans. Soon, Gabriela was crying too. *Ah*, she thought. *This is what I needed to release my stress. Not sweat, but tears*. For a long time, the two women held each other, needed each other, cried together. Eventually they pulled apart. Eve grabbed Gabriela's towel from the air and they each dried the other's tears.

"Do you know what you need right now?" Gabriela said tenderly. "Do you know what you need right now, Eve?"

Eve half expected Gabriela to say, "A joke."

"A story," Gabriela said. "You need a story. A story to believe in, to tell yourself, because other stories are forming in all our minds right now, stories that tell us we might as well shrivel up and die. You need a better story. So do we all."

"I don't know," Eve said. "I should know . . . but I don't. I don't know what that story might be. All the stories I know . . . they feel used up, Gabriela. They're failing us," Eve replied. "Refa just asked me for help, and I tried, but my words felt hollow. I didn't even know if I believed them as I said them. My stories don't feel big enough, strong enough, honest enough . . . for this."

Gabriela pulled back so they could see each other. "We are three months into this voyage. We have six months to go. You'd better get to work, *querida*. Six months is enough." Gabriela's face became tender. "You and I both know that biological evolution is slow; it depends on random mutations over long periods of time. But cultural evolution . . . it can be much faster. It can happen through intentional mutation in stories. Some tipping points are positive, you know. They are revolutions of the heart. That's your work. So, get on that bike and work up a sweat like I just did, and trust that the story will come."

"Trust?" Eve asked. "Trust what? My faith is gone. My hope is gone. And you're the only one I can tell."

Gabriela's face hardened again. Her jaw clenched. "Figure it out," she said. "Maybe faith and hope are overrated. Maybe what you need to do is to fall back on love. I know your heart is full of love, *querida*. Let it come to you. Let it rise from that deep, dark abyss of honesty, that infinite abyss where your faith and hope have gone to die."

Then her face softened into a smile. She once again pulled Eve toward her and kissed her on the forehead. "I believe in you," she said. "I have not lost faith in you. I am not lying. I am not even exaggerating. I believe in you. It is easy for me. I think you are amazing." Then Gabriela positioned her bare feet on Eve's thighs and gently pushed herself up to the hatch. She grabbed her jumpsuit and cap along the way, then disappeared into Deck 3.

Once through the door, she slipped back into her jumpsuit, but then lingered among the plants, listening to the bike's faint whir and Eve's grunting in the deck below . . . five minutes, ten, twenty, and then Gabriela heard the bike slow and stop. She quickly pushed up through Deck 2 and retrieved something from her locker. Then she sped back toward Deck 4.

"Hey!" Gabriela stuck her head through the diaphragm. "Did inspiration come yet?"

Eve tried to smile, but all she could do was shake her head. "Nothing. Not a glimmer. No feathered thing sitting in my soul. Just . . . emptiness. And fatigue. Same as before."

Gabriela pushed half her body through the diaphragm. "My mother, she used to go to see a nun at the church in the next barrio, after our church closed. Mama would pour out her many troubles and the nun always told her the same thing: *Es una noche oscura del alma*. 'It's a dark night of the soul,' she would say. This always made my mother very happy."

"Happy? That doesn't sound like something to be happy about," Eve replied, wiping her neck with Gabriela's towel.

Gabriela nodded. "I thought the same thing. But the nun also told her that the dark night of the soul was the tomb for the old you, and it was the womb for the new you. That's what made Mama happy. She liked the thought of being a new person on the other side."

Eve sighed.

Gabriela said, "I know. It sounds naive. Too good to be true. But maybe the nun was right. Maybe none of us change deeply enough until our *noche* becomes *oscura* enough so that the old version of us passes away and a new version of us can be . . . can be born. Come up here. I have something for you." Gabriela pulled back through the doggy door.

Eve pushed off the bike, pushed through the diaphragm, and met Gabriela in Deck 3. Gabriela, in her blue jumpsuit, surrounded by the humidity and viridity of Deck 3, was holding out a child's toy, a faded green cloth frog with a big smiling mouth and white plastic eyes.

"This was my toy when I was a little girl," Gabriela said. "His name is Kermit. I want you to have him, and someday I want you to give him to your own child, to your own little boy or girl."

"But shouldn't you save him for a child of your own?" Eve asked.

"When I have a child, I will tell him or her why I gave Kermit to you, and maybe our children will play with Kermit together. That will help them be *amigos cercanos*, as we are."

*

Gabriela and Eve spent the rest of the day together, doing daily chores, eating dinner, and then they tethered next to each other on the wall in the meeting space on Deck 1, watching a short vid about Martian geology on Eve's digital page.

When they were about to retire into their cocoons on Deck 2, Eve noticed the Bridge door was partially closed, which was unusual. She pointed to the door and Gabriela said, "Let's go check."

When Gabriela looked through the crack in the Bridge door, she saw Soraya and Thurman, sitting in the relative darkness, tethered into the captain's and pilot's chairs, staring out into space. Soraya turned and saw Gabriela and she pushed the door open, revealing Eve beside her.

"Thurman and I were just chatting," Soraya said. "Please join us. You should be part of this conversation."

Gabriela took the co-pilot's seat, Eve took the jump seat, and the others swiveled their seats to make a circle facing Eve. Their eight knees were practically touching.

Thurman had lost muscle mass on the flight, and Gabriela noticed how there were two small craters where his cheeks used to be. He skipped exercise some days, and even when he did work out, his exertions seemed lackluster. She made a mental note to check his vitals.

"I was telling Soraya about my . . . I don't often speak this way, about my personal life," Thurman said, barely audible. "I was saying that both of my parents were professors, part of the Black intelligentsia that emerged after the Civil Rights era. They would always remind me that my grandfather's father was the great Howard Thurman, mentor to Dr. Martin Luther King Jnr. They would tell me that Howard Thurman's grandmother was born in slavery, so I was born into a lineage of Black survivors.

"They also gave me a sense of vigilance, this constant awareness that white supremacy was still festering like a hot, swollen abscess in America's chest, that the nation could deteriorate at any moment. That's why I . . . I dressed and spoke and filed my damn fingernails as if I were a member of an aristocracy. I needed to prove to white folk that I was every bit a man they should respect. Of course, that was a losing battle, because most white people believed what they believed, whether or not any Black person was brilliant or successful or had clean fingernails."

Thurman pursed his lips , shook his head, and sighed. He looked angry . . . or was it remorseful? "Here's the thing I've never told you, any of you. Here's the thing I'm so ashamed of, especially tonight. The three of you need to know this. This voyage, this last voyage, the most important voyage of all in many ways . . . it has been rushed. We developed the Macopro Method, triple-triple checking everything through a highly developed process. But not this time. We cut some corners because . . . because we felt our time was growing short. And here we are. In this metal tube shooting like a damned bullet through space. We're at each other's throats, not sure what to do. I wanted you to know that I'm sorry. I'm very sorry. I feel responsible."

Eve interrupted. "Thurman, I'm curious. Why? Why did you rush? I'm sure you had a good reason. That feels to me like the one remaining secret. I tried to ask you about it back when you first began recruiting me in that restaurant on the Puget Sound. But you were vague, a little evasive even. I wondered if it was because you were afraid the suicide epidemic would destroy the whole colony if we didn't act fast. But I could never be sure."

"You deserve an answer," Thurman replied. "You all do. The turning point for me was a private meeting I attended in Bermuda, back in early 2055. It feels like forever ago, but what was it . . . two Earth years? I should tell you about it, if . . ." Thurman paused, and then proceeded not to tell them.

26

Global House of Lords

The silence went on long enough that Gabriela said, "We're here, Thurman. We're listening."

He nodded, as if he had finally resolved an intense internal debate about how much to reveal. "OK. Here it is. This meeting, it was invitation-only, and it involved a group that I came into contact with way back in the early 30s, when I was about forty years old. Back in those days, the world's oligarchs had periodic meetings every winter in Davos, Switzerland. They called it the World Economic Forum. I doubt you've ever heard of it because it . . . went dark, like so much else. For decades, the Board of Trustees was composed almost exclusively of white men. Gradually a few women were included, then a token Asian and Middle Easterner or two, but there was very little African representation, even less African American. So, they decided they needed to increase the racial diversity, and I was invited to be a Board member. You need to understand: being invited wasn't a compliment. It was an insult. It said something terrible about me. It meant . . ."

Thurman bit his lip and closed his eyes. It looked to Gabriela like he had run out of battery. But when he opened his eyes, they suddenly looked fierce.

"It meant that they saw me as a quiet, harmless, compliant Negro who wouldn't rock their damn boat. Plus, I gave them some moral cover because of my environmental work . . . I was becoming known as the solar panel guy, the tree planting guy. I knew I was being used. I was a harmless prop on their little stage. I hated myself for agreeing to be part of their performance.

"The only upside was that I could use my position in Forum governance to keep my eye on the bastards. I would be sitting in some restaurant in Davos with my back against the wall. There would be an arrogant asshole of a Russian oil magnate on my left, a weaselly Swiss bank manager on my right, across the table, a sweaty American retired general with bulging veins in his neck who sold illegal weapons to the world's worst humans, then next to him, a poker-faced Chinese guy who ran a disreputable genetic engineering company, and next to him, a British so-called security expert who organized and outfitted private militia to contract out to the others at the table. It was sickening, really, simply to have a seat at their table. But I suppose I learned a lot about how the world works.

"Then, in the late 30s, they could no longer meet safely in Switzerland because ecoterrorists were targeting them, and some of the oligarchs were using fake ecoterrorists to knock off their rivals. So, the Forum went dark, but the big dogs kept meeting secretly in various configurations, and I would be invited on short notice to this or that remote place . . . Iceland, Okinawa, Tristan da Cunha, the South Pacific . . . in fact, that's how I first encountered Kiribati. It struck me as the best place on Earth to hide something.

"And that's also what brought me to Bermuda just over two years ago, Earth years, I mean. That's when . . . I guess you could say I panicked." He exhaled loudly as he recalled what happened. "Look, most of the oligarchs like to drink or . . . ingest other more potent substances. I developed an ability to appear to be drinking or . . . whatever . . . without actually doing so. So, when this young fellow asked to meet privately with me, I brought along a bottle of very expensive cognac, a brand I knew he liked because I kept track of that sort of thing. We brought a couple of chairs and sat under the stars in the center of a helipad behind our hotel. I managed to endure his boorish presence until he was really drunk, and he told me more than he intended . . . as to what he was up to, along with his father, of course. I kid you not: he told me he was making me an offer I couldn't refuse, a line straight out of an old mafia movie."

Thurman appeared to be wavering as to how much more to reveal. He blinked a few times, cleared his throat and let out a long breath. "I thought that arrogant bastard was going to ask me to be chair of his political campaign, because rich young white guys like him always dream of being governors or senators or prime ministers, especially if they have rich daddies to give them an even greater sense of entitlement. And they always need some compliant person of color to give them cover, but . . . it was worse than that."

"What do you mean?" Gabriela asked, trying to keep him talking.

"Well, first I should tell you how this young man's father made his first quarter of a trillion dollars, back before the currency shift. He built massive yachts and luxury land-based survival bunkers for oligarchs back in the 20s and early 30s. People thought the yachts were just for play, but they were really oligarch lifeboats, floating survival bunkers with desalination equipment, radiation shielding, and a couple years' worth of food for their entourage. Over the years, I was invited to several floating bunkers he had designed and outfitted, in the Mediterranean, in the Arctic Ocean, in the South Pacific. I also visited more than a few of the land-based bunkers he designed and sold . . . in places like the Yukon and North Dakota, Saskatchewan and Greenland and Siberia. In fact . . . well, I won't go into that. All of these oligarchs were carrying on their businesses as if nothing was going on, but privately, they were spending billions preparing for what they knew was coming. The land-based bunkers were like small, self-contained cities, luxury fortresses really, constructed deep in the earth in old, abandoned mines, or hollowed-out mountains, or under huge domes of reinforced concrete. You may have heard of their company, but probably not: *Vivalic.*" He looked at his three companions.

Soraya replied, "I've never heard of it. Anyone else?" Her colleagues shook their heads.

"Well, that was their plan – that you wouldn't have heard of it. Vivalic put this Cognac Kid and his daddy in the position of being brokers of sorts, not just yacht or bunker brokers, but relationship brokers, you might say, introducing this oligarch to that, this cabal to that, since they knew so many of them. They did all this in the dark, of course, which is why you've never heard of the company."

Gabriela leaned in. "You said this young man made an offer to you, Thurman, but it wasn't to be part of his political committee. What was the offer?"

"He told me they were launching this bold new venture, top secret, invitation only, blah-blah-blah. He was giggling like a little boy, albeit a drunk one, beaming with pride in his own brilliance. He said that he and his father wanted me to become a partner, a very junior partner, of course, in *the greatest humanitarian project of all time*. Those were his exact words. He said it would be a successor to the World Economic Forum *and* the United Nations. That's when he started telling me details that I'm sure he wasn't supposed to mention. It was pretty horrific. It took all my self-control not to unleash some Colfax-level insults on him when he told me. But I merely nodded . . . as if I were weighing his offer. Frankly, I could choke just thinking about it."

Gabriela braced herself. She thought Thurman was going to say that Vivalic was planning a Mars colonization project of their own. Her mind raced to what that would mean . . . if, perhaps, Vivalic's colony was already elsewhere on Mars, or perhaps en route a few million miles behind them at that moment. She prepared herself for the worst.

But what Thurman said next was far worse than the worst Gabriela had imagined: "One of the labs in Vivalic's cabal was developing genetically modified viruses to kill cattle, pigs, and chickens. They had also developed an antiviral vaccine, of course.

So, the plan was, at their chosen moment, to secretly distribute their vaccine to a pre-selected group of agribusiness oligarchs who pledged allegiance to them. After secretly inoculating their livestock, they would spread the infection to the whole world, then blame it on ecoterrorists."

Soraya had been unusually quiet, but now she spoke. "What? That would unleash a food crisis that would kill millions, no, billions of humans . . . not to mention the decimated livestock. Last time I checked, cattle and pigs were eighty-one percent of Earth's mammalian biomass, and chickens were seventy-eight percent of Earth's avian biomass. To wipe them out would be . . . How's that a humanitarian project?"

Thurman nodded. "Of course it's genocidal, not humanitarian. But they can pitch it as humanitarian because when everyone is hungry, they can provide the protein. *Protein will be the new petroleum*, Cognac Kid said. His exact words. *The new petroleum*."

Soraya continued, "So they knew the collapse was coming because they had planned to precipitate it. For profit. For power. They knew. They weren't just in denial. They weren't just idiots. They were . . . I can't think of a word that is despicable enough to describe them. Of course you made this the last voyage, Thurman. You had to. Of course you had to hurry. You had no choice."

"I did have a choice," Thurman said. "My first choice was to go to some government officials somewhere, to blow the whistle on the bastards. But I didn't. I felt I couldn't. Every single government was already on their leash, one way or another. But it was worse than that. If we went to Washington or London or Moscow or Beijing and told them what Vivalic had created, their first instinct would have been to acquire the virus and vaccine for themselves. It would have been Tolkein's ring of power. When we realized that . . . that's when Kat and I decided to rush the last voyage."

Gabriela paused a beat and then asked, "Who was he, Thurman? Who was that young man who talked to you . . ."

Thurman looked down at his hands. "That drunk young fellow? He and his daddy were just like Trump, Putin, Hussein, the Kims, and all the craven politicians of the American politicult ever since. It wasn't simply that this drunk punk was extraordinarily evil. Believe me, he was absolutely banal, un-extraordinary in every possible way, the definition of mediocrity, sipping his goddamned cognac and slurring his goddamned words. He was simply . . . a typical contemporary human being. He was one of us. He was playing by the playbook of capitalism and patriarchy and . . . civilization; the same playbook that shaped all of us, including me . . ."

Then Thurman looked up and met Gabriela's gaze: "Gabriela, I will tell you who that young man was. He was the American colonists dispossessing the Indigenous peoples. He was the Maryland plantation owner raping his slaves so he could sell their children to labor camps farther South. He was the Lutheran minister and Catholic priest in Germany, lining up behind the Führer. He was an ExxonMobil, Chevron, or ConocoPhillips executive, destroying the Earth but feeling like a holy capitalist saint because he was making huge profits for shareholders, and himself too. He was the so-called tech genius making billions so he could buy social and mass media to swing public opinion to vote for politicians who would allow him to make still more billions.

"That young gentleman and his goddamned daddy knew that the global economy and the modern nation-state were failing. So, they made a simple business decision: they would flip the global economy back into feudalism. Look, among the oligarchs, it's widely known that feudalism has been the most durable arrangement of human civilization, from the time of the pyramids to the present. That's who the oligarchs have always been, really: feudal lords in disguise, dynastic lords in waiting, holding out until the democratic and capitalist interruption would end. So, they developed their plan."

Gabriela still wanted to know who the man was. She said, "But . . ." and Thurman raised his hand to signal that he wasn't finished.

"Of course," he continued, "it was a costly plan in terms of human lives. But that's not a cost that oligarchs measure. It's not a cost they even notice. So, this fellow invited me to be part of the little cabal he was forming, the *Global House of Lords*. That's what he called it. He had already recruited weapons manufacturers, food processing magnates, owners of private genetics labs, the titans of agribusiness . . . It turns out that when you control the global protein market, you are the kingpin. Which means it's good to have an ally who has a big slice of the solar panels market, especially when the conventional electric grid fails due to social unrest."

Thurman now turned to Eve. "Your father would not be happy to know that this drunk young man quoted *Dusk or Twilight?* to me, to justify what he was doing. He saw an excellent business opportunity in the disaster scenario your father described."

Eve swallowed hard. She asked, "Did he . . . did that oligarch's son . . . did he happen to run for political office last year?"

"He did."

"And?"

"He was elected U.S. President on November seventh, 2056, right around the time I was recruiting you to end your life as you knew it. I suspect he and his daddy orchestrated the attack on Macopro on December second. When I refused the offer he said I could not refuse, I knew my days were numbered. In fact, Ekaterina and I . . . we couldn't tell you this . . . but that was when we developed Code Violet. We designed those necklaces and cufflinks with cyanide inside them, realizing that we had to be ready at any moment to . . . protect the mission by ending our own lives. We knew . . . when that average little oligarch had the assets of the U.S. presidency at his disposal, there would have been nowhere for us to hide. So, we were planning our own suicides on Earth at the same time as we were recruiting you to go to Mars to stop the suicides there. I've never told anyone this. I . . ."

Una noche oscura del alma, Gabriela whispered to herself.

She glanced quickly at Eve and in her eyes she saw exhaustion.

Then she turned toward Thurman. In his hollow cheeks and forlorn face she saw defeat and despondency.

Then she turned her gaze to Soraya. She noticed that Soraya was wearing her lapis lazuli earrings. Gabriela hadn't seen them since before launch. *I wonder why? Why now?* she thought.

As their eyes met for an instant, Gabriela saw in Soraya a glimmer of something familiar, a faint spark of determination that mirrored the tiny flame flickering dimly but defiantly in her own heavy heart.

Gabriela knew what she had to do.

THE END of Book 1.

Coming

Book 2 of The Last Voyage Trilogy: The Great Rift
When the crew of the Ark arrives on Mars, they face a community riven by rivalry and distrust. They discover that wherever humans go, their greatest challenges prove to be social and personal, not simply technological. Through their struggles, a new kind of leadership emerges that sets the stage for a new way of life.

Book 3 of The Last Voyage Trilogy: Ethnogenesis
Three decades pass with no contact between Mars Base and humans on Earth. Then, a native-born Martian and some intrepid Earthlings risk restoring contact and discover that even though they are separated by over fifty million miles, their futures are inescapably interconnected.

Acknowledgments

First and deepest thanks to Laci Scott who has been my trusted colleague-at-a-distance for about twenty-five years, keeping my travel schedule organized so that I could write. I am forever grateful for such a pleasant, competent, and consistently delightful colleague.

Heartfelt thanks to my agent, Roger Freet, who didn't discourage me from changing lanes and has helped me find a good place on this crowded and crazy highway of publishing.

Thanks to Joanna Davey and the whole team at Hodder. You also gave me room to change lanes and have been a true pleasure to work with.

Thanks to Jennifer Ould and Jack Jenkins for reading very early drafts of a manuscript that eventually became this book. Their feedback encouraged me to keep crafting the story, and they steered me away from some serious pitfalls. Thanks also to my sons-in-law Owen Ryan and Jesse Stone who have helped me by sharing their love of fiction and insights on writing it.

Special thanks to Randall Curtis and then-seventeen year-old Nikko Curtis who read later drafts of the book. Nikko gave me super helpful suggestions for enhancing several characters and sharpening the story. Honestly, I've never had an editor so quickly "get" what I was trying to do and offer such insightful and detailed suggestions. Thank you, Nikko. I dedicate this book to you, and to your generation.

Thanks as always to Grace for her partnership in life for almost fifty years, and to our four adult children, their spouses, and our five grandchildren. Whatever worthwhile things I have been able to do have been empowered by the love we share.

Finally, thanks to all the science fiction writers who have inspired me. Like prophets and mystics through the centuries, they have imagined strange worlds and distant futures, warning us of present dangers and inspiring us to dream of what might still be possible here and now.